VOICES OF THE FUTURE

STORIES OF HEALING AND HOME

VOLUME 3

Cover design by Plethora Creative

Published by The Author Conservatory

TABLE OF CONTENTS

GROWN UP MAGIC | RHIANNA RING-HOWELL | 9

HOW TO FORGIVE A MERCENARY IN FIVE STEPS | GABRIELLA BANASIK | 31

SPLINTERS IN THE SEA | LYRIC ROSE | 54

OF SONGS & SWAMPS | ZOE ANASTASIA | 80

THE GLASS TREE AT THE EDGE OF THE WOOD | ZACH SOLLIE | 103

TREEFRIEND | RYAN ELIZABETH | 129

THE WOLF AND THE WILLOW | RACHEL NORTH | 151

PHONE CALL TO THE WIND | CALISSA DING | 177

SAILBOAT OF DREAMS | KRISTIANNE HASSMAN | 199

DETAILS IN THE BUTTERCREAM | JULIET ARTMAN | 225

KINDNESS IN COLOR | BAILEY GAINES | 249

FOREWORD

The eleven authors in this collection have fought for growth and belonging even in the lonely, hopeless places—and poured those hard-won lessons into the anthology you hold in your hands.

For that, we could not be more proud of them.

These short stories may span genres, characters, worlds and settings—but two key themes unite them: healing and home.

Whether you are a Kaelyn or a Jude or a Vanessa or someone else entirely, these authors have taken their own lessons and perspectives and woven a bit of their hearts into these stories.

The authors: eleven rising young creatives from the ranks of The Author Conservatory, an online college-alternative program focused on writing craft and entrepreneurship which I co-founded with Brett Harris.

They've spent countless hours working with industry professionals to bring to you short stories that are well developed and showcase the highest level of craft these students have reached thus far. The first bold step into a broader world. Showcasing the incredible storytellers they are becoming—and the chance for you to discover their voices before they become household names.

The students featured in this collection are nearing graduation. As they prepare to launch their careers with serious momentum, here are a few highlights of their accomplishments:

- Several have placed in or won contests for their writing

- Most have attended professional writing conferences

- Many already have interest from agents and publishers

- All are experienced working with professional editors and on deadline
- All have extensive training in business and marketing
- Most have run successful businesses that have provided financial security

These young writers are pursuing their dreams, courageously stepping out into an industry where it can take hundreds of rejections before you get that open door—and doing so with a desire to help others feel seen too. By holding this book in your hands, you are bolstering that courage.

Thank you for supporting their journey by purchasing a copy of their collection. One hundred percent of the proceeds of each sale go towards helping them and their classmates attend writing conferences where they can pitch their novels to agents and publishers.

On behalf of the eleven student authors, my co-founder Brett Harris, and our entire team of award-winning authors, professional editors, and successful entrepreneurs, thank you for investing in voices of the future.

Because who can possibly imagine what these young writers will become?

Kara Swanson Matsumoto

Award-winning author of the *Heirs of Neverland* series

Co-Founder of the Author Conservatory

FANTASY

GROWN UP MAGIC

RHIANNA RING-HOWELL

Hunting for unicorns isn't exactly a grown-up activity, but I couldn't bear to turn Grandma down when she invited me along this morning.

So I drag my feet along the dirt path. Orange and yellow leaves crunch under my boots. Grandma crouches down to gather some lichen off a rock, humming a jaunty tune to herself.

Her unicorn song.

I try not to roll my eyes.

The sun descends behind the trees, golden rays stretching up as if trying to grasp the blue sky. If I had it my way, I'd be cozied up by the fire working on homework. An essay on nearby flora and fauna is not really that exciting, but grown-ups get their work done.

And I know I'll get a good grade on it.

"Are you sure the unicorns are out right now? What if they went to sleep?"

Grandma drops a piece of fuzzy green moss. "Then they'll have a nice breakfast when they wake up."

I bite my tongue. I love my grandmother and spending time with her. It's better than being at my own house. Especially since Papa won't be back till later, and it's anyone's guess what mood he'll be in. But it would be nice to do something normal for a change. Something that grown-ups do. Like listening to the radio or reading books.

Or going on a hike that doesn't involve hunting for magical creatures.

I kick a pebble. It skitters across the ground and disappears into a pile of leaves. Next to it, a few tracks mark the ground. Possibly from a wolf or coyote.

They will be out soon. And I don't want to meet them when they are.

"It's getting late, maybe we should head back home?"

"We will soon." Grandma slows to walk beside me. "You haven't been very talkative. Is something wrong?"

I fix my gaze on a crooked tree ahead. How do I tell her what the other kids said to me? What they keep saying to me. And what Papa said after.

If I look at her, she'll know what I'm thinking. I don't want her to figure out that I'd rather do anything else. That part of me is embarrassed to be out here at all.

I never want to hurt her feelings. But it sure would be easier if she knew.

"I'm just tired." Not a lie, but not really the truth. Hopefully enough to make her believe me.

Grandma pats my arm. "Why don't we head back then? It's getting late, and I have a lovely pot pie waiting to be put in the oven."

My mouth waters. "That sounds so good."

I turn to stride back down the path, but Grandma grabs my elbow, holding me back for a moment as she reaches for another clump of lichen. I resist the urge to rip my arm away. Why did I agree to come? I could be at home. Instead, I'm stuck out here while my grandmother continues to collect foliage like we have all the time in the world.

Gritting my teeth, I search for a topic to pass the time. If this is the situation then I must make the best of it. "When do you think you'll finish the blanket for Mr. Cardle?"

"Oh. Probably in another few days. My hands aren't quite as quick as they used to be." She smiles in the same wistful way she does whenever she talks about "the good old days."

"Maybe I could help? I've been practicing."

"Are you sure you'd have the time? You've been awfully busy with school lately. And I'd hate to take you away from your work."

I drop my gaze. I never meant to make Grandma feel like I didn't want to spend time with her. Only that I don't want to hunt for mythical creatures. It's just hard to separate the two. "I-I'm busy. But it's 'cause I have an essay due in a few days, and I want to make sure it's good."

For a split second, I remember one of the many stories she told me while I lay curled up on her couch. Maybe she walked through one of the little portals that supposedly litter this forest. Suddenly trapped in another world. Perhaps one made entirely of pudding.

No, that's silly.

"Grandma? Where did you go?" I call again.

The birds answer me. Their twittering calls echo through the leaves. Blowing out a breath, I tramp through the bushes. The back of my grandmother's yellow sweater jumps out at me like a picture in a pop-up book. Why didn't she say anything? Grandma cups something in her hand.

As she turns to face me, her ankle twists. She yelps, crashing to the ground in a heap of arms, legs, and skirts. A light darts from her outstretched fingers.

I dash through the leaves and drop to my knees next to her. "Are you alright?"

My heart stutters in my chest. I've heard about old people and falling. Papa is constantly worried that something like that might happen to Grandma. It's one of the reasons he lets me visit so much. That way someone knows that she's still okay.

My grandmother grimaces, clutching her ankle. "I'm all right. Wasn't paying enough attention, that's all."

"What were you doing?" I peer down at her ankle. A small purple bruise is already appearing on the right side. I take a deep breath, trying to calm my frayed nerves and wild heartbeat.

"There was a fairy, didn't you see?" Grandma looks around, probably searching for the supposed sprite.

Anger simmers in my chest. It's one thing to drop lichen on a well-worn path for any unicorns that might pass by. It's an entirely other thing to risk your life to look for a magical creature. But what else can I expect from her?

Sighing, I shake my head. "No, I didn't see anything."

"Well, perhaps it will come back." My grandmother groans, holding out her hand. "Help me up, dear?"

I nod. My hands tremble as I lift her to her feet. She leans heavily against me, taking deep, shaky breaths.

"Can you walk?" My knees threaten to buckle underneath me, but I dig my heels into the ground to brace myself.

Grandma gives a stiff nod.

The sky above us burns pink and orange; darkness will be here in less than an hour. We take a few shaky steps forward. Grandma practically drags her leg, taking a labored breath with each step.

Sweat beads on my forehead. Frustration and panic build inside of me, threatening to spill out. If she had been reasonable, this wouldn't have happened.

After a few feet, Grandma shakes her head. "It's no use. I can't walk back like this."

"But we can't stay here." I lower her to the ground, my mouth drying out. I scan the undergrowth for anything Grandma could use as a walking stick, but there's nothing. Where are large branches when you need them?

Grandma tilts her head. "Of course not. You'll have to go back to the house and call your papa. He can come and help."

"By myself?" My jaw slackens.

I've never done anything like that before. Most kids are told to stay away from the forest entirely. And even though Papa takes me hunting and camping and Grandma takes me out on hikes all the time, they never let me roam on my own.

But here I am, being told to do exactly that. It's a very grown-up thing to do. Normally I'd be thrilled about that, but Grandma is focused on all the "wonderful" things found in the forest. Like "fairies" and "unicorns." She seems to be forgetting that there are very real, very dangerous things that I might encounter in the evening.

"You'll be all right. Just right back to the house. And if you need help, there are always creatures willing to lend a hand." She smiles. "Or a hoof."

I glance at the skyline between the trees. I'll have to go now if I want to make it back before it's too dark. But I'm not sure . . . can I really do this?

If I don't we'll be stuck out here until morning. And I don't want to meet up with any bears or wolves tonight. And Grandma has no way to escape from creatures like that.

The more time I waste, the worse off we'll both be. She's right. I'm responsible enough. I can do this.

"Alright. I'll go and bring Papa back." I clench and unclench my fists.

Grandma nods firmly. "Good girl. I'll be here when you get back."

I try to give her a reassuring smile, even though my stomach roils. This really isn't that big of a deal. I've taken this path all the time. Walk back to the house and Papa will come with me to rescue Grandma. No big deal. I force my feet to move.

I peer over my shoulder once more, savoring the picture of Grandma and her bright yellow cardigan. Now I do wish magic were real since it would save me a lot of walking. But unfortunately, I will have to do this using my own two feet.

So, with one last longing glance, I plunge back through the bushes onto the path.

The sky darkens faster than I anticipated. I've only made it halfway home before twilight blankets the world around me and obscures my path. I've never liked the dark. It makes it harder to see all the things that might want to eat me.

The wind bites at my arms and legs. Owls hoot in the trees. The songs of crickets and the rustling of leaves fill the forest.

Stars glitter in the distance, next to the bright, full moon. I stop, tracing my gaze over the white specks. Which constellations can I use to guide me home?

I scuff my foot on the ground, wracking my brain for the answer. Papa told me what to search for. All I have to do is remember.

I wring my hands, glancing around the forest as if that will trigger a memory. Little lightning bugs flicker around me like little bits of floating magic.

No. They're not. They're insects. Just bright insects.

Bright . . .

I can almost see it. Papa and me lying on the ground, positioned between two skinny trees.

"Do you see that?" Papa points up at the sky, tracing a little square with a handle.

I nod, biting my tongue. "That's the Little Dipper."

"Good." He moves his finger to the edge. "That's the North Star. If you follow that, you'll find your way home."

Focusing, I scan the sky until I spot it. The little lopsided square with the handle, a bright star at its tip.

My heart skips a beat, and I grin.

Papa would be proud.

I stride down the path. Confidence builds until the bushes shudder behind me. I yelp, nearly jumping out of my skin. Spinning around, I search for the source. To my left, the leaves shift and shake. I stay rooted to the spot. Bile rises in my throat. I know I should run, hide, do something, but all I can do is stare.

Am I about to get eaten by a wolf or a bear?

Something brown leaps forward. I lunge back, stifling a scream.

Two pairs of black beady eyes stare back at me. A little nose quivers. I exhale, cheeks flushing.

It's a rabbit.

Taking a few steadying breaths, I pick my way back down the path. Stepping over fallen branches. A wolf or coyote howls in the distance. A few more high-pitched whines follow, the trees around me echoing with their calls.

The hair on the back of my neck stands on end.

The forest floor disappears as the light drains from the world. Sounds fade, leaving only the shifting foliage as my feet probe through them. I kick aside rocks and little twigs.

While I know that it's a natural cycle of life, the darkness seems to prowl around me. Every little snap of a branch or shift of the wind sends my heart pattering. I long for the comforting light of my village. And I have no idea how Grandma is doing. Is she as afraid as I am?

The tinkle of bells joins the cacophony, and the clear and incandescent melody merges with the crickets, the owls, and the wolves. For a moment, my heart lifts.

If you hear silver bells, know that a unicorn is nearby. That's what Grandma used to say, anyway. I had almost forgotten what it sounded like.

Warmth spreads through my body, and the world brightens as if the music itself is shoving the darkness away.

But then the music melts into the whispering wind. A trick of nature. The darkness continues its slow crawl, closing in on me. I shiver and yank my sweater around myself.

I lift my eyes to the stars again, gaze locking on Polaris.

Grandma used to tell me that unicorn's magic came from stardust. And that like the stars, they light the darkest places. When I was younger, I longed for them. I sat on the steps of my front porch, staring at the trees, hoping unicorns would stroll by.

Until the day Mira was particularly cruel, and I came home crying. Papa told me to grow up. Grown-ups must face the darkness themselves, armed with the skills passed down from parent to child. Magic can't be trusted to fix anything.

Blowing out a breath, I trace my hand over the bark of a nearby tree. My fingertips run over the grooves in the wood, grounding me back in the world. Branches stretch out like giant craggy talons wanting to tear me from this world. They shift and sway, casting massive shadows on the ground, which morph like shape-shifting monsters.

My grandma's fireplace stories pull themselves to the front of my mind. Stories of werewolves and trolls. Stories of witches with wispy hair and warty skin, who prowl around searching for unsuspecting children to take.

But I'm not a child anymore, so I'll be fine. Right?

"You're being silly." I shake my head as if that will clear out the unsavory images. "Witches, werewolves, and trolls—they don't exist."

Papa told me time and time again not to worry about mythical creatures. He said that I should really be worried about bears or wolves. They prey on small girls like me. But I have never been able to tame my wild imagination.

Papa says that's why I believe in unicorns—because I use my imagination too much. Adults don't use their imagination like that.

Grandma told me that he, like so many others, chooses not to see the magic. That if you look hard enough, it will always be there.

Well, everyone else says that grown-ups can't believe in magic. Papa, my teachers, my classmates. Magic is only found in fairy tales, told by grown-ups to little kids to teach them lessons. To explain why they shouldn't go into the forest alone. Or why they should eat their vegetables.

I'm not sure why my grandmother hasn't let go of fairy tales. Or why she doesn't want me to either. But it doesn't matter. What matters is getting to Papa and bringing Grandma back home safe and sound. Right now, she is sitting somewhere cold and alone. She's counting on me.

I skirt around a fallen log and skip over a little brook. My gaze flicks upward. Polaris winks at me, urging me forward.

Picking up the pace, I jog through the leaves. Spiky vines grab at my ankles. My breath speeds up. My clothes stick to my skin. Old stories continue to circulate in my mind, mingling with the real reminder that wild animals are not my friends.

Something growls behind me. I freeze, slowing my breath. The thing growls again. Maybe it's simply another trick of the night?

I probably shouldn't, but I glance over my shoulder.

Far in the distance, a figure hulks in the shadows. It shifts and sways. My heart beats wildly in my chest. The figure swivels its head around to catch a better look at its surroundings.

It could be anything. Probably a bear, but perhaps something worse.

I half-walk, half-slide my way down the hill. I will not stay here any longer and risk becoming a tasty snack.

As I get farther away my legs pick up speed. Faster and faster, kicking up leaves and dirt. I know that I'll probably be fine, but I can't seem to convince my wild mind of that. I can't rid myself of pictures of glittering white teeth, powerful jaws, and sharp claws. Arms pumping, I tear through the night.

I don't stop until I'm sure I've made it far enough away.

Taking shaky breaths, I glance around. But nothing appears right anymore. The trees are sparser, and more evergreens sprout from the ground. I tip my head back to look at the sky. But the last light of the sinking sun and Polaris are gone, covered by silent clouds. There's only the white light of the moon and a few small, minor stars that I don't recognize.

Not only is the sky useless, but I have no idea how far away I am from the path.

Tears prick my eyes, and I wipe them away. I'm lost. Well and truly lost.

"Think, Wynna. Think." I rub my forehead as if I could coax knowledge from the recesses of my mind.

But nothing.

My stomach churns. The hairs on the back of my neck stand on edge. *Lost. Lost. Lost.*

My father wouldn't get lost. No real grown-up would get lost. But perhaps I was wrong. Maybe I'm not a grown-up. Maybe I can't do this.

I can't think of what my father would do. He wouldn't ever be in a situation like this. He'd tell me to scan for landmarks or to follow the stars. But there are no stars and no landmarks that I recognize.

I take a few gasping breaths, trying not to let fear overtake me.

But I don't feel grown-up anymore. I feel like a little girl. I want my grandmother. I want my papa. I'd even settle for old Miss Crowley.

Anyone.

Sniffling, I force back tears. There is one thing I haven't considered yet. What would Grandma do?

After all, she is the one who taught Papa almost everything he knows.

She said that magic could take me where I needed to go. I picture my little cabin in the woods. Topped by a shingled roof overgrown with foliage and vines. And painted pictures on each of the walls.

I let my hands rest by my sides. Chewing on my lip, I glance around. I'm not sure what to look for, or even listen for.

"If there is any sort of magic out there, now would be a really great time to help." My voice trembles.

The frogs continue their croaking. The crickets join, growing louder and louder as if trying to compete with the wailing amphibians.

Nothing about this is magical. Just frightening and disorienting.

Something buzzes in front of my face. I bat it away, but it comes back.

"Go away. I'm not food." I take a step back; the insect follows.

The heel of my shoe catches on a branch. I throw my arms behind me as my back slams into the ground. Everything around me shifts and rotates like it does when I spin in a circle too many times.

Sitting up, I blink. The world splits into a kaleidoscope before merging back into one picture. I rip up a clump of grass. Kneading the green in my hands, I take steady, deep breaths.

"This is stupid." I chuck the clod down.

Out of the corner of my eye, something flashes. Probably another pesky lightning bug. I stagger to my feet. The bug glows again, and at the same time, a thought hits me.

What if . . .

The insect, as if sensing my attention, darts a few yards away. Then it stops, hovering.

Waiting.

I take a few steps after it. It extinguishes itself. A few seconds later another light appears farther down the path. I trail after it.

This dance continues through the trees. Numerous lightning bugs create a path, which I pray is really leading me home, instead of deeper into the woods or in circles.

I follow as if pulled along by some invisible tether. The forest around me gradually grows quiet. And suddenly, a soft ringing floats by. The same silver bells from earlier.

Maybe there were bells after all. Besides, what kind of wind sounds like silver bells?

I pick up the pace. The world around me lightens with each step, even though the sky is inky black. The trees grow in clusters closer together. The trail begins to slope gently upward. Both are promising signs. One of the lights floats tantalizingly close to me and I reach out to touch it.

A high-pitched shriek reverberates through the leaves. All at once the lights go out. The silver bells fade away. My hands and feet grow cold. Fear seizes my heart with an ironclad grasp, threatening to choke me. I claw at my sweater, pulling it around me.

The terrible sound dies away, leaving nothing but empty silence.

What are you doing? You aren't a baby. Magic can't help you.

My throat tightens, and my chest shakes with suppressed frustration. I thought it was real. But I was wrong. I resist the urge to stamp my feet and scream. Because that's not what grown-ups do. Instead, I pace back and forth.

Grown-ups solve their own problems. Grown-ups know what to do. Grown-ups don't get lost. Grown-ups would—

I screech to a halt, the thought slapping me in the face like a tree branch.

I don't know what they would do.

In fact, no grown-up has told me what to do when there's nothing left to do. Because to them, being an adult means figuring it out.

I can think of only one other person who would tell me differently.

Grandma wraps a blanket around me, and I nestle close to her. The fire crackles in the hearth, sending sheets of warmth cascading toward us. Her soft voice floats above my head, and I drift in and out, eyelids drooping.

"And the moral of the story, my dear, is that magic always provides help." Stroking my hair, she finishes her story.

I crack an eye open. "So if I need help with my homework, magic can do it for me?"

Grandma laughs, leaning back. "Not exactly."

"Hmph. Then what good is it?" I wiggle further into the soft wool.

Something nudges my side, and I glance up. My grandmother smiles at me. "It can't help you with your homework. But it can help when you feel lost, or afraid, and you don't know what to do. All you have to do is choose to see it."

It's a silly memory. Only half there, since I was practically asleep. But now I can see what I couldn't before.

Maybe the realest things in the world are all around us, just waiting for us to see them.

Grandma's words from earlier pull themselves to the forefront of my mind.

She's always believed in magic. Believed that when I was lost, alone, and afraid, it would be there. If only I chose to look for it.

I kick over rocks and run my hands across the rough tree bark. My fingers brush something fuzzy. I rip it off the wood then tear a few more handfuls from rocks.

Behind me, howls rend through the night. My stomach twists. Doubt creeps back in. But I shove it away as I flop onto the ground. Sitting crisscross applesauce I place the lichen in front of me.

This will work. I have to believe it will work.

The music of the forest crescendos around me, and I shut my eyes, taking deep breaths. In through my nose. Out through my mouth. I dig through my memories for a picture of a unicorn.

Crickets sing in a chorus, joined by the owls. Frogs interject, and the wind whistles. But no silver bells, no matter how hard I focus on the picture.

So, I start humming the little tune my grandmother sang earlier. I used to call it the unicorn song because she would always sing it while looking for them. And the unicorns love the music. One of the reasons Grandma thinks they love the forest so much is because it's always making music.

Warmth creeps up from the ground beneath me. It spreads slowly, tendrils stretching down to my toes and snaking up my legs and torso. Something approaches me. A soft *thump, thump, thump*, as whatever it is comes closer. I sit up straight. My heart bounces around in my chest like a rubber ball.

My eyes flutter open.

Light cuts through the darkness, blinding me momentarily before my vision adjusts. And there, standing before me is a beautiful white unicorn with a golden horn. Amber light halos around it, and its glossy coat sparkles as if covered in moondust.

Sucking in a breath, I gape at it. It's right there. In front of me. For the first time in over a year.

Bowing its head, it snuffles around on the ground and its lips part as it finds the lichen. It munches away, tail swishing lazily. I smile despite myself. My grandmother was right, like she always is.

Rising carefully, I take a few tentative steps forward. The unicorn picks its head up and whinnies quietly. I swallow hard, before blowing out a long, slow breath.

"Can you help me get to Grandma's house?"

As if in reply, the unicorn bobs its head and takes a few steps back. I walk up beside it and place a hand on its silky mane. It smells like the candy from the shop in the square. A mix of melted chocolate and sweet sugar drops.

Magic. Pure, unbridled magic.

Without warning, the unicorn kneels to the ground. I laugh, shaking my head. Despite the language barrier, I know exactly what it means.

Grabbing a fistful of its mane, I jump, attempting to swing my leg over its massive back. After a few tries, my leg manages to wrap around its belly. I hoist myself up. My heart leaps in my chest, and I grin.

The unicorn stands, and its muscled back shifts beneath my thighs. Despite being dizzyingly high off the ground, I feel more at peace than I did before.

The halo around the unicorn envelops me. It drives away the dark, and the world comes alive in a burst of color and light.

Then the magnificent beast takes off. The autumn wind whips through my hair as we barrel through the forest. Night curls back, fleeing as the equine flies across the ground. My knuckles turn white like the unicorn's coat as I cling to its mane, yet never once do I feel myself slipping.

It slows to a trot along a riverbank. Disappointment seizes me for a moment at the sudden stop. But then it hits me. The sound of rushing water.

The river runs right along the side of Grandma's house.

And a few moments later, a little orange pops out of the landscape. My grandmother's lamp sits on a windowsill, shining through the warped glass.

I was nearly here. I simply needed a little bit of help.

A little bit of magic.

I hug the unicorn's neck, pressing my face into its mane. "Thank you."

The unicorn whinnies softly. I slide off, landing on the ground with a *thud*. And with one last glance over my shoulder, I take off toward the porch.

Grandma still needs rescuing after all.

Papa was already inside the house. He'd been calling everyone he knew, hoping to track us down. I walked him back to the spot where Grandma was waiting. It doesn't take nearly as long. Perhaps that's because I'm not by myself.

We are still yards away when I see her bright yellow cardigan—the color is washed out in the darkness, but I know it. Little lights sit in the trees and bushes beside her, and she seems perfectly content.

"The cavalry has arrived." She grins.

Papa scolds her for this, that, and the other, but I don't hear what he says. My eyes are locked on the things surrounding my grandmother. I thought they were lightning bugs, but instead, I am met with little wings and tiny faces.

Fairies.

As Papa wraps Grandma's ankle, she catches my gaze. She glances at the fairies around her, and a slow smile spreads across her face.

She knows what they are too. She knows I can see them.

All around us, the trees light up, as if strings of Christmas lights were threaded through them. And the breeze carries the faint sound of silver bells.

In that beautiful moment, as Papa hoists her to her feet, I vow never to forget. Even as the lights and sounds fade away as we walk back toward her house.

Because though I can't see it, I know the magic is there. Little glimmers of it, if I only know where to look.

RHIANNA RING-HOWELL

Rhianna Ring-Howell was diagnosed with ADHD and anxiety at seventeen, but somehow, she managed to complete over a dozen novels and novellas as a teenager and graduate high school with honors while in the Author Conservatory. Now she writes stories for young women who feel broken, incapable, or worthless, reminding them they are stronger than they've been told and more valuable than they know. When not writing, she spends her time teaching kids Taekwondo, singing classical music onstage and Taylor Swift in the car, and searching for dragons to tame.

ACHIEVEMENTS

- Completed three novels, ten novellas, and a short story.

- Attended Realm Makers (2022) and the Writer's Digest Conference (2023).

- Implemented edits on an 80k-word manuscript in two months.

- Graduated high school with honors while also enrolled in The Author Conservatory.

- Received extensive training in platform building, focusing on email marketing.

PITCHES

- *Loki* meets *Clockwork Angel* in a YA fantasy about a girl with ADHD, a time-traveling train, and a race to save the conductor's missing six-year-old daughter.

- *Over the Moon* meets *Caraval* in a YA fantasy about a young star catcher who teams up with two magical siblings to rescue the stolen sun from a dark sorcerer.

- A Mediterranean-inspired retelling of *The Little Mermaid* where a young siren races to find the lost city of Atlantis before the mer-king destroys the last remnants of her people.

How to Forgive a Mercenary in Five Steps

Gabriella Banasik

"You can't go back and change the beginning, but you can start where you are and change the ending." - C.S. Lewis

Back straight. Shoulders back. You have a plan. Own it.

Sucking in a breath, I study the room, my gaze landing on the portrait of my mother in the place of honor. A crowd of both supernaturals and humans alike mill about, adorned in finery of satin with lace overtures and fine suits of all colors. The ball is already in full throttle, laughter drifting from even the furthest corners of the castle. My home, which doesn't even seem historic anymore, has been transformed into an elaborate modern ballroom.

I won't be sad. It is good to remember.

Despite being a known shifter, men usually line up to ask me to dance, but I keep to myself tonight.

Even in this crowded room, I'm alone. None of my old friends are here. Parents are long in the grave. And no *brother*—I hadn't seen him since he cost me my team and companions.

I'm not even the hostess because the city council has taken over this celebratory tradition. I'm a part of the decor. But I still dressed the part, to blend in with all the other ladies.

Making sure no one is watching, I spin, letting the past few bad months fade away for a moment. My silvery blue ball gown seems to float like clouds right after a storm. The perfect contrast to the pale pink banners signifying the 40th anniversary of my mother saving the city from the elder dragon. The anniversary of her being given the key to the city, a key with the power to unlock any door within the town.

A tickle of loss flutters in my chest, but I push it back. This night is not about me. I might lose everything I have left.

Step one: bring the remainder of my old mercenary crew here.

But I have a plan. Tonight, I can't fail. I will *get my brother back. And then, I will have my team back.*

Hopefully it's worth it. Hopefully he doesn't let me down—again.

I catch a whiff of cedar and oregano, *his* signature smell, and stiffen my spine. But I don't know if I can bear to glance at my ex-boyfriend . . .

"*Arlae* Skipper." The warm voice tickles my ear, but I withhold my shiver. He knows how to affect me. He always has. My heart hurts at the reminder of the loss of him.

Here it goes.

"Silver," I whisper back, staring across the crowded ballroom, unable to meet his eyes. Even if this meeting is my doing, I couldn't prepare myself enough for the pain of being next to him again. My fingers tingle in remembrance of his firm grip holding my hands close. Music reaches its crescendo and begins its descent as the dancers beam, cheeks rosy and faces bright.

In one more hour, the key will be brought out, then the trap will be laid, a plan set in motion. And he doesn't know. My ex-boyfriend used to know everything about me—it's complicated.

"We were hired as extra security detail." I can hear the unspoken questions in his voice and paste on a surprised expression. My poker face has improved over the last few months, not that he would know. Not that he would care to dig deeper anymore.

My gaze tracks the other security guards, older men who retired from the military decades ago.

"Interesting. No one asked *me* to hire mercenaries." *Because I hired you myself.* I wait a moment before I start to walk away from him. But apparently Zayden Silver is not done with me. He grabs my arm to halt me as he lowers his head to my ear.

"Are you not going to look at me, love?" Silver brushes back a piece of my black hair from my neck. His other hand lowers to the small of my back.

I stiffen, knowing he can feel the twin blades cleverly woven into my dress's back.

Lifelong habits don't die in a matter of months . . . and I want to be prepared.

He raises an eyebrow, but he doesn't say anything as he lets his hand fall away. "You're stunning, darling."

My cheeks flush, and I push down the reaction. He isn't allowed to say things like that anymore.

I'm about to respond, to come up with anything, but my eye catches a familiar pixie standing at the outskirts of the room, glaring at the endless array of fake plants as if they offend her very being.

Rosie, the last member of our once-legendary mercenary team. We had done well for ourselves monetarily. Gotten into places where we could act more like heroes than mindless guns-for-hire. Until the last job, when my brother took off with every cent and left a bigger hole in our team than we knew what to do with.

We had trusted and trained together for years—for nothing. And they assumed I was part of his deception.

But tonight is about redemption, and not only for me.

Suck it up and deal with it.

"I wish I could explain everything." The softness in his tone finally has me spinning to my fellow shifter.

"What—" The words die in my throat at the sight of him.

"Happened?" He answers for me. Silver eyes to match his name dance with hidden mirth. "I lost a bet with Rosie and this"—he shakes out his *navy* locks of hair—"was the punishment. Don't bet against a pixie."

"I learned that lesson a long time ago." I shake my head, trying to regain my composure. The last thing I expected tonight was for Silver to show up with blue hair.

His face stills. "Of course you did." His hand rises to cup my cheek. "Skip, I don't . . ."

I push him off. I don't want to listen. He was the one who turned on me, ghosted me, completely shut me out of his life. I hadn't just lost my team and brother that day. I had lost the man I love.

Loved. If only I could rewrite our story.

The lights lower into something trying too hard to be romantic, signally the top of the hour. I skirt around the bodies to gain a better view of the security team bringing the pedestal covered by a satin curtain into the middle of the room. Silver follows me.

As the pedestal is carried in further, the mayor of the city steps up. "It is with great honor we remember a great warrior of our city and hearts . . . ." Before he can lift the red cloth, it slides off, revealing a white pillow—and *only* a pillow.

"Where's—" Silver begins.

The key is gone.

My heart is pounding, and I don't know how to feel.

It's time.

I hold up my hand and press the button attached to the bracelet on my wrist. An ancient alarm blares through the room, red lights beginning to flash. Startled supernaturals scream and screech as humans begin running toward the exit. The chaos makes my head rattle, the noises almost too much for my amplified hearing. I would wince, but I'm trying to control my smile.

They will be safe.

The mayor goes white. The entire security team spins in a flurry, bumping into people, and adding to the mayhem. I can hear my mother's voice in my head. *"Arlae, the key."*

The only heads cool enough to work are my old team—and me. Silver passes me with a flash of speed in his wolfish form. Rosie snaps her fingers and is gone in a gold flash.

I don't know if they will even accept help from me, but instinct takes over and I take off all the same, picking up my skirts so I don't trip as I sprint past the guests.

The metal locks slide on all the windows and the doors, locking everyone but us three into the ballroom and bringing the castle into lockdown.

The treasury is splat in the middle of the castle, the ballroom being in the East Wing. I am the last to reach it, having been ignoring my fitness routine in order to mope better for the last few months.

Way to go, Arlae.

Mental exercise doesn't make up for the lack of physical movement.

Now isn't the time to berate yourself. You can do it well enough later.

Rosie and Silver's expressions don't spell good news, glaring with similar expressions that clearly mark them as cousins, as they stare at the empty case.

The usual resting place of the key is empty. It's gone.

Please don't let something permanent happen to it.

The key my brother and I would stare at in awe when Mother told the story for the sixtieth time. Another piece of my childhood and past *gone.*

Someone stole it.

And I know who.

Step two: use the key as bait.

Silver starts sniffing the space out in his werewolf form. Rosie pulls out her favorite fingerprint dusting kit, her pixie features intent on the podium that the key used to rest on.

"We'll nab him, Skip." Silver manages to shift back without me noticing and watches me now worried and haunted.

I nod, pushing past him, not wanting any of *the past us* intruding on this evening. I loved, I lost, I need to move on.

Rubbing my forehead, I stalk toward the small security room off to the side of our treasury. Maybe technology will prove better than our magic for once.

Give me an idea of what's going to happen next.

The screaming alarm is even louder here. The security cameras are running, and I sense my old team filing into the room behind me.

"This is quite the setup." Silver runs his fingers over the monitors.

"Don't mess anything up," I mutter, scanning the computers.

I click the button to shut off the alarm. The screens go black.

Lookie there.

"No." Rosie glares at the monitors. "Ugh. We are going to have to go old school."

A little mix of supernatural and old school never hurt anyone.

"Suck it up, buttercup," Silver grunts.

"Be nice, kids." I tap the screen at the upper right corner. The thrill of being back together, working together, is intoxicating.

I am a part of something again . . . but don't get too used to it.

"Why are you assuming it's a he?" Rosie snarks, breaking through my mental hash.

Silver rolls his eyes. "Because a woman would be a little more discreet about when she stole it."

"Where should we start? Should we split up to cut him off or stay together? Silver seems distracted so Rosie waves a hand in front of him to capture his attention.

"Do you have any idea who would steal the key?" He pushes back his blue bangs.

Silent, I wait for him to speak up again. I'm not giving anything away. I make sure to keep my expression neutral.

"Rosie, I want you scouting it out. Be careful. Skip, you're with me. Let's try to see if we can find and cut off the thief before he gets out of this castle." Silver tightens his gloves and stretches his fingers out before fishing a communication device out of his pocket and tossing it to me. I fumble with it and manage not to drop it.

Score.

But . . .

I don't want to be teamed with Silver. Well, I do, and I don't. Complicated feelings are going to make a mess of this. If I could make him explain why he dumped me like a hot coal—but no. Tonight isn't about the two of us.

"Fair enough. We do use our brains better." Rosie grins at me, and I match it, watching as she catches herself.

I have missed watching them raze each other.

Another thing to add to the building list.

This still feels so bittersweet. I shift, hoping to ease the pressure in my chest, and trip on my hem.

Silver grabs my arm as I teeter on my heels. "We will get the key back, Skipper." His voice is low and certain. I see an unspoken plea, but I don't understand it.

Rosie nods viciously behind him, her skin beginning to glitter. "This thief will regret messing with you."

Caught off guard, I search their faces, trying to figure out why they're being nice to me. Seeing nothing suspicious, I smile weakly. "Thank you."

Silver pulls me forward. "Be ready to run." His brow darkens with excitement as he tilts his chin.

I clutch the comm to my chest for a split second, staring around me. "You want me to be a part of this?" Even with all my planning, the shock of seeing them and the knowledge they were the ones to turn their back doesn't discount the fact I want them to want *me* with them again.

Rosie presses her lips together, a flash of pain shooting across her face before she smooths it out. I wasn't the only one who had been hurt in our split. We had been the closest of friends. I had hoped she would become my cousin-in-law. She'd almost become my sister-in-law before my brother messed their engagement and *everything* up.

Roe musters through. "Of course we do, Arlae. Once a team, always a team. Now hurry."

She snaps her fingers. A golden mist settles over her, and she is a tiny, winged fairy. A poof of dust, and then she's gone.

This better work.

The fear it could fail. That *I* would fail once more, hurting those I loved—and to be honest, still love. The thought makes my heart pound in fear.

Silver grasps my hand.

Ready. Set. Go.

I'm not ready.

Silver yanks me out of the room by my hand, almost dragging me behind him as I struggle to push my comm in my ear. "Come on, Skip."

"I'm coming," I groan, slipping in my heels. They aren't made for running.

"Come faster," Silver barks, sprinting around a corner.

I pull to a stop, causing Silver to stare at me in shock. "Why are you helping me?"

Don't do this now, Arlae. Don't step into the mushy gushy.

A flicker of shadow shows in his silver gaze. "We haven't forgotten you. We miss what we used to be. Anything important for you, is also important to us."

All the "we" and "us" are annoying. But then his voice drops into a growl. "And I will do anything to protect what you value."

The passion threaded in his voice almost moves me to tears. The key was a memory of my family from long ago. Despite its magic, and the danger it poses in the wrong hands, I would lose it a hundred times to get back the people I built my life with, my family.

"Zay." The word comes as a croak.

But words couldn't do the emotions justice.

He waits, knowing there's more.

"I don't deserve it," I manage. "I feel like I let both of you down when I failed to see what my brother was becoming." And now, I needed a chance to show him the error of leaving.

He grips my shoulder. Nose to nose, he watches me for a moment. "You believe that, don't you?" The depth of the grief covering him like a clock shocks me.

My puzzlement must show in my eyes because he pulls me to him, gripping me in a hug. "Did you make your brother become a criminal?" His voice rumbles against my cheek.

"I didn't stop him."

Silver groans. "You are so hard on yourself. At some point, you are going to need to separate your life from his."

Warmth spreads through my chest at the revelation. *He says he doesn't blame me. But how can I know if it's true?* We were getting off track.

I push him back. "Thank you, but we have a key to get."

The shutters fall across his face, and he starts forward. "Yes, let's."

"Let's keep going." I stammer to his back, trying to reorient myself. *I am Arlae. I am doing this to fix what is broken. I am doing this to help the ones I love. The plan is in motion.*

We run again, feet pounding against the empty cement passages through the castle. It is too big. The candles on the wall do little to light the way, the darkness of the night encroaching as a taunting threat of what is to come.

Time to meet with our thief.

The comms in our ears buzz.

"Come in, Silver. This is Rosie."

He presses a finger on his to respond. *"Have you found anything?"*

"I'm on his trail. The thief is heading for the West Tower. Hurry, this guy is fast."

Silver meets my gaze as he responds. *"We will meet you there."*

I spin on my heel, round the nearest corner, and push into the West Wing. Once upon a time, it had housed a happy family. Now it was a graveyard of memories. Running would be faster in our wolf forms, but we need the comms and can't use them in the other form. Still, we have our amplified senses.

I sniff, the familiar scent of wood and citrus invading my nostrils. Silver follows suit. "Do you smell that?" I ask in a hushed voice.

Silver nods, serious.

He knows now.

The comms come to life once more, a growly voice pirating our link to Rosie. *"Did you think I wouldn't find your pixie? Well, maybe you didn't. Because you don't know me at all."*

The hair at the back of my neck stood straight up. That voice. Even with him trying to disguise it, I know who it is. *It's part of the plan. Fix what is broken.*

Rosie's high voice cracks on the comm, coming at a distance. "*Silver. He is still in the tower. It's Wil—*" The comm goes to static before an overly rough chuckle takes over, an enraged shriek echoing behind him.

"What are you doing splitting your team up, stupid?" The dark voice continues, and I stare in horror as Silver readies himself. It's too quiet now. No alarms. No screams. And no Rosie.

"Rosie? Roe!" Silver hits the comm over and over, both of us waiting. I stand there, heart frozen.

This wasn't part of the plan.

Did I make a mistake? He wasn't supposed to capture Rosie. He wouldn't hurt her, would he?

Silver lost contact with his cousin—we already lost our team—and now we could all end up worse off . . . because of one stupid overpowered key. *And one big-headed plan.*

The silence is too heavy.

I lean against the wall for a moment to catch my breath. "This is my fault. I failed again."

This wasn't part of the plan.

"You didn't fail," he says quietly.

"Then what would you call it?" I snap. But he doesn't answer.

We are still for a moment.

I missed his laugh. I missed our team. I missed *us.*

Now to take back the key. To save Rosie. The finish line is in sight. Once we have a chance to talk it out . . . if Wilder doesn't make it worse.

I reach behind me and pull out one of my long knives.

The knife gives me an air of fierceness. Of confidence. But mentally I'm crumbling.

This isn't going to work.

How could you be so stupid?

You are only hurting them worse.

I couldn't breathe. This isn't happening. I can't fall apart.

"I'm sorry." The words choke in my throat as the first tear escapes.

Silver stares down at me in frustration. "This isn't your fault, Skip."

"No, but everything else was. And then this had to happen as well." I covered my face with my hands and sobbed.

It is only a moment before he grabs my shoulder, fingers hard enough to capture my attention. "Get it together. We don't know for sure she's gone. There isn't a thing you should feel bad about. We were the ones to send you away. Your brother was the one to—" He breaks off, staring into the distance for a moment before shaking off the weird daze. "Let go. Forgive us. Forgive your brother. Forgive yourself." He pleads with me now, breaths coming in pants, and he leans over to grab my knife from my hand. "I'm going to take care of this. Once and for all. We are here for you, not the key. Watch my back. I'm getting that stupid key for *you*. I'm getting Rosie back for me. And then you never have to deal with this again."

But this isn't only about a key. I want . . .

"I can help," I mutter, straightening my dress, and fingering my other knife.

"No, you stay here. He is still in the castle, having too much fun with his games. I can't have you be a part of that." Silver has never sounded so firm. Emotions flash across his face faster than I can identify them. "I can't lose you again."

It's almost like you still love me. But why did you push me away?

"But—" I try to breathe.

"*Arlae.* I can't deal with this right now, and neither can you." He shifts into a wolf, causing the comm in my ear to shriek while its partner shatters during the shift. I yank it out and throw it to the ground as Silver sprints through the corridor.

And I watch him go—wondering if I'm making a mistake. But if they can understand how weak we are apart. Maybe they will remember why we should be together.

Bending, I finally remove the toe-pinching heels and then I run after him.

He's always been too fast for me. I don't remember doing all this running before. A werewolf shifter who doesn't like to run . . . go figure.

Up ahead there is a muted conversation, growling, snarling, the clang of metal upon metal, and finally a gunshot. My heart skips a beat, my steps stuttering.

No matter what you come across, Arlae . . .

I will be brave. I won't fail again.

I skid to a halt, my gaze landing on the sight before me, and suddenly, I can't catch my breath.

Step three: confront *him*.

My brother.

He stands there, the tip of his gun pointed to Silver's temple. A shining lantern sits a few feet away, Rosie's form barely visible, trapped inside. Anger shines in every line of his body, but I know it's hiding his pain.

Is it weird that a scene so dreary gives me such hope? The four of us, in the same room again, after six long months apart.

"Wilder." My voice is far calmer than I feel.

His stature is full of pain and anger. "Come here for your team, did you?"

His black hair stands straight up, his blue eyes the perfect mirror of mine. His face is like my father's, but his smile is all my mother's. *It's not right for him to appear this way. Family isn't supposed to bring so much pain.*

As I continue to stay silent, he lets out a hiss, jabbing the gun harder into Silver.

I stare at my ex, seeing the defeat in his position, the guilt.

This is my chance.

"I'm not here for a fight, Wilder." I throw my knife down and stare him in the eye.

He lets out a bitter laugh. "Then why am I here? Why the bait? Why the trap? It *is* a trap, isn't it? Usually, the key isn't shown at the anniversary celebration. Mother couldn't risk it."

Silver jolts. I keep my focus on my brother.

"I'm here for the truth." The words escape me in a growl and Wilder's face smooths. I used to read him so well, but now I wonder if I am interpreting the flicker of his eyebrows and the stubborn tilt of his chin correctly. He seems frustrated but also done, tired, and lonely.

"Oh, the truth." His tone is vicious, his eyebrows raised. "I don't think you want that, *sissy*."

But I do. I'm willing to do anything for it because it is the only way.

"What happened with the Greendale Manor job? Why did you steal that money?" I spit out, hands clenched.

"I *didn't* steal it."

And there it is. Truth. I can feel it settle in my bones and feel my body almost melt in relief.

Wilder seems calmer now. He glances between Silver and me and shoves Silver away from him. "Why don't *you* tell her, Sil. Tell her what you did to me, to all of us. I would like to know the truth too. The whole truth."

Silver stumbles against the wall and slumps there, taking no notice of the blood trickling down his temple.

Our heavy breaths echo in the cold hall.

No. Not possible. Not Silver. He loved us. Loved this team. Loved me.

Rosie bangs on her lantern, trying to draw our attention.

Wilder dips to let her out. "Sorry, darling. Thank you for waiting there."

A flash of gold light, and she is human size again. She glares at each of us before bending a withering glare on Wilder. "I hate you!" She screams, leaping forward and beginning to pound him with her tiny fists, not doing any damage, even in her rage.

He stands there and takes it, staring down at her. Without taking his gaze off Rosie, he speaks once more. "Tell them, Silver. Tell them what you did." Rosie freezes, wide green eyes fixed on my brother with *hope.*

Because it's not her world that's shattering.

Mine is.

Not Silver. Please no.

I wanted the truth. But what I thought I knew partway, I do not know at all.

But I have one more step. My plan got us this far.

Step four: get my brother back.

Silver isn't listening, dulled. Not even the blue hair can make him appear livelier.

If it wasn't my brother's fault. If it wasn't my fault . . . was it *his* fault?

"Speak, *Zayden*," I snap. The three of us stand, facing our last teammate. The thrill of adventure is gone.

He finally peeks at me, squaring his shoulders. "Lord Greendale's son went missing soon after our protection detail job with him. The payment had already gone through. Three pouches of gold coins." At this, we all nodded. It had been fun to count them. "But as soon as he found out his son was gone, he decided we must be the ones to blame. So, he began sending threatening notes to me. He sent a hitman, who almost got you, Arlae. And then he twisted his sights to Wilder. Poisoning, snipers, sneaking into our apartments."

I didn't remember until that moment the night we woke up to a gunshot. We had laughed it off, thinking one of our "for show" pistols had fallen.

"I had had enough. I couldn't protect either of you, and I didn't know how far he would go. He is a powerful man. Not to mention, Wilder is too foolhardy to care about his own well-being. So, I came up with a plan."

Wilder's face reddens. "You betrayed me because you were chicken?"

Why? At least he was scared on my behalf.

Silver ignores the interruption. "I got rid of you to give me more time to figure something out. I placed the payment on Wilder's bed and as soon as he was picking them up, wondering how they got there, I led you girls in, making it appear like he was counting his own stolen loot to warp the girls against him. Then all I had to do was speak over any defense he tried to give and send him away. We don't keep dishonest members in our team. I then told Rosie we needed to regroup and Arlae needed a break, effectively sending her away too." He finishes with a sigh. "So, I got you out of there, Rosie disappeared for a while like she tends to do, and I left to find Greendale's son."

"You set me up because you were trying to handle it in your own twisted way?" Wilder hisses.

"You ghosted me, chose not to trust us," I whispered. "We have always been a team, able to trust and depend on each other. You took that away from us."

Wilder moves before I can, whipping out a fist and landing a solid punch into Silver's nose. "You set me up, abandoned my sister, and then waltzed back in here? The only reason I didn't fight harder for the truth is because I was sure you had a good reason to protect Arlae. But you went and hurt her worse than anyone else." The fury in his face was something I had seen very few times, and only when others hurt those he cared about.

My brother stayed away because he thought Silver and I were still together.

Silver betrayed my brother so he could send me away.

The two thoughts rampage in my mind.

Rosie spins away from the men, her face filled with pain, and places a hand on my arm. "I . . . I need to go." I nod brokenly as she disappears in a gold flash. She will always come back after her emotions settle. *I don't blame her. Her cousin and her fiancé—if I could call him that—in fisticuffs.*

Silver has enough and kicks out at Wilder's knees. Back and forth. Hit after punch.

"Leave." I hiss. I only mean Silver, but the moment I press the button on my bracelet, opening the iron clad windows, Wilder wraps his arm around Silver's neck.

"We need to talk," he tells me, as Silver thrashes against him.

"We will," I promise. I am not losing my brother again.

"Here." He swipes the key to the city out of his pocket and throws it at me. "Good job setting the trap." I barely catch it, my finger throbbing with its power. Studying him, I take in the new lines of his face. The months haven't been any easier on him.

"Thank you. Take care." I press my hand to my heart as he flings himself backward, knocking him and Silver out the two-story window.

But they will survive. They will be okay.

I don't know if I will be okay.

I got my brother back. I know the truth. But at what cost? I'd said no matter what . . . but maybe I hadn't meant it.

I ruined us. I broke us even worse than it was before.

Our story doesn't seem like it is going to be rewritten.

Step five: forgive one another.

Two weeks later...

I still can't believe Wilder just let him go.

I can hear their giggles and soft mumblings before they come tromping around the corner. I stand at the same window that I last saw Silver.

Rosie and Wilder rush to my side the moment they catch sight of me. "Arlae, you won't believe it." Rose gushes. "We have our first client since regrouping." She pushes an ornate contract into my hands.

I blink down at it, trying to figure out how to feel about this. On one hand, our business is finally starting to look up again. We are mercenaries for hire once more.

But one person is missing.

With some overly fancy wording and names, I nod up at the eager pair. "This contract states the job starts tonight."

Wilder chuckles, running a hand through his hair. "We have just enough time to check our gear." He gives me an understanding smile and my numb heart thaws slightly.

I force myself to grin back. "It looks like we have work to do." I stand, Rosie and Wilder giving each other a high five.

This is good.

We arrive at sunset, just as the contract stated, to a shadowy mansion. Wilder and Rosie flank me as we knock on the dark and are gestured inside by a solemn butler.

Okay then.

We follow him through the grand entry towards the ballroom. I freeze at the doorway, everything else fading away except the candlelit room, with a key on the pedestal in the middle. Right beside it, stands Zayden Silver.

So this was just some farce to lure us here. What now?

Everything hurts where it should be numb. My ears roar with hurt as my hands clutch into fists.

Cedar and oregano. Blue hair. Silver eyes. He is too much.

I whirl back around for back up but Wilder, Rosie, and the butler have disappeared.

How could they?

"Please, Arlae," he whispers.

I shake my head, refusing to spin back.

Silver walks around me, fingers tilting my chin up. "I messed up big time."

"You think?" I mutter.

He chuckles grimly. "Believe me, I know. But here I am. I'm hiring you to protect this key." Silver gestures towards the pedestal, and I pivot towards it, pulling out of his reach.

The key glitters in a twist of blue and silver metals, lying on a satin pillow. "Why? What is important about this key?"

I feel him press up behind me, his hand reaching past me to pick it up. "This is the key to my heart. The key to my secrets. The key to our future. It's the key to my trust, because I *do* trust you."

I want to roll my eyes, but my heart is pounding too hard.

"I want to hire you to protect this, Arlae Skipper. Because I know with you, it will be safe." Silver whispers it in my ear as he tucks it into my hand, wrapping my fingers around it.

"I can't." I find myself saying as I pull it closer.

"I'm sorry. I cannot apologize enough for what I did to you, Wilder, and Rosie. These months have been torture. I shouldn't have been high handed. I shouldn't have gone behind your backs." He falls to his knees, hands outreached towards me. "You worked so hard to bring us back together, let's all be a team again." A single tear trails down his cheek but I ignore it, fury erupting in its place.

"That's right. I worked hard. I poured sweat and tears and sleepless nights into trying to figure out how to fix what was broken, not even understanding where the cracks had come from. I blamed *myself!* And in the end, it wasn't enough. Because you were the piece tearing us all apart. How could you?" I seeth, shuddering in full body sobs.

So this is what it really feels like to be broken.

Silver cries with me, still on his knees. "Please forgive me." He breaths.

Red-hot anger hums in my chest. "How can I?" I scream in his face. "You broke us."

His eyes go bleak, hopeless. "I will never stop trying to make it right. I promise I will never do it, or anything like it, again."

"How can I trust you?" I murmur, deflating.

He stands. "Because I have never broken a single promise to you and I'm not about to start now."

That's true. But what about the unspoken promises?

I watch him walk away through misty eyes. The key digs into my palm and I glare down at him, a tear running off the tip of my nose.

Is this it? What would happen if I gave him one more chance? Do I even want to? Would I regret it if I didn't?

All I know is that I don't know if I can handle him disappearing from my life again. There is a piece missing in all of us.

I'm exhausted from the past couple weeks. No, make that the last six and a half months. This isn't right. We are a team and we can try again. He is ready to make amends.

"Zay." I call him back.

He shudders, turning back. Hope shines through every pour in his being.

The moment he stands before me, I know it is time to put the past to rest. To forgive. To move on and make something better. We can't go back. More importantly, we *won't* go back.

Wilder and Rosie appear behind him, eyes bright in expectation. They must have known. Just waiting in the hall for the right moment.

Grr. Those two.

Well, it's time we *all* forgive each other.

I hold up the key. "I'll hold you to your promises and keep watch over your key, Silver. But only if you rejoin the team." My voice comes out as a croak but he understands me.

Silver wraps me up in a tight hug before I can get anything else out. Wilder and Rosie pile on top.

We are going to be okay.

I was missing one step in that grand plan of mine, but it was the most important of all: forgiveness.

Thank goodness the plan worked. We aren't all the way there yet. Maybe we aren't even close. But we are at the start of rewriting our ending. And I can tell it is going to be our favorite story yet.

Step five: check.

GABRIELLA BANASIK

Gabriella Banasik fell in love the moment she heard her first story, opening infinite new worlds. She writes stories filled with fun banter, light overcoming the darkness, and characters who learn they are never alone.

With a pile of throwing knives hidden around her room and an overactive imagination, Gabriella sometimes takes breaks from reading to enjoy boating, traveling the world, and dancing in the kitchen to worship songs.

Achievements

- Completed two novels, drafting an 81,000-word novel in 40 days, and a novella.

- Received intensive writing training and edits from industry professionals including Kara Swanson, S.D. Grimm, Sara Ella, and Joanne Bischof.

- Pitched and received a book proposal request and manuscript request.

- Started three businesses as a teenager to practice marketing and networking skills, including sold-out summer swim lessons serving dozens of students.

- Attended Realm Makers (2021-2023) and The Young Writer's Workshop Conference (2021).

Pitches

- *Hansel and Gretel* meets *Pirates of the Caribbean* in a YA retelling set ten years after the cottage where Gretel lost her memories, Hansel is missing, and she must voyage back to where it all started to recover what's lost.

SPLINTERS IN THE SEA

Lyric Rose

Thalasseus.

The Sea's voice echoes in my head. Distant, yet close by. Real, yet merely my imagination. I shove the voice to the back of my head, even as it tugs on my heartstrings. I have to honor my promise to myself. I agreed to help her tomorrow. Today is for me and my friends—my *family.*

Mac tugs on my hand, braids flying as she runs toward the next food stall. "Dad's getting *bananas!* We've gotta hurry."

I chuckle and clutch the bag in my hand tighter as I follow. The moment we get back on our ship, I can give it to her. A brand-new outfit, her first one in a year, with pants that will actually reach her ankles. It took four months of saving, but her smile will be worth it.

I slow to a stop after Mac finds her father. She tugs at his worn sleeve and bounces in anticipation. They have matching dimpled smiles and dark hair, the picture of a perfect family, despite their worn clothes.

He laughs and pats her head. "Yes, you can have one."

"Yay!" She snatches a banana from his hand, peeling it and stuffing it all into her mouth at once.

I share a smile with Kai. He's near my age, in his mid-twenties. Yet, despite his youth, he's been a great father, a friend, and a wonderful captain.

He steps closer, pulling a small box out of his pocket. When Mac sees the box, her expression somehow lights up more. I raise an eyebrow, my own smile growing as well.

"What's this, then?"

Kai offers a simple wooden box with a ribbon tied around it. "For you. Mac and I made it together."

I unwrap the ribbon and remove the top, eyes widening slightly as I do. Inside sits a small ring of metal. It's somewhat disfigured, but a squished semi-inaccurate representation of Ursa Major has been hand carved in the metal. And in the place of the north star is a small, gleaming gem.

I'm unsure of what to say, but I slip the ring on my pointer finger quickly. It blends in with the vast amounts of jewelry I've found over the years.

"Do you like it?" Kai asks, voice soft. Almost uncertain. "We wanted to show our appreciation, and I thought, well . . . wearing something to remind you of us—"

"It's wonderful, Kai, Mac. Thank you." I breathe in, reveling in being with them. I watch the ring for a moment more as the sun's dying rays make it glitter. Mac gives me a tight hug before running off to talk to the other sailors scattered on the street.

Once she's out of earshot, I ask, "How much longer do we have at this town?"

He glances at the sun as it disappears behind the rooftops. "A few hours. There's a festival in the square. I thought you and Mac would enjoy going to it."

I grin, opening my mouth to reply, but—

The Sea's voice echoes in my head before I can. *Thalasseus. Are you listening?*

Words die in my throat.

I need your help. She sounds desperate.

My shoulders droop ever so slightly. Another outing taken away. I can't remember the last time I had a peaceful day with Kai and Mac. "I have some business to take care of, but I'm sure Mac will love it."

His smile vanishes, but he nods. "Meet at the ship before the sun sets?"

"Sounds good." I shift to merge into the crowd, in the hopes Mac won't see me go. She has a habit of following. But she can't go where I'm going.

I follow the trail down to the beach and the shimmering green-blue ocean. My shoulder bumps into a woman on the way, and she cries out. I mumble an apology under my breath.

Sometimes, I wish I could remember what it's like to be human. To feel pain, have a heartbeat. To be alive.

Thalasseus, where are you?

"I'm on my way." My murmur escapes my lips, softer than the wind. But I know she heard. She *always* hears.

I step down the last few stairs to the beach. Empty, unlike the warmer months. It's a relief, after months of being surrounded by humans, to have these moments of solitude. Sand clings to my shoes. The water laps at the sand beneath my feet. I let my gaze rest on the horizon for a moment, the spray of the ocean surrounding me. White foam contrasts the sea's green-blue.

I stall on the shore, glancing back at the town where I left Kai and Mac. The sun paints the rooftops golden, with clouds hanging low, like freshly picked pieces of cotton. The buildings stand in the glow, nestled in the rolling hills, their walls turned the color of honey. The food stands—special for this festival—stand out against the buildings. They're heaped with different foods—some fresh produce, some exotic treats. Streamers decorate the entire town, the myriad of colors representing pure joy.

As flawed as they can be, humans truly have created beauty.

But my concentration breaks as the waves lap at my feet. All I can visualize is the current grabbing me. Dragging me back into the depths. Back to the darkness, away from everything. Keeping me captive. My breath catches in my throat, and I shake the feeling away.

Yet it's still strong enough that the Sea picks up on it.

Surely you don't see me like that, Thalasseus. You know more than anyone how much I love you, my son.

I shake my head. "I don't. I have no idea where that came from."

Good. Now, hurry to me.

With a nod, I walk into the ocean, pausing as it reaches my waist. I glance back at the shore one final time. The lantern lights beckon, the festival roaring to life. The sounds of human joy light on my ears, and a deep emptiness echoes back.

One day, the Sea will be able to do this alone. I'm only helping for a little longer. Then maybe I can finally be with Kai and Mac. Join them in their festivities—finally be *with them.*

I sink under the water, not bothering to pretend to take a breath as the water propels me deeper, faster than any human could hope to descend.

It doesn't take long to arrive at her "palace." A massive coral reef, dripping with treasures taken from sunken ships. Pearls and other shining treasures of the ocean are scattered through the coral. Despite how little the sun rays penetrate structures as deep as this, her palace glows with what little light it gets. As I float through the entrance, the bracelets lining my arms glow faintly as the human illusion fades away. The Sea resents the form, and I don't want to anger her.

For a moment, I can only stare at my wooden arms.

This is what I must always remember. I am not human. I'm just a broken hull of a ship that the Sea breathed life into.

I push myself toward the Sea's perch.

She sits on a chair in the middle of the room, the deep blue water forming a body with a humanlike visage. Her chair is massive, forcing me to tilt my head up to see her. Fish swim through the soft currents making up her body and the sea foam standing in for hair. The currents form a grand, rippling dress that hugs her form. Pearls drip from her arms, starfish adorn her bodice, and coral creates a grand crown.

A grin-like ripple spreads through her face. She hops down from her chair, shrinking nearer to my size. "Thalasseus, you made it."

I stay where I am, even as she approaches and throws her arms wide.

"Come, come, sit. You must be exhausted from all of the time spent on land."

"Sea, what do you need? I wasn't supposed to come until tomorrow." My tone is sharper than I intended.

She peers up at me, almost appearing to pout. "I missed you."

For a moment, I can only stare. Something dark bubbles up in my chest, but I push it away. The Sea is lonely, She's told me countless times. It's unfair of me to be angry.

I owe her too much.

But I still have promises to Kai I must keep. I soften my voice and meet the Sea's gaze. "You said you needed help. I'm here to help."

A flash of pain crosses the Sea's features. She backs away, hugging herself. "No, you clearly don't want me here. Go, if I'm such a bother."

I wince and follow after her. "I'm sorry, I didn't mean it. Please, let me help."

She watches me for a moment before her expression lightens and she smothers me in a hug. The pressure of her embrace pounds on my skull, and the world seems to spin for a moment. I wonder if this is what it feels like to drown. For a moment, every bit of my body feels as if it's on fire as I tense up beyond belief. My chest feels like it's splintering into a million pieces.

I barely hear the Sea say, "I knew I could depend on you."

The Sea drags me down a familiar path to where the ocean spirits live.

I frown at the Sea. "You said you could handle them today. They'll listen if you only—"

She scowls. "They *never* listen, Thalasseus. They hate me."

"They don't hate you."

She shakes her head and sighs. "They think I'm cruel. No one understands me like you do." She fully turns to me, clasping my hands in her own. "You're my only hope."

I sigh. "Okay. I'll wrangle them, but I need to go back right after."

"Must you?"

"Yes. I have a life up there to attend to as well."

"Right, of course you do." She shifts to leave, then peers at me. "Just don't forget little old me while you're off living your adventurous life, all right?"

I offer a smile, hiding the unfair bitterness behind it. "I would never."

She beams at me, then floats off. I force the smile to stay as I swim into the ocean spirits' home. I will never be free of the Sea.

I don't know how much longer I can take this.

I drift through the opening of the cavern, then up to the trapped air inside the cave. It's simple, the stone of the cave shining in a way that's simple but still so beautiful. The spirits look like human children, made of bubbles of air and stray ocean currents. Their eyes sparkle with playfulness, and I've hardly ever seen them without a grin. The fakeness of my smile melts into something real as I watch the spirits play in the waves, their childlike giggles reverberating around the cave.

They remind me of Mac. Young, innocent, free.

I wade to the rocky shore of the cave, catching the attention of a few of the spirits.

"Thal!" They cry in unison, flocking towards me. "You didn't say you'd be coming today."

I grin, not letting any of the anger show. "I didn't know I would be."

One of the spirits pouts, tilting her head. "The Sea made you. She's a bully."

Could they tell that the Sea upset me? I keep my voice soft as I say, "Please don't call her names. She means well."

The spirit drapes herself on a rock, peering at me upside down. "She yells at us when we don't do what she wants."

I exhale. "I'm aware, but you guys need to start listening. You're the only ones who can bring in the tides. *All* of the spirits of the Ocean need to work together, or it'll fall apart. You guys are the most important piece."

"But it's not fun."

I raise an eyebrow. "You're doing something with your friends and family. I'm sure you guys can make it fun."

One of the older ones pops up out of the water. "Really?"

With a smile, I nod. "You don't have to do it the same exact way the rest of your life. As long as the tide rolls in, you've done it right. So, how about you try to do it without me today, and have fun? And listen to the Sea next time?"

They share a look, nod, and jump into the water.

The eldest, however, remains. She looks at me a moment longer. "You should listen to your own words, Thal. Sometimes our old way of doing things no longer serves us as it once did, and we have to figure out our own way—have fun. You're stronger than you think." Her gaze rests on my many bracelets, the artifacts I've pieced together to power the illusion of my humanity. "But thank you. I'll ensure we keep the tides in check. For you."

With a salute, she sinks back into the water, racing to join her sisters.

I smile until she's gone, then let out a breath, turning my face toward the bits of the sky filtering through the opening at the top of the cavern. I'm not unused to the eldest spirit's words. She often tries to break me away from the Sea. But I think she's viewing the Sea incorrectly. Nothing is changing.

Nothing, except me.

The spirits still find joy amongst themselves. The Sea still strives to keep order and balance. So what issue do I have that I can't be content with my place like them? Why did I have to go chasing after the human world?

To escape the Sea. To have my own life.

I shake my head, taking a deep breath. There's nothing to escape from. She cares for me. I promised I'd be gradual and wouldn't leave her all at once. I need to be content with that.

The light in the cavern is dimming with the sunset. I need to return to Kai before he worries. I slide into the water and swim out of the Sea's palace as quickly as I can manage, and propel myself towards the shore as my human illusion pieces itself back together.

But as I reach the shore, I lose my momentum. The water presses on me, and it's almost like I'm fighting against the very will of the ocean to keep moving. I kick my legs hard, straining against the current.

It's worse every time. It's like the Sea's desperation for me is preventing me from leaving. No. I know it *is* the Sea.

But why would she do this?

I keep straining, my vision blurring slightly from the pure force I'm fighting against. But the surface is mere feet away. If I break the surface, it'll all stop. It has to stop.

I strain, and the pressure skyrockets. If I needed air, I would be dead now. I keep kicking, pushing against the water, and finally break the surface. As I strain against the last bits of pressure, there's a loud, resounding *crack.* I freeze, whipping my head around. A sinkhole of darkness forms in my chest, dragging all other feelings in. Nothing's there. And the sun is setting—fast. I get onto shore, shaking the water off of me. I'll be mostly dry by the time I get to the dock. Let's hope Kai doesn't question anything.

I set off running towards the dock, off the sand quickly so it doesn't stick to my shoes. But a strange *twinge* from my shoulder slows me to a stop. Then, it amplifies to a burning sensation filling my whole body. I fall to a knee, gasping out a cry. I shouldn't have felt that. I shouldn't feel pain. I've *never* felt pain—I'm made of wood!

I tug my shirt aside, hands shaking.

The illusion around my shoulder is shattering. And the wood underneath is warped and cracked. I curse under my breath, and fiddle with the bracelets on that arm. My vision blurs as I do, the burning pain only getting worse. The Sea tied her magic to these bracelets, they should be keeping the illusion alive.

But what could have happened? There was no impact. Nothing happened. Not until I was struggling to escape the ocean.

It was the pressure. It shattered the wood. The bracelets aren't strong enough. I take a deep breath, re-covering the injury. The longer it goes, the less the pain bothers me. I keep my focus away from the pain, praying it will fade away. If Kai or Mac sees—how will they react? Mac would be terrified, wouldn't she? Her dad's best friend is a wooden man.

Thalasseus, what happened?

I don't respond to the Sea as I pick up the pace again, racing towards Kai's ship as the sun dips towards the horizon.

You're injured.

Yes, I know I'm injured. It's her fault. It's her fault the illusion I pieced together is breaking. I'll have to get another artifact from the shipwreck the Sea found me in. Then, I can twine it into a bracelet to fix the illusion. The wreck isn't that far from here—but I can't let Kai or Mac get caught in the backlash. The Sea doesn't like me being there. She doesn't want me to dwell on the past.

But I have no other choice. I hope I can return unscathed.

Come back. That illusion does not matter with me. I can fix the wood.

But then, I would lose my family. So, I keep pretending I can't hear her, jogging until I reach the dock, where Kai is waiting. He smiles when he sees me, exhaling in relief. "You're actually on time for once."

I offer a tight smile, biting back the throbbing pain. "Yeah. I'm sorry, the business was last minute. I couldn't avoid it."

"Will you finally tell me what this business is?" His tone is light, but he's watching me closely. Expecting an answer. An answer that I cannot give him.

"I will one day. I just can't right now."

He studies me a moment, then sighs. He knows by now I won't give him another answer. "Did you already eat? Mac and I had dinner at the festival, but I can whip something up for you."

"I'm all right." I don't need to eat like they do. I've done it when I've *had* to, so Kai won't take too much notice, but it's wasteful. Kai nods, and I follow him onto our ship.

"We're leaving in the morning, so rest up. You're the best navigator here, so we'll need you bright and early if we want to get to Dernath on time."

I nod, descending into the hull. I'll have to leave when everyone's asleep. I'll find Kai and Mac at Dernath. The shipwreck is a few hours away from there at the speed I can row, and I'll write a note to tell them where to meet me. But first, I have to fix this illusion.

I lay in my hammock until the entire cabin is full of the crew's snores. Carefully, I set my feet on the ground, each step intentional to avoid a creak, then lift my full satchel, scarf, and jacket. I drape them over my arm, creeping into the halls of the hull and towards the opening.

Before I get onto the deck, I pause before a small mirror and move my shirt aside. The break in the illusion is spreading. The wood is clearly exposed by the base of my neck, and across my shoulder, creeping towards my arm. I don't have much time.

I pull on my jacket, followed by the strap of my satchel over my shoulder.

Thalasseus. I've presented you with a solution. Why won't you take it? The desperation in the Sea's words is overpowering. But there's also a certain anger that hasn't been there before. She's hurt that I'm ignoring her.

But how can she not understand that this was her fault?

I've found my own solution. I'm going back to the wreck, finding another relic, and using it to keep the illusion alive.

"Thal?"

I whirl to face Kai. He sits cross-legged on the deck, a map in front of him, a candle at his side, and a compass in his hand.

I work my jaw for a moment before sighing. "Hi."

Kai raises an eyebrow and sets the compass down next to him. "Where are you going?"

I press my lips together, shifting my weight. "Out."

He watches me for a moment, gaze once again piercing my soul. Then, with a defeated breath, he whispers, "Why won't you talk to us?"

The circles under his eyes are more pronounced, his shoulders bowed, his hands are restless, fidgeting with his sleeves.

I hurt him. I neglected him and Mac while I ran to the Sea. *I hurt him.*

"I do talk to you."

He laughs, a weak sound, and leans back against the bench.

"No, you don't. You joke with us, you work hard, you tell us what anyone can see." He shakes his head. "You know nearly everything about Mac and I. But we know nothing about you. And now you're sneaking off in the middle of the night, and for what? What reward?"

"It's—"

He slams his book closed. "Don't say it's important. I understand that it's *important,* but I don't even know *what's* important for you."

"You guys are." It comes out quietly, almost as if a plea.

Kai finally meets my gaze.

He's not just hurt.

He's angry.

"Then tell me why you're really doing this. Tell me where you're from, why you randomly *disappear.* Tell me *something* about yourself."

I quiet, my breath catching for a moment. I can't tell him *anything* without telling him everything. I don't even know what to say anymore.

I meet his gaze. "I'll use the money to pay you back."

"I don't want your stupid *money,* Thal! I want to know I can trust you when you say you'll be *okay.*" His voice cracks, and he closes his eyes.

"You can—" I slide my hand through my hair, the end of my sentence falling short.

"Why are you going, Thal? Are you in trouble?" Instead of being demanding, like I had expected . . . he's kind. Caring.

I still for a moment, almost reaching for my jacket, almost showing what I am.

But I'm going to fix the magic. I don't need to tell Kai. I don't need to risk his hatred—it'll be back to normal soon. I need an excuse to buy more time. Some reason to be so desperate to go. Maybe I can say a bit of the truth.

"My parents died at sea. I barely survived the wreck." I didn't survive. The Sea saved me, put my soul into this wooden form. I exhale, letting the regret, the wondering of what a different life would be weigh down my words. "I'm looking for it. We haven't been this close for months."

Kai softens, watching me for a moment. My breath stills in my throat as thousands of worries flood my head. What if he doesn't believe me? What if he asks more questions? What if something about that angers him more?

He starts speaking several times before shaking his head and landing on a simple, unobtrusive question.

"Are you sure that you can't wait? There's signs of a storm—"

My shoulders collapse in relief. "It won't get safer before our ship leaves for Dernath. I'll meet you there."

He exhales, part defeated, part something else. He drops his head and returns his gaze to the map.

"Okay. But Thal?"

I look at him, my grip tight on my satchel.

"Don't destroy yourself over this."

"I won't."

He watches me another moment, then nods. "Good luck. Be safe."

I nod in return. I wish luck were real. Because I need all I can get.

I walk to the far end of a dock where a fully prepared sailboat awaits me. I paid a deckhand to secure it yesterday. She's probably the reason that Kai knew I would be sneaking out. I lower myself into the sailboat, then I untie it and push away from the dock, rowing until the wind is able to take over. I slump against the side, trying to ignore the throbs of my shoulder.

I don't think I've ever felt pain before. This is . . . *overwhelming.*

Thalasseus, you're on my waters. Why don't you pay me a visit?

I don't have time to pay her a visit.

The wind carries my whisper to her. "I can't come for a while. I talked to the spirits, they should listen to you."

"Spirits?"

At the voice, I straighten.

Mac climbs out from under a tarp, a devilish grin on her face. My eyes widen and I stand, looking towards the dock. It's already almost out of sight. The wind is *strong* tonight—it'll take forever to get back.

"Mac? How did you—"

"Shelia told my dad you were leaving! I wanted to go with you."

I grit my teeth. This is beyond risky. Now not only do I have to watch out for and protect her, but I also need to make sure she won't see the breaks in my illusion. "Okay. I don't have time to take you back. But you need to *listen,* okay?"

She puffs out her cheeks, but nods after I send her a firm glance.

I settle back down, though the tenseness of my shoulders doesn't fade. "You should get some sleep. It'll be a few hours before we can make it there."

She plops down next to me, mirroring my body language as she closes her eyes. "Okay!"

I smile, looking up at the stars. It's not optimal, but I get to spend time with my family, so maybe this isn't all bad.

Kai's going to kill me when we get back, though.

The ship cuts through the ocean, the waves rippling away. The morning light sparkles off of the water, making an almost magical scene. I exhale a soft breath as Mac guzzles a canteen of water. I hope she told someone what she was doing, or at least left a note.

Thalasseus, why won't you come to me? This plea is more desperate than the last.

I glance at the ocean with a frown, keeping my mouth firmly closed. Mac has already heard me speak to her. I can't explain away anymore.

Yet the Sea's voice is louder. Harder to push away.

I must be near the wreck.

Yes. The one that I *saved you from. The one you* died *in.*

With a sigh, I pull the sail up and pull out the oars so I can go exactly where I need to go.

With the sun lighting up the sky, I can't judge where the wreck would be from the stars, and it's too far from land to use a reef as any sort of marker. But I can use the Sea to guide me. The louder her voice grows, the closer I must be. I should have realized she'd know where I was.

Mac pads behind me, yawning. "Why are we out here anyway?"

I glance at her then look over the open water for another moment. "I need to go on a dive."

"Can I go with you?"

"No."

She scoffs and plops down in a shadow. "It's so hot out here, and boring. I want to learn to dive!"

"You can't."

"Why not? I can learn to hold my breath like you."

I shake my head. "It's not safe."

"I don't want to be safe. I want to go on dives with you. I want to adventure and explore too."

The determination in the set of her jaw and glimmer of her eyes almost makes me pause.

I shift in my seat, touching the skin of my arm. The illusion is fading alarmingly fast. "Diving is dangerous. I don't want you to do it." I take the oars back up, starting again, the movement of pulling them through the water almost therapeutic. As I row, the water almost sparkles under the oars—a sign of magic. I smile a bit. It's most likely the sea spirits. They love accompanying me on these journeys.

But all of a sudden, the wind changes direction. It's . . . *cold,* stinging against us, rid of the usual salty smell. Dark clouds spread rapidly on the horizon. A curse falls from my lips, and I row faster.

Thalasseus. I told you. Come to me.

The Sea is angry. Angry I am not going to her.

Mac sits up, frowning. "What's happening?"

"Storm." My voice catches in my throat after I get the word out. I have to get Mac out, and I have to stay calm to do it.

So why are my hands shaking?

I know the Sea is causing this. I know she's upset I've been ignoring her. But I don't have the time to calm her down.

Mac's eyes go wide, then she starts looking around the floor of the dinghy. "I wanna help."

I force a breath in and out. *Stay calm.* "Stay still. Keep yourself in the boat, no matter the cost. If it tips, get onto the top. If I fall, do not come after me."

Wind roars in my ears. The waves—so calm mere seconds ago—rise up to meet the side of the dinghy. The boat rocks, and Mac barely holds back a scream as heavy clouds torrent ever closer. I keep rowing, forcing the oars against the Sea's tide, away from the storm, and towards the shipwreck. For some reason, the Sea can't touch the wreck itself. Mac should be safe there.

The rain starts, first a drizzle, then a downpour. Still, we're on the edge. We have a chance. I keep pushing at the oars.

"Please," the words—the prayer—fall from my lips before I truly realize, "don't take her from me."

The storm does not relent.

I force the dinghy atop a wave with all the strength I can muster, and it coasts back to the edge of the rain, the drizzle. I don't stop, manipulating the boat with every trick I can think of. Pain begins throbbing through my shoulder anew, but I can't give it a second of thought. Not with Mac's life on the line.

Mac stares at me the entire time, eyes wider than sand dollars. I keep pushing the dinghy up, riding the water out, over and over trying to get to the eye of the storm.

Please. Keep her safe. Take me if you must, but do not harm Mac.

I don't stop until the water calms, and we're in the center of the eye.

Mac stares at me, jaw dropped. Her face is twisted in . . . horror. *Fear.* I blink, then follow her gaze.

My entire arm is wood. I reach up for my face, feeling wood under my fingertips. I stiffen, looking over the rest of myself. My entire body is wood.

The illusion is gone.

Not only is it gone, but the wood is splitting. A chunk falls off my finger, even as I stare at it.

"Thal—" Her voice is hoarse. Small.

I open and close my mouth, over and over, nothing coming out.

Splitting pain echoes up my arm as a large section of the outer wood of my bicep falls, hitting the bottom of the dinghy with a thud. I flinch away from it. The fear on Mac's features is greater than when she saw the storm. Greater than when Kai went missing for a few days. Greater than I've ever seen.

Nausea rises at the edge of my throat. I'm losing her. I'm losing one of the last people I have.

I close my eyes, exhaling a shaky breath.

"What are . . . what's—" She chokes on her words.

I force my expression to blank. She thinks I'm a monster now. But maybe if I can explain—maybe if I can fix the illusion, I can convince her it was a dream. No . . . no, I'll come clean to Kai. Maybe he won't immediately reject me, maybe I can convince him—

The what ifs aren't important now.

"Thal! What's going—what's going on?" Her voice is sharp, high pitched.

I have nothing to hide anymore. It's cruel to leave her with so much unknown. I need her to trust me long enough for me to dive. I'll get an artifact. I'll bargain with the Sea.

Even so, I can't look at her as I speak. Instead, I watch the waves flow past her. "I am a creation of the Sea." My voice is strained, fading out at the end.

Silence spreads over the space, thick, smothering.

"Why are you—why are you breaking?"

"I couldn't fix it fast enough." The strain of the storm probably broke it further too.

"For Dad and me?"

I only nod.

"Why did you hide it?"

There it is. The accusation. The hurt. Why did I hide it? Because I love them. Because I want to be with them. I don't want them to look at me like I'm different. But I *am* different.

The words fall from my lips before I can stop them. Anger, not directed towards Mac, infusing each word. "I'm just a piece of wood. What do I know?"

She frowns and tilts her head. I wonder if she even understands the scope of all of this. She's young. But she'll understand one day. Kai will keep her away once he finds out.

A strike of lightning illuminates her face. The fear is still etched in her expression. I stand, boat rocking beneath my feet. "I need to dive. I'm going to try to get the Sea to drop the storm. If I don't come back . . . I'll make sure you get to Dernath. Kai will know to wait for you there."

"I'm not staying here."

"It's dangerous, Mac!" It comes out in a yell, her name cracking in my voice. "Let me do this. I'll be back as fast as I can. Don't leave the boat."

And with that, I'm over the side, propelling myself towards the ocean floor. The deeper I go, the darker the water, void of the slight light of the fading sunlight. Fish which would usually love the tropical warm water avoid this area more than shark-infested reefs. The Sea is here too often, always angry, her presence powerful and encompassing. Just along the border of the wreck. The only place she cannot reach.

It doesn't take long to come across it. A towering ship, the sails in tatters, the entire hull covered in barnacles. The ship lies on its side, the anchor uselessly sprawled atop dead coral. One of the doors to the cabin still holds onto its hinges, shifting every so often as the current hits it.

I drift through the openings in the ship, each movement more familiar than my own name. I've spent so much time here, finding artifacts and creating an illusion with them.

At the bottom of the boat, rusted pieces of gold and coins glimmer. I root through the metals until one glows at my touch. A bangle. I study it for a moment. It's made of a slightly dulled gold, with emerald etchings along the side that create a winding pattern unfamiliar to this region. Some exotic export, perhaps from some noble family. I clasp it on my arm, and the illusion stitches itself back together. As if it were never gone.

Familiar wondering crosses my mind for but a moment. Of what my parents were doing on a ship like this. What my life would have been if not for the shipwreck. If I would have even believed in the Sea.

But I can't waste time wishing for them. I hardly knew them. I need to get to the surface, I need to get Mac home.

I propel myself off the ship as fast as I can, swimming towards the surface. The currents drag me away from the wreck as I do. And, before I break the surface, the Sea appears.

She smiles, floating towards me as if in the air. She looks different here. Darker. Sharper. Her hair, bioluminescent like the fish in the depths, pools around her face, matched by her eyes. Her sea-foam dress has been replaced with heavy seaweeds, darker in hue. Bioluminescent algae is wrapped in tight tendrils, coiling around her like a jellyfish's tendrils, tangling around her every time she moves. She reaches a hand out.

"Thalasseus."

I tighten my jaw, pushing away from her. "I need to go. Your storm could hurt Mac. Let me get her home."

"Why won't you let me help you? You know I always welcome you in my waters, and it hurts me to see you suffer." Her voice is soft, loving. But behind it, I can feel her distaste at the fact I'm here. And with that, my own anger.

I'm trying to return to my family. Why is she so intent on *controlling* me?

"No, Sea. I'm going."

She tilts her head. "But your home is here, Thalasseus. I love you, the ocean spirits love you. We need you. Why do you act like you hate us?"

I don't hate them. Maybe I've been too harsh. Maybe I've shown my frustration too much.

"Please, come home. I'll make sure the child gets home. They'll move on. They have all of humanity to love. I only have you."

"I can't abandon them."

She frowns, her very form getting stormier. "Oh, but abandoning *me* doesn't bother you at all? Do you not remember how I found you there? How I *saved you*? I know you better than any human ever could, or will. Do you think such a young child could comprehend what you are?"

Any response I can hope for dies in my throat, and I close my mouth. Kai knows me . . . but *does he?*

The Sea smiles. "Look at you, Thalasseus. My perfect boy."

She's right, isn't she? Kai doesn't know me. Even if Mac accepts me, he'll know I'm a monster. I can't return to them.

Sensing my defeat, the Sea reaches out to me. As I reach to take her hand, Kai and Mac's ring on my finger gleams back at me, the gem sparkling in the slight beams of light penetrating the water.

A sign of their unconditional love.

And is that not what it's truly always been? No matter how many times I've disappeared, or how many delays they've had because of me needing to see the Sea. They don't demand anything of me, even though they have the right to.

Not like the Sea.

She demands all of my time, all of my energy. She wants me to be hers, just as I have always been.

I pull my hand back, and her expression darkens. "Thalasseus?"

"I'm not staying with you. We made a deal, Sea. I've helped you plenty, so you need to let me be free."

"But you haven't cared for me like you promised." Her voice rises in pitch.

"You hate me now and think I've been a horrid mother."

I shake my head. "I've tried, Sea. But you promised I could live on land. I'm barely even with my family anymore. I'm leaving."

"No, Thalasseus. You need to *stay.*"

I scoff and try to swim away. The water changes. It's cold, thick. The currents tighten around me, pulling me back towards the Sea no matter how hard I fight. The deeper I go into the water, the more my ears ring, the more my heart races.

And that's when I see, far above me, the telltale eruption of bubbles as Mac jumps in after me. I try to scream, but the sound doesn't escape my throat. A current catches her, dragging her down, past me, faster than I can hope to follow. But I try anyway.

Can humans even survive this far down?

With her focus on Mac, the Sea's currents around me lessen enough for me to break through. I keep swimming, the water harder and harder to see through, fewer fish swim around me. Then, I'm at the ocean floor. I float near the bottom.

There.

Mac is there, losing consciousness quickly. But even as she does, she's fighting with all her might. She reaches out for me, desperate, the plea for help in her eyes. The Sea looms over her with a scowl.

She looks *terrifying.*

The water making up her form is dark and murky, flashing out like lightning, whirling around her. Kelp and seaweed expand out in a billowing skirt. She's missing her normal adornment of pearls. Her crown is full of spikes of rocks and shells. Every bit of her is dark and sharp.

I propel myself towards them, gasping in a panic. I have to save Mac. I have to get her out. I'll let the Sea keep me if that's what it takes.

As I get closer, the Sea turns to me, holding Mac closer as her hum cuts through the water. "See, I've captured the child. With her here, you can no longer run from me." She meets my gaze with a smile, one that's colder than the currents circulating around me.

And even as I'm speeding towards them, Mac's body begins to change. Wood crawls up her arms and legs as she stops breathing. She's slowly going more and more rigid. Currents grab me, stopping me in my tracks, no matter how hard I thrash against them.

"Stop it. Stop whatever you're doing to her."

"Can't you see, I'm making her like you. She's dying, after all. So I can claim her as my own."

"Claim her? You can *save* her! You only need to get her to the surface."

The Sea laughs as I fight a futile fight against the currents to get to Mac. "Why would sending her back to the humans save her? I *am* saving her. You are abandoning me, and she's here to take your place."

The wood has claimed Mac's legs completely.

"Take my place? That's stupid—I'll stay, just let her go."

Even as I fight, the Sea's words echo in my head.

Why would humans save her?

It's the same as all those years ago, when I was a child. She held me close, the same as she did with Mac. She told me she saved me from the shipwreck.

But could she not have gotten me to the surface before I died?

She can be anywhere. If she truly wanted to save me, she could have.

I look at the Sea, eyes wide. "You lied to me—"

She tilts her head, but her smile is sharp. "What do you mean?"

"You didn't save me!"

"Yes, I did. You were dying, and I wanted a child. I tried and tried. I was a perfect mother. I loved you, I gave you everything. But you had to *hate* me in return."

I freeze for a moment. But out of the corner of my eye, I see a soft glow coming from behind the Sea. A familiar glow. That of the ocean spirits, their bubbles foreign in such deep water. They can feel my desperation. I can feel their love.

I need to make sure the Sea doesn't notice them.

"Perfect mother?" I scoff. "You're nothing like a mother. You're cruel and demanding. Nothing I can do pleases you, and I've *tried* more than anything."

"You just wanted to run away to your fake little family."

"A family that loves me more than you ever will. You are not my family. You have not saved me."

The spirits are almost upon us. They hold out their hands, and the water around me begins to warm and loosen from the Sea's icy grasp. The leader gives me a wide grin.

I straighten. The more confident I seem, the more the Sea will focus on me. She won't notice the spirits, not with how angry she is. "I'm taking Mac, and we're going to return to my real family together."

She starts laughing, even as the wood creeps ever closer to Mac's heart. "How do you plan to do that, child?"

"I've made friends. I've loved people while you've only ever controlled them."

"How does that matter?" She scowls.

"Because when you love people, they're *happy* to love you back."

The spirits flock around the Sea, using her rage against her. They pull Mac out of the currents and rush us towards the surface, towards the shore. I wrap myself around Mac, sliding the shipwreck's relics onto her arms in the desperate hope of slowing her transformation. If we can get out of the water, it should stop. It hasn't turned her completely.

The spirits propel me faster than I've ever gone before, until I'm tumbling onto the sand, shielding Mac with my body. I scramble to my feet as soon as I can and set her down gently.

As I hoped, the wood begins to melt away. But her eyes don't open.

"No, no. Mac—"

I drop to her side, pumping my hands into her chest. It doesn't take long for her to spit up water, and she chokes awake, eyes flying open. She sits up, coughing water out.

I look over at the spirits as I pat Mac's back. "Thank you."

The spirits stand at the edge of the waves, the oldest of them smiling at me. "No, Thal. Thank *you*. You have stood up to the Sea. You have given us true freedom—away from a tyrant who has held us captive for years."

"Has she always been so cruel?" I know the answer before she says it, but I still don't know how well I can believe it.

"She has. But you've weakened her. We can be free, thanks to you."

"And *I* can be free thanks to *you*."

She smiles and waves as the spirits melt back into the ocean.

I exhale a breath of relief, bending to lift Mac. She trembles, clinging to me as the cold air brushes her skin.

"Thal?" Her voice is small, weak.

I look at her, beginning to climb the steps back to the docks. "Yeah?"

"Please don't leave us."

Her words strike a chord in my heart. She doesn't fear me. If nothing else, if Kai hates me, at least Mac had faith in me until the end. I smile. "I won't, Mac. I promise."

As I climb the steps, I hear a panicked, "Thal?"

I run to the shout, smiling. "I have Mac. She's okay."

Kai skids around the corner, gasping in relief before stilling, grip tightening on his satchel as his gaze flicks between Mac and me.

That's when I remember. I'm made of wood. I look like a monster. I should leave. Before everything's over. I should maintain a good last memory of them. I take a half step back.

But instead of screaming, instead of taking Mac and shunning me, Kai pulls the three of us into a hug. "You're home."

My vision mists, and I close my eyes, melting into the hug.

And as I melt in, I begin to . . . *feel* it. Their skin against mine, Mac's trembles, the wetness of my clothes. I feel the *warmth* of the skin. I've never felt warmth before.

I open my eyes, looking at myself.

The wood is gone.

I'm *human.*

An echo of the elder ocean spirit's voice sounds through my head. *You have found it. Your home, those who love you. You have released yourself from your burdens. Your soul belongs to you again. As you heal, you are finally your own, untainted by the Sea.*

A grin breaks out on my face.

"Yeah. I'm *home.*"

LYRIC ROSE

Lyric Rose grew up in classical education, and has spent her whole life obsessed with mythology and classics. Today, she strives for the same depth and wonder she grew up with. She writes adult and YA fiction that exposes the dark realities of life while still valuing hope and joy. She loves crafting characters readers can connect to and stories they can get lost in. When not writing, Lyric spends time exploring her worlds through art or curling up to read a good comic or fan fiction.

Achievements

- Drafted five full length novels and one novella.
- Received mentorship and manuscript edits from award-winning authors and editors.
- Learned email marketing from the Author Conservatory.
- Attended Realm Makers in 2022 and 2023.
- Graduated high school with honors a year early.
- Completed and publicly presented a high school capstone on how religion can affect art.

Pitches

- A YA fantasy retelling of *Swan Lake* about a black swanshifter whose touch causes death and the prince she's been sent to kill.

OF SONGS & SWAMPS

Zoe Anastasia

Father once said that of all the magic in the world, music is the only kind that can tug on your heartstrings. The only kind that can add a bounce in your step or lull you into a blissful dream. He went as far as to say it could relieve the sickly, if only for a moment.

Yet as I sit beside Mother in our cottage, his words fade into the background. As if the truth he believed has gathered a layer of dust. Tucked behind a row of medicine bottles and forgotten.

Everyone knows music can't heal illness. And without Father here, I no longer know how to believe in magic at all.

I sag against the wooden bed frame and dip my hands into a pail of water. My fingertips brush against the ragged cloth at the bottom. I wring it out, and the water droplets plink into the pail.

It sounds like notes in a song.

My throat tightens as tears threaten to rise. Father would have pointed out the melody with a soft smile. He would have taken out his ocarina, cupped it in his palm, and tried to mimic the song. And I would have closed my eyes, soaking it all in, pretending time had stopped and we could stay here for eternity.

The heaviness of my own ocarina weighs down my dress pocket. I'm more aware of it than ever. If it didn't feel like betrayal, I'd bury it in a box behind my woodcarving tools.

Instead I drape the damp rag against Mother's creased forehead. Her skin burns underneath her tangle of dark tresses, yet she curls up on the thin sheets, hands close to her chest.

I ease away. *What if she doesn't get better?*

Spring air warms the tiny cottage while wood shavings skitter across the floor. A twinkle of laughter drifts from the swamp. Through the open doorway, I can see my little sister skip across the sinking logs that form a makeshift bridge through the mire.

"Oh my dear, oh my darling," she sings, "have I a story for you. There was a small frog, that nobody loved, and yet he's still singing his song..."

I wave, trying to catch her attention. Her singing will wake Mother if she doesn't quiet down. Ari slows, her mud-splattered skirt billowing around her like swamp lilies in the wind. I place a finger to my lips. She sighs and hums instead.

Turning to Mother, I feel her skin one more time. Cooler. Her breaths barely pass between her lips. "Kaelyn..."

I grip her hand in mine. "Yes, Mother?"

"Can you play the song your father used to play?" She opens her eyes, just enough that I can see the faint glimmer of her blue irises. "The one about the crickets in the swamp?"

"W-well, I—" The lump in my pocket grows heavier. I haven't played it in weeks.

But if it brings her happiness, who am I to say no?

I drag the instrument from my pocket. Memories linger in its woody scent. Father taught me on a simple four-hole ocarina, but after a few years, he made me one with twelve. Each of a different size, they decorate the ocarina's ebony surface. I cover a couple of the holes with my fingers.

Gently blowing into the mouthpiece, I begin the tune.

"A Cricket's Lullaby," Father called it when I was tiny. Although it doesn't have sharp, sudden notes like the creature it was named after, the song carries the same lilting comfort of a night full of insect songs. Mother's eyes glow.

My fingers dance across the small holes in the ocarina, chasing away the suffocating silence with the melody.

It doesn't feel the same as it did when I was younger, however. The sounds, the song, feel forced despite my best efforts to smooth out my movements. My fingers fumble. I accidentally cover the wrong hole and an odd note warbles inside the hollow instrument.

The tune is dull, the "magic" only a ghost whispering along. Instead of warmth kindling in my heart, I feel nothing but ashes long gone cold.

My knuckles turn white as I grip the ocarina too tight. When I release one final breath into the instrument, the wood crackles. So quiet I almost miss it.

I tense. *What was that?*

Turning it over, I study every nook and cranny. The wood slides across my skin, so polished I know only Father could have crafted it. When he taught me how to carve instruments, he always meticulously sanded them until they felt like water trickling against your fingertips.

"One day, Kaelyn," he had promised when he'd given the ocarina to me on the first day of spring, "you shall understand the true magic hidden within music. You'll learn to listen for its gentle sound."

My hands graze against a hairline crack.

I suck in a breath.

A fissure cuts through my heart, leaving me as hollow as the inside of the instrument. What have I done?

I've neglected my ocarina's care. The last thing Father left for me.

"Is something wrong?" Mother's bed creaks as she shifts toward me, then bursts into a fit of watery coughs.

"It's nothing." Before she can see, I slip the ocarina into my pocket and offer her a teacup, instead. Only to find it empty.

Ari slips inside the cottage and plops onto her bed. "I made something for you in the swamp!" Her voice, like a ray of sunshine, startles me. With a flourish, she produces a set of reeds tied together. "Panpipes!"

I take the delicate instrument into my own hands and kiss my sister's forehead. "It's lovely, Ari." I swallow. "I shall cherish it."

She falls still, her gaze on Mother. As if she'd been too distracted to realize she's awake.

Mother reaches for the panpipes, a small smile stretching across her weary skin. "Father taught you well, dear."

I ruffle Ari's pale curls. "Can you please fetch a pail of water?"

She nods and disappears. Mother manages to pat my hand before sinking into another bout of sickly sleep.

After I set a fresh log into the hearth, Ari returns.

"Kaelyn?" Her voice is hesitant and she tilts her head in that far-too-innocent way.

I bristle. Not this again. I fill the kettle and hang it above the fire. "Yes?"

"Won't you come visit the swamp with me?" she pleads. "I always go alone, but it's more fun with two."

I stoke the fire to avoid her gaze. A tendril of flame bursts to life. "I'm sorry, but I must stay with Mother. Besides, I need to carve several ladles for a family in the village."

Ari clasps her hands. "You could take a break from carving. Then you could meet my swamp friends, and they'll help you take care of Mother."

I release a frustrated sigh. Her imagination is wild and untamable. Like Father's. I don't want to douse it, but this isn't the time for stories. "Ari, we need that money. How else are we going to eat?"

She shrugs. "We could find some berries in the swamp. I know a few places—"

"No." I step back from the fire to face her. "Someday I promise I'll visit the swamp with you. But you must wait until Mother feels better."

When she feels better. Not if.

I try to convince myself of those words, but that's as impossible as magic.

Ari tucks one foot behind the other. "Don't you remember all the stories Father told us? They aren't simply fairy tales, Kaelyn. They're true and they'll help Mother." Her tone drops a note, her gaze on the knotted floor. "If only you'd listen."

Before I can respond, she takes off, running back into her swamp. I grip the fire poker, my heart twisting. It looks like my ocarina isn't the only thing I've broken today. The last thing we need right now is to argue with each other. There's too much work to do, too much at stake.

The kettle whistles. I force myself to turn back to the fire and remove the boiling water.

Ari's song picks up again, quieter this time. She splashes into the reeds. "In the midst of a thunderstorm, can you hear its hidden melody? Let the sweet sound soothe thee." Her voice wobbles. "The rain may fall, but fear not, my dear, for I will hold you near."

I let a sad smile slip onto my lips.

Maybe there is whimsy lurking somewhere in the swamp, like Ari says. When rain drums against the swamp's green surface and wind plucks at the reeds like strings on a lyre, it's hard not to wonder if there's a conductor.

Father chose to make instruments for a living. He chose for our family to live beside the swamp, at the heart of nature's music. Why?

And would it really hurt if I visited the swamp once?

I hold my hands to my chest, watching Mother. Her fever could spike at any moment. What if she needed a doctor and no one was there to help? I can't risk her health for a child's bedtime story.

Lowering my gaze to the mortar and pestle on the table, I grind yarrow into an herbal tea. Each repetitive motion wears on my wrist. Pain flares. I grit my teeth. I've spent too much time carving ladles and bowls and chairs, making just enough coin to scrape by.

The sunset casts an amber hue across the garden outside, the heat dwindling. Frogs croak, a cacophony more than a symphony. I slowly exhale. Father used to joke that he knew more about music than any humans around, but he'd forever be an apprentice of the tiny swamp creatures.

I set the pestle aside, the yarrow flowers thoroughly mashed. Lifting the kettle, I pour hot water into a teacup and let the herbs steep. The steam wafts into the air and fills the room with its pungent odor. I wrinkle my nose. At least that means I prepared it properly.

A blue light flickers in the corner of my vision.

I swivel.

It slips behind a tree.

Goodness, what was that? I shake my head. I do need to rest. How long has it been since I've gotten a full night of sleep?

As I tiptoe back to Mother's side, another light flickers in the willows.

It hovers in the trees, growing smaller as it bobs up and down. After a few moments, it extinguishes like a mystery flame from one of Father's fairy tales.

Scalding liquid splashes across my foot. I yelp, jolting the teacup up. Tea dribbles into the saucer. I blow a strand of hair out of my face and glare at the swamp.

Only the lights of tiny fireflies blink back.

Those are real. The familiar golden sparks, like little suns speckling the twilight hour.

But then the faint blue light ignites once more, tugging me to my feet and down the porch steps. The ground squishes beneath my slippers. Murky water stretches as far as the eye can see, only interrupted by crisscrossing bridges. Some lie half-submerged, others rotting.

"Hello?" I call, as if the lights can speak.

Such a silly thought.

My sister materializes from around a tree, her arms overflowing with wildflowers. I can only see the tips of her eyebrows. "Hello, sister! I'm bringing the outdoors to Mother." Her tone is airy as if she'd forgotten our previous conversation, but she doesn't quite meet my gaze.

Did you see a blue light? The question is on the tip of my tongue before I think better of it. Ari climbs the porch steps, a few stray flowers slipping from her stack, and disappears inside.

I watch the color fade from the swamp as night blankets the waters. Father told stories of strange blue lights. Creatures named Will o' the Wisps that would bob to the beat of a song, like they were orchestrating it. Through their motions, they coaxed lost travelers deeper into the swamp. Father's voice always held a note of awe, the crinkle to his smile hinting he knew more than he let on. But whenever Ari asked him where the Wisps led people, he'd only say that we'd have to find out together.

A light flickers before me. In the growing darkness, it shines as bright as a blue sky. I squint, taking a step closer. Is that what this creature is?

My leg sinks into the mire.

I splash backward and slam into the earth. My ocarina tumbles from my pocket and lands in the reeds, while muddy water slides down my skin. My left slipper, now damp and brown, hangs from my foot.

I dump the dirty water out, but not before it seeps into the fabric. I groan. Have I ruined my only pair of slippers? Will soaking and scrubbing them even help?

The light disappears around a tree. I pick up my soiled shoes and ocarina before trudging up the hill instead, back into the cottage. *It's a story. Nothing more.*

When I shut and lock the door, Ari is plucking wildflowers from a vase beside Mother's bed. She weaves them into a crown. Her eyes twinkle mischievously.

I ignore that look, pecking a kiss on her cheek. "Time for bed."

In the corner of our small cottage, Mother shivers. She's tucked her single blanket all the way to her chin. I drape my own around her for when the night grows cold. That won't be too warm, will it?

Ari begins to hum "The Lost Woods." I take the candle beside Mother's bed, light it with the help of the dying fire, and set it on my woodcarving table. Hesitating, I draw the ocarina from my pocket with a sigh and place it down too. *I'm sorry, Father.*

Damp humidity clings to my skin. Crickets chirp outside. With the remaining pail water, I scrub the mud off my shoes. The stains remain. I place my slippers on the hearth, scrape warm ashes into a bin, and arrange fresh logs in the fireplace for morning.

Ari continues to weave wildflowers into a crown, like a mosaic of colors. Her song flows like a breeze through the quiet cottage.

I yawn and sit down at the worktable. Weariness sinks into my skin as I pick up one of my knives and a half-carved ladle. I have the basic shape of the spoon, but it's clunky.

Once I finish this set, I can sleep. At least, that's what I promise myself. But I'm bad at keeping promises.

Shadows creep across the floor as I work by candlelight. I fall into the rhythm of guiding the blade through the wood. Tiny pieces skitter onto the table. A pile of shavings grows. My wrist slowly begins to throb and I bite my tongue.

In the corner of my vision, Ari tiptoes to Mother's side. She rests the finished flower crown on her head.

Mother sighs in her sleep. The wrinkles in her face even out.

I lower the knife. *How is that possible? Do the flowers have some sort of medicinal property?*

Ari slips into bed. "What happened to it?"

I frown. She's pointing at my ocarina. Starlight illuminates the hairline crack.

"Not sure."

Ari leans forward, teetering precariously as she reaches for my instrument. She rests it against her lips and breathes into it. An odd whistle escapes.

I snatch it away. "Shh. I told you, it's broken."

Ari glances at Mother to make sure she's still asleep, then lifts her chin. "If you go to the swamp, perhaps my friends can help."

I open my mouth to say "no," but stop. It's hard to read Ari's shadowed expression. How did she know those flowers would ease Mother's breathing? Does she know something I don't? What if she followed the blue lights? Discovered a secret Father left for both of us?

Warmth kindles inside me at the thought.

"It's also the perfect time." Ari scampers to the window. "They're... What's the word? When they stay up at night?"

"Nocturnal?"

"Yes! We have to go. Just for a little bit?" She tugs on my hand.

I glance at Mother, her chest rising and falling gently. Would it be okay to leave her for a short time? Would she need me?

I look down at the chisels and gouges on my desk. The flicker of hope fades. Even if I did go to the swamp, I'd discover nothing but reeds and floppy fish. The hollow in my chest would cut deeper than ever, and I'd be left with a broken ocarina and no music for Mother.

I shouldn't even be thinking about this.

"It's not safe to leave Mother." I slide my hand from Ari's and shave another piece of wood from the ladle's bowl. "I can't go. I'm sorry."

Ari's lip quivers. She crosses her arms. "Well, then—" Her gaze flickers to the ocarina on the nightstand. "I'm sorry too."

She snatches the ocarina and darts through the door.

I gasp, stumbling out of my chair. "Ari!" My dress trips me. I slam into the doorframe. "What are—?"

She's already disappeared into the tree line.

I swivel to look at Mother. I can't leave her. But I can't let Ari run into the swamp in the dark either.

Sucking in a breath, I shove on my sturdy boots. Despite the full moon that spins tall grass into threads of pure silver and the willows into diamonds, I can't make out Ari's silhouette.

I burst into a run.

Blue lights blink like eyes in between branches. The faint tinkle of my sister's voice drifts farther and farther from our cottage.

What is she thinking?

My heart is a music sheet stamped with a forte. Each heartbeat pounds louder in my chest. The makeshift bridge creaks and cackles beneath my thundering steps. A shadow skips ahead.

"Ari, stop!" My foot slips off the path into the slippery mud. I stagger to the side, barely catching a tree branch before I tumble off the opposite edge. My heart lurches.

Father's story of Will o' the Wisps echoes in my head. What if the true danger lies not in their ability to lure people into the swamp at night, but the swamp itself? What if they're trying to drown us?

I stumble forward. Willow branches, ghostly pale with moonlight, reach out to brush my skin. I flinch. Ari hums a fairytale song—one Mother always sang when we were little, before she became too weak to even raise her head.

A brilliant turquoise radiance appears before me, as if someone has captured the sky. It blinds me. The shadows darken as my vision struggles to adjust.

The light springs away. Whispers follow, but I can't make out Ari's words. A frog croaks in response.

I step gingerly toward the glowing mist, into the sprouts of grass poking above the water before shifting to dry ground. A glade.

I glance around a tree.

Speckles of blue peek between the leaves and grass, but there's no sign of Ari. I wring my hands. *Where is she?*

A flash of light lands on the tree beside me. Giant eyes peer up, blink, and then the blob of light expands.

"*Ribbit.*"

I gasp, stumbling toward the center of the glade, and trip. I hit the ground hard. The small light crawls across the tree, its webbed feet holding it in place. It tilts its head. "*Ribbit?*"

"Aha! My plan worked."

My sister emerges from the trees and kneels on the ground. A dozen bioluminescent amphibians hop around her skirt, while she cradles a few in her arms—tucked beside my ocarina.

Words fail me. Her swamp friends are... "*Frogs?*"

"Yes." Ari lifts her chin.

I manage to sit up and blink at the tiniest amphibian as it leaps onto my knee. Silver dots speckle its skin like stars. But instead of in the sky, the stars are here. At my feet.

"His name is Freckles," Ari muses.

This *can't* be real.

Can it?

"Why didn't you tell me?" I demand.

This time Ari purses her lips. "Would you have believed me if I'd told you frogs could fix your instrument?"

I release a huff. Of course not. That sounds ridiculous.

My sister turns to the brightest frog perched in the tree. The one who led me here. "Oh," she says, brushing the dirt off my arm, "she's okay, don't you worry."

They understand Ari? Or is this another make-believe game?

"*Ribbit...?*"

Ari's smile brightens. "They can help us," she translates. "I told them Father taught you to play many songs, including Mother's favorite, but your ocarina broke."

All the frogs croak in discordant harmony.

She bites her lip. "I-I think Father and Mother knew about them. The 'Wisps.' But I was too little to go into the swamp, and then Mother got too sick to even sing..." Ari grasps my hand. "Maybe if your ocarina is fixed, you can play her favorite song with the frogs. A swamp orchestra! She'll love it. It... it could lift her spirits. Give her strength."

I release a shaky breath as all the pieces of Ari's past behavior click into place. "Is that why you asked me to come?"

Her eyes water as she nods.

My throat tightens at the idea of Mother sitting on one of the makeshift paths years ago, smiling and listening to the magical frogs croak in the night. A tear slips down my cheek.

Is Ari right? Could we bring back Mother's smile by playing her favorite song with all the swamp creatures?

Ari leans forward and drops the ocarina into my lap, while a frog climbs along the sleeve of her dress. I turn the instrument over, finding Father's signature carved into the bottom and the hairline crack beside it.

There's still a problem. Despite all Father taught me, I don't know how to fix an instrument.

The little frog on my knee croaks.

My sister shifts. "Freckles wants to hear its sound."

An audience of amphibians blinks up at me. I swallow as I lift the ocarina to my lips. When I breathe into the mouthpiece, an odd trill escapes.

Covering several tune holes, I play. A tiny semblance of Mother's favorite song echoes throughout as muscle memory guides me. It's not beautiful. It's not even pleasant. The warbling sound whispers then screeches.

I've heard these sounds before. On the first day of spring when Father was carving my ocarina, we sat beneath the rustling swamp trees. He took his knife to the bark, peeling it away and cutting a hollow into the instrument, as toads croaked mere feet away in the underbrush.

When he lifted it to his whiskery lips and softly blew into the mouthpiece, it warbled. Not at all like the polished sound I expected.

"Need to keep adjusting it, don't I?" He smiled and played a string of wobbly notes. "But I rather like its silly sounds, don't you?"

Ari burst into giggles, but I shrugged and asked him questions about all his tools instead—to which Ari responded, "That's boring stuff. Play again!"

And he did, echoing the same odd notes. But then he tuned the ocarina until the notes were as smooth as a raindrop.

Several frogs croak at each other, drawing me out of the memory. I blink. All the notes are broken.

"That," Ari says, "without a doubt, needs fixing."

"But how *can* we fix it?"

Freckles hops across my dress and clings to the side of my ocarina. After croaking a single note, he waits. A line of seven frogs hops forward.

"And?"

Ari claps her hands. "I think I know where this is going."

Each frog croaks, one at a time, with each sound higher than the last. I arch a brow. They're playing the seven notes of music.

Freckles tilts his head, as if to say, "*Your turn.*"

The frogs begin the pattern again. I try to follow along, but fumble. My notes sound nothing alike. Only cracked and broken. But Ari adds in her own string of music to complement ours, humming along. She winks at me. When I try again, the sounds begin to blend with the frog song.

I soak in the music. The basic notes that form all songs. Did Father ever come to the woods simply to tune his instruments with the frogs' help?

Another frog hops forward, this time joining in to time each beat like the metronome Father built for us. But instead of using sound, his luminous skin blinks on and off.

The rhythm shifts as the frogs sing out of order, this time playing a real song. One I know well. "A Cricket's Lullaby." I suck in a breath and try to keep up, my fingers dancing against the tune holes. The music of the night wraps around me as we all play together. After the first song, we move onto another, and another.

The Metronome Frog quickens the beat once more, playing faster than I've ever played.

My fingers fall into the rhythm. The familiarity of the instrument rushes back to me, along with the realization… *I've missed this.* The hum beneath my fingertips, the weight of the notes, the spark of memories.

I want to soak in it forever.

When the frogs bring the final song to a close, I try to draw in a decent breath. My sides heave. Warmth fills me to the brim as I beam at my sister.

Ari tucks her knees to her chin and smiles back. "A round of applause to my dear sister, Kaelyn, for joining our symphony tonight."

The frogs burst into a cacophony of croaks and ribbits. Ari herself claps—a dainty ladylike clap that contrasts the little amphibians surrounding her.

She giggles. "It sounds a little better, doesn't it?"

Eyeing the ocarina, I nod. Does the crack seem smaller too? Or is that only my imagination?

"Now you can play the song for Mother."

A breeze rustles the trees and sends a shiver down my spine. Darkness hovers beyond our safe, cozy glade. Mother. She's all alone. How many songs did we play? How long have I been gone?

My hands begin to shake. I've made a mistake. I should've been paying attention to how much time had passed, instead of getting caught up in a song.

"Ari, we must leave." My voice is strained. I grip a low hanging tree branch, ducking beneath it to reach the makeshift path. *Foolish.* Older sisters aren't supposed to drift into daydreams.

Ari kisses a few frogs on their tiny heads. As if she doesn't understand how serious this could be. "Farewell, my loves. I will see you in the morn."

I grab her wrist. "We must hurry!"

Frogs hop into the underbrush, their blue lights dying. Ari gives me a wounded look, but I shake my head and pull her toward the bridges.

As we run along the rickety path, I try to take deep breaths. What if Mother woke up to find us both missing and it scared her? She'd have no idea where we were. Or what if she tried to find medicine in the cabinet and collapsed?

The path blurs beneath me, the darkness encroaching. But the slices of moonlight keep me from stumbling into the swamp.

The cottage slides into view. I force myself to slow, my heart thundering in my chest. If Mother's still asleep, I don't want to wake her. Ari's hand slips from mine as we climb the stairs and duck inside.

The dying embers of the fire cast a faint glow across the floor. Mother is still in bed. *Thank goodness.*

I tiptoe to her side, praying she'll be tucked into a dream.

Her chest rises and falls, each breath rattling as it passes her lips. She clutches an extra blanket to her chest. I kneel beside her and touch her forehead. It burns.

I suck in a breath.

"Kaelyn?" Ari's voice hitches.

I try to tug the blankets away from Mother, but they're curled tight around her body. I shake her shoulder. "Mother, wake up. You're too hot."

She doesn't stir.

I shake her harder. She's struggling to breathe.

Why won't she wake?

I shoot to my feet and tear a cloak from the wall hook. "Ari, stay with her. I'm going to fetch the doctor."

Before she can respond, I rip open the door and plow into the night.

It takes far too long stumbling through the dark to reach the village and find the doctor. When he meets me, I explain the situation between gasping breaths. But he understands and saddles his horse in a matter of minutes.

We race all the way to the cottage. With every *thud* of the horse's hooves, blue lights blink on and off. The trees blur together. I try to ignore the melody of crickets drifting from the undergrowth. What does it matter if I found musical frogs when Mother is ill in bed? Dying?

My shoulders tremble.

The horse slows to a halt outside the cottage.

I dismount and stumble up the steps while the doctor tethers his horse to a tree. My hands shake so violently, the tarnished doorknob rattles. My knees threaten to give in.

The doctor hurries inside. Ari is sitting at Mother's side, her face stricken with tears. The faint moonlight illuminates Mother's silvery hair. I can't bring myself to look at her pale face.

"Is she going to...?" Ari whispers.

The doctor kneels beside the bed and feels Mother's forehead. I lift Ari from the floor and wrap her in my arms. She presses her watery cheek against my nightgown, holding me tight.

I don't know what to tell her.

Everything blurs and fades. The crickets chirping outside, the shadows of leaves dancing across the floor, the sound of Mother's ragged breathing. Instead, a numbing cold sinks all the way to my bones, until all I can think about is the hollow ocarina in my pocket.

I let my imagination get the best of me, let it feed me fantastical ideas—and now Mother is suffering because of it.

How silly of me to think playing a song with frogs would make her feel better.

How *childish*.

I bite back a sob. The flicker of hope that arose in the woods, as a small group of amphibians connected me to the greater song Father believed in, extinguishes.

I slide my arms away from Ari. Stray hairs fall from my braids and stick to my damp cheeks as I lift my ocarina from my pocket. I can't bring myself to meet my sister's gaze, although I can feel her watching me.

The croaking of frogs outside taunts me.

Father was wrong. There is no greater song, no sweet symphony. There's only the whine of reeds and the click of the doctor's bag and the weight of my sister's hope upon my shoulders.

Nothing about this is magical, and I was foolish to think otherwise.

I cast the ocarina to the floor. The impact splits the instrument in two.

Ari gasps, but I simply bury my head in my hands.

After what seems like hours, the doctor rises and sets an apothecary jar on the bedside table. "Give this to your mother four times a day. It should help her fever fade." He gives me instructions for how much to give her as well as symptoms to look for. I take it all in, somehow storing the information in the back of my mind. My head swims.

Without moving from my spot on the bed, I drop coins into his palm. He disappears.

My eyes must be bloodshot. I rub them, trying to get the room to sharpen into view. There's work to do. I should refill Mother's teacup. Slice cheese for breakfast. Finish carving a set of ladles. But I can't bring myself to move.

My gaze rests on the broken ocarina. Silver light pools inside the hollowed-out surface, illuminating a dark image in the wood.

I kneel on the floor. Lift it.

A rough sketch of a frog gazes up at me. Father must have whittled it. Spots decorate its skin—spots that look just like freckles.

Why would he...?

The answer dawns on me as I trace the frog's outline. He hid it inside, not knowing if I'd ever see it. But if I did, he knew I'd need it.

It was Father once again pointing me toward the swamp. Toward its music.

My lip trembles.

Holding the pieces of the ocarina in one hand, I rise.

Mother draws in a ragged breath. Petals from Ari's flower crown litter the sheets around her pillow.

Thoughts war inside me. She needs rest. And yet, I can't forget the soft smile that had spread across her lips when I'd played a song for her. Or the way Ari lit up when she'd asked me to put together a swamp orchestra.

How can I bring the music to our cottage?

How do I get the frogs to come back?

I turn in a circle. No lights illuminate the willows.

Ari is slumped against the side of Mother's bed with her blanket tucked around her, her mouth open as she drifts into an uncomfortable sleep. Something slips from her hand and clatters onto the floor.

Her panpipes. The ones she'd made for me.

An idea flickers to life. The frogs would know the sound of the panpipes—Ari probably made them from the reeds surrounding the glade. Surely they'd listen for its music. But would it bring them out after I'd scared them away?

I hesitate. It's been too long since I've played this instrument—the only song I can think of is "The Song of Frogs," the one Ari always sings while she skips through the woods.

Slipping onto the porch, I lift the panpipes and play the first notes. As my fingers warm up and mold to the curves of the instrument, the music smooths out. Echoes through the swamp. *"Oh my dear, oh my darling, have I a story for you..."*

I let the notes drift like wind through the hollows of trees. My breath catches.

Nothing happens.

What if this isn't the way to reach them?

Something shimmers in the distance. A frog, bobbing up and down like beats to the song as he leaps from tree to tree. Another follows.

I play two more verses. Lights dance through the swamp, like glimmers on waves, and the frogs multiply. I stand on my tiptoes and grin. How is it possible to feel light as a breeze?

When the spotted frog from the glade hops onto my boot, I lower the panpipes. "Freckles. Would you like to play another song?"

Freckles ribbits quietly.

I slip into the cottage, glancing back to see a trail of bioluminescence. I prop open the door and tuck my arm around my sister. "Ari."

She startles. "What—?"

"Shh."

Still clutching the panpipes, I sit on the edge of Mother's bed. Ari huddles beside me, her skin covered in goosebumps.

When I gesture outside, she draws in a sharp breath. "Are we going to play?"

I nod.

Beyond me, the reeds on the edge of the swamp rustle, while the bark on the trees appears to move. It's the other frogs, leaping down and gathering on the porch. They sit on the railings and windowsill, on the muddy fabric of my skirt and the water pail. One even splashes into Mother's teacup.

Freckles leaps onto my shoulder and blinks up at me. *"Ribbit!"*

Mother stirs. Something flickers in her eyes when she sees both me and Ari sitting with her. She glances at the amphibians all around. "W-what is going on?"

A smile dances across my lips and I raise the panpipes. "You wanted us to play your favorite song, remember?"

I blow softly into the reeds, skimming their surface with my lips. The frogs' throats expand in a ribbit as we start "The Cricket's Lullaby." The song wavers at first, and then smooths out. It's as soft as the ripples across the swamp waters, as gentle as a lily petal. Ari begins to whistle, mimicking the insects, and the frog song wraps around us to create our own little symphony.

Mother sits straighter, the bed frame creaking beneath us. The blanket falls from her shoulders and she begins to hum weakly to the song.

My heart flutters at the sound.

When a frog starts another tune, I follow along. All the different swamp songs weave together like strands of vibrant yarn, from the owl cooing in the tree branches to the crickets chirping at the roots. But nothing compares to the symphony of the lilting panpipes blending with the deep croaks of the frogs.

As the song comes to a close, the last notes echo in the hollows of the makeshift instrument.

Mother wraps her arms around both me and Ari.

"Thank you," she whispers, her voice watery. "How did I get the best daughters in the world?"

Tears well in my eyes. I lower the panpipes and hug her back. As the three of us huddle on the bed, the music of the swamp drifts onward.

Like time has been captured in the notes.

Is this what Father meant when he said I'd one day learn the true magic hidden within music?

I tousle Ari's curls. "It was Ari's idea. To bring the frogs to you."

Mother smiles. The glimmer in her eyes is real. It's as real as the glow from the magical frogs hopping onto the porch steps.

She whispers something to Ari. Something about a box. Kneeling on the floor, my sister unearths a tiny chest from underneath the bed, the thin detailed wood from a long-ago memory.

I reach forward to lift the lid. Moonlight catches on Father's messy scrawl. His notes. Dust covers the paper, but when I blow against it, the particles swirl in the air.

"Perhaps, if you wanted," Mother says, her voice still frail as she picks up a small notebook from the bottom, "you could continue your father's work?"

I flip through the crinkled pages and sketches of ocarinas in-the-making.

How had I not known about this? That Father wrote every detail about how he carved his instruments?

As if sensing my question, Mother lightly squeezes my hand. "He wanted me to give it to you once you were ready."

I draw in a breath. From the fractured pieces of my ocarina, the frog sketch smiles.

If frogs helped Father master his craft, perhaps they can help me mend my ocarina too. Perhaps I'll be able to play songs on it for Mother and Ari once more.

I smile at her. "I'd love to."

"I have an idea," Ari says, cradling a frog close to her chest. "To make your instruments extra special."

I tilt my head. "What's that?"

She taps the frog sketch. "Whittle art into all your instruments. To remind others where the heart of music belongs."

I run my finger along the smooth wood, imagining it. Traces of wind and ripples of water. Etches of willow trees, musical notes, and tiny frogs.

It will be a tale of their music. Of light and laughter and loved ones cradled close.

Of songs and swamps.

ZOE ANASTASIA

Zoe Anastasia grew up in an Army family, moved all over the country, and discovered along the way that whimsical fantasy stories feel like home to her. She writes to illuminate the darkness and show the girl tucked in the corner that she is seen and belongs.

When Zoe isn't daydreaming about magical humpback whales and butterflies who can speak, she's usually wandering through nature or making apple cider donuts at her local pumpkin farm. Wary of crafty, book-thieving monsters, she also runs The Fable Fortress, a shop filled with bookmarks and sleeves to protect your precious tomes from harm.

Achievements

- Drafted seven novels, two novellas, and dozens of short stories.
- Received two professional edit letters, including one from award-winning YA author Nadine Brandes.
- Launched The Fable Fortress and sold thousands of bookmarks and book sleeves.
- Published three flash fiction stories with Havok Publishing in the past year.
- Received manuscript requests from multiple publishers.
- Attended the Realm Makers Writing Conference for six years in a row, as well as Write to Publish and HopeWords.

Pitches

- *Fable* meets *Winter, White & Wicked* in a YA fantasy about a dreamer who must defeat a storm-wielding Leviathan to protect her little sister, even as she battles her own sleep disorder.
- *The Legend of Zelda: Twilight Princess* meets *Frozen* in a YA fantasy where a telepathic princess and her chess-prodigy sister must find a star fragment in order to banish the Shadow Wolves from their kingdom—if their own secrets don't destroy them first.
- *Wishtress* meets *The Legend of Zelda: Breath of the Wild* in a YA fantasy where a healer and her moss monsters must unearth the secrets of the spreading ice plague, before it can freeze her own brother's heart.

THE GLASS TREE AT THE EDGE OF THE WOOD

ZACH SOLLIE

Immaculate. That was how he needed to appear. Immaculate and invisible.

Rylan tucked a loose strand of dark hair back under his yellow headband. Thankfully, there wasn't anyone around to have noticed the slip. He returned his hands to a folded position in front of himself as he walked deeper into the citadel.

Most of the hallways had been void of people so far, thank the gods—

Did he really want to thank one of the gods today? He was, in fact, sneaking into one of the holy citadels to steal their divine words for personal gain. Maybe he'd hold off from thanking them for now. For today, he'd thank his luck.

He rounded a corner and almost ran into one of the sage apprentices. The young man's eyes went wide and he gave a low bow to Rylan before hurrying off.

It must be true that no one questions those who appear like they belong.

A small smile played at the corner of Rylan's mouth. He used to think the bold yellow robes of the sages were gaudy and an eyesore, but after donning the outfit, he rather enjoyed that people only saw the color and not the person wearing it. Very convenient for a thief.

Last night, the sages lit the purple flame, signaling that the Oracle had received the location of the latest Glass Tree from the gods, the first one in months. In a few short hours they'd announce the location at the citadel's Proclamation Grounds.

They said the public announcement kept everything fair, so no one person would have an advantage. Not the truest of statements. Those with access to wealth, horses, and connections were the ones who reached the Tree first and received a divine gift.

Rylan's plan was simple: steal the information before the announcement and get a head start. Not the wisest idea in his thirty years of life, but the Oracle did say that many of the gods favored the bold; and his plan was definitely bold.

I'll get it for us, Leah. He touched his pocket where a small, leaf-shaped locket sat. *I'll make sure others can get a happy ending.*

The trickiest part was knowing where to look. Not a single room bore any sign or marking that would indicate what lay inside. Rylan's best guess was something as important as the location of the Tree would be kept deep within the citadel.

He continued forward until the hallway opened into a large circular room with an enclosed chamber in the center, like a pit at the center of a peach.

The chamber had a single door on one side, carved from the auburn wood of an azarth tree, considered to be the most sacred of plants. Only sages could cut them down for use. If that didn't signal a holy place, nothing would.

Patience.

He couldn't rush. If he was caught, then all his careful planning would be for nothing, and someone else would reach the Tree first and pluck a leaf from it. Then the magic would cease and everyone would wait for the gods to plant another Glass Tree somewhere.

Rylan glanced around. Four other halls led to this room, but a quick walk around the central chamber ensured he was alone.

He approached the door and tried the handle.

Locked.

Excellent. That meant whatever was kept inside was worth locking away.

Rylan withdrew two thin pieces of metal from his sleeve and inserted them into the lock. There should be an internal latch that he could—

"Um, what are you doing?"

Rylan spun around and found himself staring at a young girl, maybe fourteen or fifteen, and a good head shorter than himself. She wore a poorly fitted blue robe—the mark of a sage's apprentice—with the hood barely covering her red hair. At her side, she carried a bulky leather bag.

"Who are you?" Rylan hissed. He straightened and crossed the distance between them in two swift strides. Behind her, the hallway was empty.

Good.

"You don't belong here," he said, trying his best to sound like one of the sages. "I should—"

"Call the guards? Me too," the girl said. "You're clearly trying to break in." She pointed at the lockpick set that he'd forgotten he was still holding. "I think we're after the same thing. Friend."

Rylan's neck tensed and he bit his lip as he stared at the girl. "How did you get in?" he asked.

And how can I get you to leave?

She shrugged. "I just bowed to every sage I saw. They seemed too busy to deal with a humble apprentice."

She pushed past him and walked to the door. Dropping her bag on the ground, she massaged her shoulder before pulling out a small glass vial.

"What are you doing?" Rylan grabbed it from her hand.

"Hey."

"Quiet, kid. I got here first."

The vial was a beautifully designed glass container with an interweaving pattern of blue and green stripes. Inside, he saw a murky silver liquid.

The girl snatched it back. "As a co-thief, I think we should work together. It's not gonna hurt you if we both see the location. Besides, you clearly have longer legs than I do, so you'll get to wherever the Tree is first. And if you try to stop me, I'll scream. Then we'll both get caught." She gave him a wide smile and uncorked the vial.

Rylan tried to seize her hand, but she ducked under his arms and poured the metallic liquid on the door handle. It sparked and crackled, the noise echoing through the room and down the halls. The girl's eyes went wide as she stepped back.

"What were you thinking?" Rylan hissed.

He pushed her out of the way and reached out to wipe away the sparking liquid with his sleeve. He clenched his teeth, praying it wouldn't burn his arm off. Thankfully, the liquid didn't react to his clothes. He glared at the girl.

"Splinters! That wasn't supposed to happen," she said. "It was supposed to melt the handle off. Aghhh—" She pressed her palms against her forehead. "I can't believe I got it wrong."

"Keep your voice down."

"I worked for a whole week getting every stupid measurement right."

"Shut up."

"It's like I can't even—"

Rylan covered her mouth and listened.

The unmistakable sound of footfalls broke the silence. The girl's gaze darted to the nearest hallway. Rylan swiped at the still sparking handle with his sleeve, eliminating any indication of their presence, before grabbing the girl's arm and shoving her toward the backside of the central chamber.

The footsteps stopped as someone entered the large room. If whoever it was decided to walk the perimeter of the room, they'd be seen.

The girl tried to keep her bag steady, but it shifted and whatever she had in there clinked. She bit her lip.

The footfalls began again, this time heading in their direction.

Rylan tore a button off his robe and threw it down a side hallway, causing a soft *plink*, *plink* as it bounced away. He grabbed the girl's bag, keeping it still, and inched around the central chamber. He risked a glance and watched as a sage followed the sound of the button down the side hallway.

Rylan counted to twenty before dashing back to the door.

"Quick." He inserted his lockpicks into the handle.

"We should run," the girl said.

"Feel free."

"The sage is bound to come back."

"Almost there." Rylan shut his eyes and twisted his tools.

Click.

He grabbed the handle and turned. The door opened, and the girl rushed into the dark of the room ahead of him. He shut the door behind himself, trying not to make a sound, and relocked it.

Rylan let his breath out in a long sigh. Finally, something worked. Those weeks of practice picking locks actually paid off.

He straightened and faced the room, sight adjusting to the darkness.

The space was far more simple than he would have guessed. There were no furnishings except a glass pedestal in the center of the room. He took a reverent step toward it. Best not offend any gods who might be watching by rushing forward.

Atop the pedestal lay an old, weathered book. Lines of elegant text covered both pages. The last few lines were dated today:

> I received a vision from the god Poldac. He has blessed the world with another Glass Tree and placed it at the far edge of the Withering Wood. I saw that one must enter the wood, cross the river, and ascend to reach it. May Poldac's favor rest upon us.

"Wonderful," Rylan muttered. He stepped away from the book and closed his eyes. Of all the places the gods could place it . . . the Withering Wood? His head start now felt foolish.

"What'd it say?" The girl scurried over and read the page. "Oh, splinters. That's not good."

"Brilliant observation, kid."

"So, how're we gonna do it?"

Rylan gave her a flat stare. "We? We are not going to do anything but leave before they find us. With a bit of luck, no one will know anyone's been in here."

"But—"

"Save it till we're outside."

Rylan pulled out a small piece of paper from a pocket and copied the text. When he finished, he walked over to the door and placed his ear against it.

Silence. Good.

He opened the door and motioned for the girl to follow him. They slipped out and started walking away from the central chamber.

Each time they came across another sage, Rylan grabbed the girl by the arm and quickened his pace, trying to make it appear like a sage dragging his apprentice along to receive punishment.

Once outside the citadel, Rylan hurried into an alley near the docks. He stripped off the yellow robes from his traveling clothes he wore underneath then bundled the robes up with a rock and dropped them into the river.

He searched behind a few discarded crates until he found the one with a loose back and withdrew a travel satchel he'd hidden there, packed and ready. From inside, he took out a weathered jacket and boots and put them on. He checked to make sure he had everything: rope, hunting knife, extra shirt, waterskin, notebook, enough dried meat and bread for three days of travel, and coin to buy a night of lodging if needed.

"I'm Emie, by the way."

Rylan stopped and looked up. The girl stood there with her red hair, bright green eyes, and a dumb grin on her face. She'd changed into traveling clothes as well, a rugged vest and green cloak. Apparently, she, too, had packed everything needed to quickly leave town into her obnoxiously bulky bag—a bag which she still struggled to carry with anything resembling ease.

"You're still here?" Rylan walked to the end of the alley and looked around to see if she'd been followed. "Go away, please."

"I think I'm gonna stick with you."

"No, thank you."

"Yes, thank you." She hefted her bag higher on her shoulder. The contents clinked together again.

What on earth does she have in there?

"You seem like you have a plan," Emie said. "I'm definitely not interested in going into the Withering Wood by myself."

"Sorry if I wasn't clear." Rylan put a hand on her shoulder and bent down to stare her straight in the eyes. "I do not need, nor do I want, help. Have a lovely day."

He started walking away.

"I'll tell on you."

He stopped, jaw tightening.

"If you don't let me tag along, I'll tell the sages about how you broke in and stole the information. Even with a head start, you won't get very far."

"You'd be in trouble too."

Emie shrugged. "I'll be in trouble if I don't find the Glass Tree. I need it."

He turned back to her. For the first time this morning, the girl's face darkened and she pressed her lips together in a paper-thin line.

His head start was slowly ticking away.

There's no way she'll keep up with me, he thought. *And after walking for an hour carrying that bag, she'll likely give up.*

"Fine," he said. "Just don't slow me down."

Slinging his satchel over his shoulder, Rylan strode away from the docks with the girl trailing in his wake. They passed by the fishermen hauling their catches from the morning and wove through the market square where the scents of fresh bread and cooking meat mixed in the air. Once outside of town, they quickened their pace until they arrived at the edge of the Withering Wood as the sun reached its height.

Rylan let out a long, controlled breath as he stared at the forest. The surface of each tree looked more like thorny black shards than bark. Inky, barbed vines snaked up their trunks as if the wood was on the verge of consuming itself.

Rylan shut his eyes and focused on the memory of Leah. She put on a brave face despite the illness. She held on to her belief of happy endings despite her pain.

He opened his eyes and stepped into the forest.

Branches intertwined like a dark woven blanket, and the sunlight struggled to reach the forest floor. A pair of ravens broke the silence with sharp calls that almost sounded like they were saying, "Run Away."

"You ever been here before?" Emie asked, following close behind him.

Of course he hadn't. He wasn't an idiot. Rylan stepped over a fallen branch that looked way too much like an arm and ignored the girl.

"Because that would be helpful if you knew your way around in here," she continued. "Before today, I'd never met anyone dumb enough to set foot in the wood. But I guess we're both desperate."

"Is this how it's going to be with you?" Rylan cast her a glare.

"What?"

"The talking. Are you one of those kids who continually has to make conversation?"

Emie bristled and set her hands on her hips.

"First off, I'm not a kid."

Rylan cocked an eyebrow.

"I'm fifteen! Well, okay. I'm fourteen, but my birthday is in a couple months. So, basically fifteen. Which puts me at least three years out from being a kid." She held up three fingers as if Rylan couldn't do the math in his own head.

"We clearly have different definitions on what kid means."

"And I'm only asking questions so I have a better idea of what I'm getting into."

"You didn't bother thinking ahead on that one?" Rylan shook his head and examined the directions he'd written down: Enter the Wood, Cross the River, Ascend to reach the Tree.

Rylan paused to listen for the sound of a river, but aside from the ravens, the woods remained silent, as if making noise invited unwanted attention.

Emie tried adjusting her pack as they walked, but it slid off her shoulder. A colorful vial dropped out and fell to the ground. "Splinters." She bent down and shoved it back inside.

Rylan nodded to her bag. "What were you expecting? A traveling pack should be small and easy to carry. Emphasis on easy."

"Sorry if my being prepared bothers you." Emie finished repacking and hefted the bag back onto her shoulder.

"What do you even have in there?"

"Food, potions, extra—"

"Potions?" Rylan asked. "Is that what you used on the door back there? A potion?"

Emie blew out a long breath. "Yes," she muttered. "It didn't work like I planned. But I have others. In case we're in a fight or something. Ya never know."

"A fight?" Rylan looked her up and down. "You'd better pray it doesn't come to that. And what's a potion going to do? Spark like the last one? I don't think that's going to help."

"What's your plan if we run into someone out here? Steal another robe and pretend you're a sage?"

"My plan is to keep my head start and not run into anyone. Unless I'm wrong, that's your best chance too. So I'd appreciate a little silence as I try to find the way."

Searching the ground, Rylan noticed what seemed like a path deer might make leading deeper into the woods. And if this was traveled by deer, they would need to stop and drink . . .

The bark on the trees had grown darker and more cracked. Rylan expected to smell rot or decaying flesh, but the forest smelled like any other woods—earthy and alive. It was like the Withering Wood kept trying to confuse those foolish enough to enter by playing with their senses.

"Not the most welcoming place, eh?" Emie said, clearly giving up on her promise to remain quiet.

He glanced at her and saw apprehension on her face. Leah had that same look near the end.

"You mean you don't find the eerie silence encouraging?" he said, trying to lighten the mood like he'd done with his sister.

"And you do?" Emie scrunched up her brow.

"I'm joking."

"Wow." Emie pushed past Rylan. "If you're making light of things, then it must really be bad."

As the day progressed, so did Rylan's concern that they were traveling in the wrong direction. The path kept weaving around trees like it forgot that paths were supposed to lead somewhere.

The first step was to enter the wood. They'd certainly done that. The Oracle's writing said they must cross a river, but he hadn't seen as much as a stream since setting foot in here.

Was this the challenge?

Every person who reached a Glass Tree said they faced a challenge along their journey. No two had been identical. One man from the southern regions said he had to venture deep underground with no light for two days before finding the Tree. Another said he had to outwit a bear. Getting lost in the Withering Wood fit the concept of a challenge.

Rylan paused, studying a particularly gnarled tree that looked like a drowning man reaching out for help.

"Did we pass this before?" he breathed out softly.

Emie stepped up and wiped her brow. "Now that you mention it, it kinda looks familiar. Should we try a different direction?"

Rylan watched as a raven landed on a branch and stared at them. "We need a better vantage point." He walked over to a tree and began to climb.

It wasn't hard making his way up. With so many twisting and bent limbs, there were almost too many options.

He reached the top and took a deep breath of air. The trees didn't appear as blackened from here, bathed in the soft glow of the setting sun. Off to the west he saw a break in the trees and caught sight of a river. Good. They were heading in the right direction.

Rylan paused before climbing back down. The first stars would come out soon. The last time he'd watched the stars, he and Leah had been out on the hill behind their house. They'd made up fake constellations, each trying to outdo the other with silliness.

He hadn't watched the stars since.

"What'd you see?" Emie asked before Rylan made it all the way down.

"The river's near. Maybe two more hours."

They kept walking until the light began to fade. Rylan didn't want to trek through the Withering Wood at night and risk getting completely turned around when he was so close. And by the way Emie kept glancing at their darkening surroundings, he guessed she'd heard the tales of nocturnal monsters that lived out here. Most likely only stories, but maybe best to light a campfire and wait until morning.

They found a small clearing and made camp. Rylan gathered a few sticks together and started digging around in his bag for a piece of flint when Emie withdrew two small bottles. She emptied the first over the sticks, coating them in a clear liquid. Then she uncorked the second bottle and let a thick yellowish substance drop onto the wood. It sparked twice then caught fire. She looked up at Rylan, a huge grin covering her face.

"It worked!"

"Yes," he said, offering her a piece of bread and dried fish, thankful the fire hadn't exploded in their faces.

They started eating in silence. Emie nibbled at her food, but kept glancing around into the darkness.

"Do you work for a potion maker?" he asked, trying to distract her.

Emie nodded. "Yeah, well. I guess it's more complicated than that. I was an apprentice."

"Was?"

"That's why I need to find the Tree." Emie took a sip out of her waterskin. "I messed up on some of the potions and Master Wielind . . ." She set her water down and stared daggers at the fire.

"We can talk about something else."

"No. It's all right. He said I was the worst apprentice he'd ever seen and my parents should be ashamed to have me as a daughter." Emie shrugged like it was no big deal and went back to staring at the fire, her eyes burning hotter than the orange flames.

"You could always find another master to train under," Rylan ventured.

Emie turned from the fire and shook her head. "I tried that already. Master Wielind told all the potion shops how much I messed everything up and now no one will take me on. But if I receive the blessing from the gods and become a great potion maker, he'll have to take me back and my parents will be proud of me."

"I'm sure your family isn't ashamed of you."

"Yeah, well . . ."

Rylan reached out, took one of the vials, and examined it. Colorful swirls of red and gold accented the bluish liquid inside. He smiled. It was like the colors of Leah's favorite type of sunsets; the ones where the sky was clear and you could watch as the warm colors shifted to blue and the stars came out. He looked up, but the dark patchwork of branches blocked out any stars.

"Why the colors? Does it tell you what potion's inside?"

"No," Emie said, voice hesitant. "I just like designing the glass myself." She withdrew another bottle and ran her fingers over it. It had tiny silver bird-shaped patterns inlaid onto the glass. The images rose around the vial like birds taking flight on a summer's day.

"Master Wielind said I was tricking people into buying non-working potions by sticking them in fancy glassware," she said with a pained scowl.

"They're beautiful," Rylan said. Leah would have loved them.

"Thanks." Emie's face softened, and her smile was like the sun peeking through the clouds. "I used to draw as a kid, then one day I realized that I had the equipment at Master Wielind's shop to create the bottles myself, so I started experimenting with it." Her face lit up. "I once made this bottle that looked like a thunderstorm with lightning flashing in the clouds."

"And you never considered finding a glassblower master?"

"A potion apprentice holds higher status than a glassblower," Emie said. "That's what my parents wanted. And I'm not completely useless at potions. These" —she patted her bag— "should work perfectly. Not that it matters now.

"No one will take me on after what Master Wielind said. Now you know why I need to find the Tree."

She straightened up and looked around their campsite, clearly done talking about herself. "What about you? What's your story?"

"You mean besides camping out in the Withering Wood with a kid?"

"I said don't call me—"

"I know, I know." He reached into his pocket and took out a small leaf-shaped locket. "I had a little sister, Leah." His smile faded as he said her name, like how the shadows of the Withering Wood consumed anything bright or hopeful.

"She got sick," he continued. "I did my best to help her, telling her stories. I thought distracting her from her pain might help, might give her enough strength to get better, but in the end it didn't matter. She died." Rylan met Emie's eyes. "That's why I'm here. I will find the Tree and ask for the gift of healing so no one ever has to suffer like my sister did."

"I'm sorry," Emie breathed, and let her gaze fall to the dirt.

"Get some sleep," Rylan said. "I'm going to take another look around."

Emie nodded and lay down.

Rylan found another tree and climbed up, breathing in the fresh air from above the dark canopy of the Withering Wood. The moon cast a pale light across the tops of the trees.

If everything went well, tomorrow they'd find their prize and he'd get his gift of healing. Then he could stop others from hurting like he had.

He paused.

A trail of smoke rose from the treetops a couple miles back, far too close. It had to be another campfire. The proclamation had gone out and others were on the trail of the Glass Tree.

"Rylan." Emie's voice pulled him out of sleep., surprised to find it still dark out. "We should go."

The two set off. Rylan set a fast pace, trying to keep his head start. If Emie hadn't woken him up . . . He set his jaw and pressed on.

They reached the edge of the river as the first rays of morning light pierced the canopy of leaves. The waters roared and churned, jagged rocks poking through like dozens of unsheathed blades ready to tear apart anyone crazy enough to cross.

A derelict bridge made from frail-looking ropes and planks of wood spanned the distance to the other side.

"Splinters," Emie muttered. "Looks like it was made hundreds of years ago. Think it's safe?"

"Doesn't really matter now." He couldn't see another way across and they needed to keep moving to stay ahead.

The gods favored the bold.

Rylan placed a foot on the bridge expecting to hear a snap. It held. He put one foot in front of the other and started inching his way to the other side. This was worse than the time he'd tried climbing up a tree to knock down a beehive. The bridge shifted under him, and he spun around to find Emie stepping out.

"Wait till I'm across!"

"No, thanks," she said, taking a few more steps out onto the rickety bridge. "I'm not waiting around for the bridge to remember how old it is and break on us."

He wanted to say more, but she had a point. "Just be careful," he said, continuing forward. He crossed the rest of the distance without issue and waited for Emie.

"Why don't you two stop right there?" a gruff voice said.

Rylan glanced back and saw a man with a long hunting knife strapped to his side standing on the riverbank behind them.

So much for the head start.

"Greetings, fellow traveler," Rylan said with a smile. "Lovely day."

He didn't need to see Emie's raised eyebrows to know how stupid that sounded. It didn't need to sound eloquent, it only had to keep the man talking long enough to figure out a plan.

"I would love to discuss the day from this side of the river," the man said. "Join me over here, would you?" The man rested a hand on his knife, focus shifting between Rylan and Emie.

The knife.

I have a knife!

The bridge was the one way to cross the river and it was ready to fall . . . This was it. He could cut it and stop anyone else from following them. The Glass Tree would be his.

How fast could he draw his own knife and cut the ropes? But Emie was only halfway across. Her bulky bag kept throwing her off balance and preventing her from moving fast.

Emie pressed forward.

The man on the far bank shook his head and strode forward. "I don't want to resort to force, but I will." He took his first careful step out onto the old wood.

Rylan had to act. If he cut the rope now, then both Emie and their pursuer would be out of the picture. He had to turn on her at some point, right? She was a liability. A flaw in his plan.

His fingers curled around his knife.

She'd fall into the river.

He stopped, gaze darting to the waters below.

The wet rocks pierced the top of the river like the teeth of a starving wolf.

His grip on the knife loosened. Was he really willing to do anything to reach the Tree first?

"Rylan!" Emie called out, still struggling with her bag. The man behind was gaining on her.

Blast.

Rylan rushed back onto the bridge. He shoved Emie ahead of himself and drew out the knife.

"Go!" he shouted.

Once they were safely across, he'd cut the ropes and let their pursuer fall along with the bridge. He risked a glance back. The man was halfway to them. Rylan placed his blade against one of the ropes used for holding on to.

"What are you doing?" Emie hissed, nearly dropping her bag.

"Stopping anyone from following us."

He sliced through the rope. The entire bridge shook. Rylan locked eyes with the man following them.

The man raised his hands in a gesture of peace. "Don't do anything brash."

Rylan continued moving toward the bank. Behind him, Emie was nearly across.

"Destroying the bridge won't stop me or others from following you," the man said. He took a step forward.

Rylan glanced down at the sword-like rocks in the water. "I think it might." He shot a look back to see Emie make it to the bank. He gave her a small nod and started cutting through the next rope. This one snapped quickly, like it had been waiting years for someone to relieve the tension. The man behind remained on his feet and continued toward them, scowl deepening across his face.

Without thinking, Rylan slid his knife through the last few ropes holding the base of the bridge together. As the last one snapped, he leapt with all his strength toward the bank. His body hit the side, and he clung to dirt, rock, or root, anything he could hold.

Emie grabbed onto his arm and did her best to pull him up. After a few flailing tries, Rylan managed to find a foothold and used the leverage to hoist himself up.

He lay on his back, chest heaving. Across the river, their pursuer had made it back to the far bank and was mouthing some choice words at them.

"I knew it would work," Rylan lied as he stood up and brushed the dirt from his clothes.

"That wasn't exactly how I was hoping to make it to the other side," Emie said. "You almost fell."

"Well, if the gods are watching, they now know how dedicated we are to finding their Tree," he said. "Let's keep moving."

Rylan chose a direction that felt like it went deeper into the Withering Wood and away from the river. After spending a day here, the ominous nature of the place had lessened. Although he still avoided stepping too close to any plant sprouting spiky black thorns or touching the decayed rot that covered most of the trees.

The river must have been the challenge. That fit the description of those who had found previous Glass Trees. He'd risked falling down to the rocks and drowning to get across. If the challenge was over, that meant the Tree had to be close.

As they walked, Rylan replayed the list of steps in his head.

Enter the Wood. Cross the River. Ascend.

And reach the Tree before Emie.

He'd added the last one. He needed to start planning how he would do it. The girl was quick. But he was stronger. He just needed enough time to grab her before she could touch the tree. He had rope in his pack. He could tie her up if that's what it took.

Rylan touched Leah's locket. She would have insisted they find a way to share the Tree's power. She always believed in happy endings. Unfortunately, that wasn't how life worked. Only one person could ask the gods for a gift, and asking for a gift to heal others was infinitely more useful and benevolent than becoming a potion master to gain approval.

Emie would understand.

She'd been voluntarily quiet since leaving the river. Her eyes focused on the path ahead and pointedly not looking at him.

Was she thinking the same thing? How to betray him and take the Tree for herself?

She hadn't told him what other potions she kept in her bag. Separating her from it might be a good idea if he didn't want to risk another surprise.

If he offered to carry her bag, she'll suspect him. He could try and take it by force. He tightened his fist around the locket.

"Why not try talking to her?"

Leah's voice pierced his mind. It was as if she stood next to him. Of course, his sister would have wanted him to try talking. Find a compromise.

"Fine," Rylan said, barely audible. "I'll do it for you, Leah."

He hurried forward, matching Emie's pace.

"Hey, kid," he started, trying to find the right words. How did one go about asking someone to give up on their dream? "We need to talk about what we're going to do—"

"Rylan, look," Emie interjected. She pointed ahead where the ground started to rise into a large mound the size of a small house, bare of any trees.

This was it. He raced forward, Emie at his side, and ascended. At the top, the mound ended in a ledge sticking out over a small cavern. And there, sitting right below the ledge they stood on, was the most beautiful sight Rylan had ever seen.

The Glass Tree.

It stood the height of two men with transparent branches and leaves sparkling in the afternoon sunlight. The Tree was far grander than any statue Rylan had ever seen. No other vegetation grew nearby. It was as if the forest knew this was a divine gift and not worthy to be touched except by the bravest of seekers.

"We found it," Emie breathed at his side. "How do we get down?"

There was no path leading down into the cavern. Rylan pulled out the rope he brought and tied it to the nearest tree then fastened the other end into a loop.

"You can lower me down there to pluck a leaf off the Tree," he said.

"No."

Rylan turned to her.

Emie stood, eyes narrowed at him. "I need this, Rylan."

"How long were you an apprentice?" he asked. "Six months? A year? You have so many more chances to make something of yourself, but this is my only chance to save others from suffering the same fate as Leah."

Emie pulled out a small vial. "I don't have other chances. My parents are ashamed of me! The leaf is the one way to make them proud."

"You wouldn't have gotten this far without me." Rylan closed his hand around the rope. He could see the Tree, calling out to him to take a leaf.

"Stop." She raised the vial to throw it.

"Emie, only one of us can get the power. I can help you find another apprenticeship somewhere else. But I need to be the one to take a leaf."

She shook her head, lip trembling and eyes filling with tears. "Rylan, please."

He hesitated.

This was the challenge. It wasn't the river. It was betraying her.

Rylan looked from the Tree to Emie. She had the same face Leah did when the pain got worse.

He could help others. No one had to go through that type of pain again.

Rylan took a step forward. "I'm truly sorry about your apprenticeship, but I can't let you take the leaf."

Emie opened her mouth to reply, but a snap of a branch caused them to spin around. The man from the river emerged from the woods, a long hunting knife pointing at Rylan.

He'd found them again.

"Don't try anything," the man said. He stole a glance over the side of the cavern and grinned. He gestured away from the edge with his knife. "Step away."

Rylan studied the man as he backed up. If he could get close enough, he could tackle him. Or disarm him. Anything to keep him from touching the Tree.

To the side, Rylan saw Emie move. He ducked out of the way as she threw the vial at the newcomer's feet. The glass shattered, and a small cloud of greenish gray smoke filled the air, engulfing both Emie and the man. Rylan dove to the side, narrowly escaping it.

Emie's eyes went wide. She put a hand over her nose and mouth and tried to move out from the cloud, but whatever it was took effect faster than her reflexes. The man dropped to the ground. Emie staggered a few feet before falling to her knees and then rolling onto her side, eyes closed.

Rylan waited for the smoke to fade away before rushing over to Emie. She was breathing deeply. Alive, but asleep. What kind of potion was that?

His gaze drifted to the rope, still affixed to the tree. There was no one to argue with now. No decision to be made except to take what he came for.

Rylan stared down at his prize. The Glass Tree sparkled like a treasure beckoning him to come and take it.

He dropped the end of the rope off the ledge and began his descent. As he climbed, he kept his focus fixed on the Tree.

Within each glass leaf, Rylan saw himself.

He saw himself plucking a leaf and receiving his gift.

He saw himself returning home to the praise of the town.

He saw himself bringing actual healing to those sick and dying.

He saw families reunited.

He saw smiles.

He saw laughter.

Emie's pained face flashed in his mind. Her tears as she'd begged him for the Tree.

Rylan shook his head. She'd understand. He didn't owe her anything. She didn't know the pain of losing a sister. She didn't know the pain of knowing you were helpless to save her.

Hand over hand, inch by inch. The rope swayed with his movements, but Rylan held on. As he drew closer, the glow of the Tree grew brighter.

He could finally make a difference.

He could finally help people.

Rylan reached out his hand. His finger brushed the nearest glass leaf.

Snap!

The rope broke free and Rylan fell. His body met the Glass Tree like a wave striking the shoreline. It shattered beneath him.

Glass shards and broken pieces scattered in every direction. Rylan lay on his side staring blankly at the destruction, a dozen little cuts across his body throbbed.

No. He had it. This was his.

He sat up and frantically scavenged the wreckage for any leaf that remained intact. Glass cut his hands, staining the gods' creation with his blood. He ignored the pain and continued searching.

There had to be one leaf left to salvage!

But each piece he found was broken. No magic of the gods remained in this place. He'd ruined his only chance.

The rope lay near him, the end frayed from scraping against the rock ledge. Why didn't he double-check it before descending? Why didn't he find a place to climb down that wasn't directly over the tree?

"Fool."

Rylan glanced up to see the man looking down at him shaking his head. Without anything to gain, the man left.

Then another face appeared at the edge. Emie.

She stared at Rylan. Her mouth hung open, but no words came. He met her tear-filled eyes. She pressed her lips tight and turned away, leaving Rylan alone.

He sat there, letting time drift by like fog on a spring morning. He pulled out Leah's locket and clenched his fist around it until it hurt.

Each broken piece of glass now reflected a different image.

He saw the doctor telling his parents Leah was sick.

He saw Leah putting on a brave face as she got worse.

He saw her suffer from the pain.

He saw the fear in her eyes as she approached the end.

He saw her frail, lifeless body in the casket.

He saw Emie's crestfallen stare.

Why did he think he could take a leaf? He'd lost the most important person in his life. Why did he think he could change the future? The gods obviously destined him to fail.

He kicked a few pieces of glass across the cavern floor. Others he stomped on, crushing them to dust. Rylan dropped the locket and grabbed the nearest fist-sized piece of shattered Tree and lifted it to throw against the rock wall of the cavern.

Sunlight caught the broken shard. The light pierced the glass like a prism, casting a dazzling display of colors on the forest floor. A mosaic of beauty.

Rylan froze and stared at the patterns of color at his feet.

No. He'd failed. Nothing beautiful could come out of this wreckage. He'd ruined it. Leah was gone and so was the Tree.

But no matter how many times he blinked, the colorful display remained dancing on the ground. It shimmered with a kaleidoscope of light. He didn't know how long he stood transfixed on the sight. But eventually, Rylan lowered the shard of glass.

"It's broken," he breathed. "I failed."

Rylan dropped his head and stared at the pieces scattered across the ground. Leah's locket lay among the glass. It was as if she stared back up at him, reminding him of the things she'd taught him during her last few months of life.

"Can't the story have a happy ending?"

He saw himself holding Leah's hand as she battled through the pain.

He saw her eyes fill with wonder as they watched the stars together.

He saw her smile as he told her one of his many stories.

He saw Emie's face light up as he complimented her glasswork.

Maybe he could still help people heal.

He tore off a corner of his shirt and carefully wrapped the fist-sized piece in it. He then gathered up a number of other pieces of the Tree and placed them in his satchel. With his new treasures packed, Rylan found an area with enough handholds to try and climb out. It took most of the afternoon to get out of the cavern, and once he had, Rylan hurried along the path they'd taken.

He found Emie's discarded bag on the ground. A number of her potion bottles lay shattered near it. Rylan gathered up the bag and continued until he caught sight of a figure sitting at the base of a tree.

Emie.

She clearly hadn't been walking fast. She looked up to him, eyes red, and stood.

"Before you say anything," Rylan started, "I wanted to say I'm sorry. I shouldn't have gone after the Tree on my own." He held out her bulky bag.

"I don't want it," Emie said. "Master Wielind was right about me. I ruined my only chance at proving I'm worth anything."

Rylan ran a finger over Leah's locket. "I once knew someone who believed that even the darkest story could have a happy ending." He took out the wrapped shard of the Tree and held it out.

Emie took it. "What is it?"

"I had an idea," he said, watching Emie open the wrapping and hold up the fragment of broken glass. "You make such beautiful glassware, I'd like to see what you can do with it. Maybe we can change the endings to our stories."

The afternoon sun caught the shard in Emie's hand and she stared wide-eyed as the light danced across the ground like a million fireflies and stars.

She smiled.

ZACH SOLLIE

Zach Sollie has battled the monster of anxiety and depression for over a decade. Now, whether he's writing a middle-grade adventure or an epic fantasy, Zach is motivated by three primary things:

1. Entertaining people, especially making them laugh, is real-life magic.

2. No matter how dark things get "Even darkness must pass. A new day will come." (Thanks Samwise!)

3. Outsiders have a place to belong.

In his free time, you can find Zach playing tabletop games, donning a new costume for the Renaissance Festival, or wishing sarcasm and movie trivia were marketable skills.

Achievements

- Drafted five novels and wrote seven screenplays for short films, including one that was selected for a college showcase.
- Built an email list with over 130 subscribers in two months.
- Consistently develops networking and speaking skills by running a podcast, www.story516.com, and YouTube channel, www.youtube.com/@ZachSollie
- Received interest from multiple publishers, including a request for a book proposal.
- Works in a middle school library.
- Worked for a college journal reviewing new children's books.

Pitches

- *A Series of Unfortunate Events* meets *The Spiderwick Chronicles* in a middle-grade fantasy/mystery where a group of siblings must uncover the secrets behind cryptic poems and a mysterious old manor.
- *Cam Jansen* meets *Julie B. Jones* in a middle-grade novel where a quirky young girl dons her fedora and works to solve a mystery to prove herself responsible enough to own a parrot.
- *Castle in the Sky* meets Jack and Locke from *LOST* in an adult fantasy where magic begins to die off, and an old mage and a young scientist must work together to find a solution before the floating island they call home falls from the sky.

TREEFRIEND

RYAN Elizabeth

With shaking hands and a blend of anticipation and music coursing through his veins, August ripped the envelope open.

This couldn't happen. Could it?

He slipped his fingers around the paper inside but hesitated before taking it out.

Three weeks ago—the day before he secretly sent in an application and portfolio—his mother had glimpsed a painting of his while passing the kitchen table. She'd reminded him that while his work was lovely as ever, "It's not gonna pay the bills. You've got to figure out what you're doing, hon . . ."

"I know, I know." He remembered letting out a sigh, a folder that held some of his other pieces of art tucked behind his back.

August felt the paper on his skin now—the paper that just might hold his future inside—as his favorite Tears for Fears song faded inside his earphones. The odds didn't give him a reason to dare wish anything could come of it; they were stacked against him.

He slipped the earphones down his neck.

Despite that, hope flickered inside of him. August had fallen into that familiar pattern time and time again throughout his eighteen whirlwind years. Leaning back against the mailbox, he closed his eyes.

He couldn't help but dream anyway.

August blinked the world back into focus. As he unfolded the letter, the hope inside threatened to unfold with it. With a sharp breath, he clicked off the Walkman clipped to his jean pocket.

Dear August, the letter started.

Reality could take the hope inside away in another mere sentence. August knew it well, and he paused—breathing in his dream—before the inevitable slap in the face could even start to sting.

Thank you for applying for the studio art program at Steel City University of the Arts.

Congratulations!

The printed word leapt out at him. August stared at it until it didn't look like a word anymore, and it somehow lost and gained all of its meaning at once.

Welcome to the class of 1999. It is with great pleasure that we inform you of your acceptance to our highly acclaimed studio art program. The admissions team receives hundreds of applications each year, and your impressive portfolio as well as your academic achievements truly stood out as exemplary.

"What?" he breathed into a whisper. Then a laugh spilled out of his mouth. "*What?*" He repeated to himself, out loud. He fell against the mailbox, sunlight hitting his face as his father's words circled in his mind—*getting into an art school is one thing, but paying for it's a whole 'nother ball game.* August unfolded the bottom third of the paper, then put a hand over his messy, golden hair as he read.

Due to your exceptional application and portfolio, we are also pleased to announce you as one of five recipients of this year's SCUA Warhol Scholarship.

August's breath caught in his chest, like a wave frozen midcrash, suspended in disbelief. As he read on, he realized that this seemed to practically be a full-ride scholarship.

But before he could even try to breathe again, he stuffed the paper back inside its envelope and raced back up the driveway, his Chuck Taylors smacking against the pavement.

Only his sketchbooks and his tree were on his mind now.

"Will, just wait 'til . . . you hear this," he called up the hill, struggling for breath as he made his way toward the tree.

He stopped, panting for air, in front of the enormous tree in his yard—the home of his only true friend: his treefriend.

The weeping willow's roots spread far and wide over the open yard, and the branches were covered with light. The tree rested in the front to the side of the driveway, a short distance from the green cottage huddled in shadow.

"Will?" He listened for his friend's voice at the base of the tree, but found no response except for the chirping of birds nearby and the hum of cicadas in the fields.

"C'mon, Willow, I have something to show you." August managed to steady his breathing enough to avoid pausing in between words, but his heart raced on. The combination of his uphill sprint, exhilarating news, and sudden twinge of fear he couldn't quite explain or understand made his heartbeat keep quickening. As he placed a hand on the side of the trunk, the familar feeling of rough bark on his skin steadied him.

Still nothing. He took the letter back out from the envelope, reading the entire thing this time, just to make sure it was real.

A Carolina wren—one of August's favorite birds to draw—flew overhead, exuberantly singing its way into another nearby tree.

He stuck the letter back inside and waited another minute, tapping the toe of his left sneaker. "Alright, I know you can hear me."

A rustle of branches shook above August's head, and next thing he knew, a figure fell from a low branch to the ground. The figure landed gracefully on his feet, without a sound.

Dusting off his knees, the treefriend grinned.

August never knew for sure how it happened, but it was as if the leaves above melted into Willow as he fell to the ground—a real boy, just ever so slightly green and ghostly.

"*There* you are, kid." August smiled back. "Guess what?"

"What?" Willow's voice was small, even with the giddy grin still on his face, but he drenched the word in curiosity.

"Something came in the mail today." He clutched the envelope.

"What?" He scratched his head of wild brown curls as he stepped forward, a spark of eagerness in his eye.

August handed him the envelope. "Read it for yourself." The thrill of the acceptance letter had him tapping his fingers against each other. He still couldn't believe he made it. This letter had already changed the trajectory of his day, his next four years . . . his life, even.

Willow took the envelope with his spirit-like hand. August still didn't quite understand how Will could interact with things and people just the same as any person could with his green-tinted, nearly see-through form. But maybe that was why August never saw him as anything less than human, despite his appearance.

Growing up, August's parents had always shook their heads while they talked about "that extraordinary imagination of his," but he had always known Willow was a whole lot more than that.

He watched his friend's gaze glide across the page, line after line. August was still proud of how he managed to teach Willow to read—over a decade ago, now—at the same time as he himself learned in kindergarten. August's treefriend grew up with him, both literally and figuratively.

Willow handed the piece of paper back but still held the envelope in his other hand, his eyes toward the ground and roots below. The birds quieted.

"Whatcha think?" August gave his unresponsive treefriend a hesitant smile. He noticed a distant look clouding Willow's normally bright emerald eyes. "Exciting, isn't it?"

"Yes." Willow handed the envelope back, his expression still lost somewhere else, outside of August and maybe what these words meant for him.

August cleared his throat. He wondered if Willow just couldn't sense his excitement; sometimes, things like that got lost in human-to-treefriend translation. "Remember my art?"

A sudden smile emerged on Willow's face again. "I love your art."

He exhaled, relief washing over him. "Then I'm sure you'll know how important this is for me."

"Steel City?" Willow said after a few seconds, his tone turning the words into a question.

"It's a nickname for Pittsburgh, that's where the school is. Pretty far from here . . ." He counted states on his fingers as he thought of them. "Six states away. Maybe seven." August reoriented himself, then pointed north, past the house. "It's that way. It'd take a day or two for us to get there. We'd find a place to stop and stay overnight." He paused, glancing up into the tree. "And we could make other stops. We could find forests, get out and be with the trees after being stuck in the truck for hours, yeah?" He looked off toward his favorite earthly possession, his old, midnight blue F-150. "I knew it was bound to happen someday—you'll have to ride in my truck with me." August grinned and tilted his head down to meet Willow's eyes.

With a start, he realized that he never had to do that before. For the first time he could remember, they weren't the same height. He'd grown taller.

"Are you going?" With that question, it was like Willow had returned to the real world again. But his gaze remained elsewhere.

August laughed. "Of course I'm going. It's what I've always wanted, deep down. You know how Mom and Dad always hoped I'd want to be a doctor or just . . . something that'd be sure to make good money. But now I've got my chance. Art matters more than money to me." He cleared his throat, then continued, "I wanna keep learning and making. I'll find a way to make money too. They'll see."

Willow's grin had long vanished into oblivion. He bent down and plucked a fluffy dandelion from the ground, resting his skinny arms over his knees.

August swallowed. "This is my chance right here. Right, Will?"

Willow turned the dandelion in his hand and glanced at August, wordlessly rotating the flower over and over again.

August's sense of exhilaration began to wane. He took a couple of extra steps closer and sat next to Willow under the tree in the cool grass. He crossed his legs and sighed. "C'mon. Please. I'm really excited about this, aren't you?" August pulled out the acceptance letter and showed it to him once more.

Willow's eyes were glued to the dandelion, unblinking.

Nerves began to shiver up his spine. August stuck his hands in his pockets. "You know, it's like a week until we leave. That's really, really soon. I should start planning and packing up some things tonight. And quit my job at the store. I won't be able to give them two weeks, but one'll have to do." He forced a smirk, trying not to stumble over the words that scared him as he spoke. "Oh, and I've gotta call the school right away, tell them I'm enrolling and all that. I wonder if the letter's late."

Willow audibly inhaled, then blew all of the dandelion's seeds off the stem in one try. As soon as they floated away, Willow vanished.

He didn't do that often.

"Willow? What's wrong?" August paced around the tree, peering through the branches above him.

His fingers turned into icicles as he called, "You're coming with me, right?"

The only answer was the buzz of cicadas and the chirp of a frog.

August opened his mouth again, but it took a few seconds before the words would follow. "Aren't you gonna watch me make more art?" His heart began to pound more frantically again. "That's what I'll be doing at school. I can keep drawing trees, but I'll draw lots of other things too. Remember how much fun we had making artwork over the years? We were crazy kids." Memories flooded in of Willow with his paint-drenched head of curls. He never knew how Willow managed to get so many shades of colors on at once.

Still no answer. August glanced around the yard to be merely met by more green.

"Hey, Willow?" his voice squeaked, but he tried again after a minute. "You know, I don't wanna go inside right now. I won't start packing until later. The house is empty, anyway. Mom and Dad aren't getting back from their trip until late tonight, and who knows if they'll even go through with that." The thought of the broken promises and dark rooms fogged his mind for a moment. "So I'm just gonna wait until you let me know what's wrong . . ." He let his voice trail into silence.

August rose and went inside for a sketchbook. With the screech of the side door, he came back out and drew under the tree for minutes that turned into hours. As the sun cast an orange glow over the horizon and the first stars began to speckle the sky, he checked the willow's branches one more time. But no one sat in the tree.

Alone, August meandered around his cluttered bedroom, searching the pictures that covered the walls. Each and every piece of art depicted something that surrounded him in life.

There was the yard he spent more time in than his own bedroom, the swamp Willow liked to visit right next to the property line, the swerving driveway and his truck that gave him a new sense of freedom. The garden Dad had planted and then forgot about, August's favorite pair of shoes he wore for miles of hikes, dozens of trees . . . *his* tree, his treefriend—they all hung on the walls.

These were the things he would leave behind.

Is growing up supposed to feel this sad?

He fell backward onto his bed to stare at the ceiling, which was also covered with artwork. He could feel the memories through the sketches, but they somehow weren't rooted in a place as much as they were in a person.

Willow might not have been human, but he was realer than real.

Blinking, he forced himself to get up. He needed to start packing, but he needed to talk to his treefriend more.

August shoved open the screen door, prompting a loud creak. He flipped on the front porch light that flickered on to a low haze, then stepped out and onto the top stair, barefoot. He didn't bother to even glance down the driveway for headlights reflecting up the road.

All he could see was the dark silhouetted shadow of the sweeping willow tree in the yard. No faint laughter or rustling of branches with magic hiding behind it. Just the tree.

He took a deep breath.

Why would my friend August leave?

The treefriend sat hunched over his knees in a high branch. Home. If he was not a spirit—whatever that meant, he did not know, but if he was like his friend August—he knew he would have scraped knees and bruised legs from all of the climbing and jumping.

The treefriend wanted to call out and speak back to his friend August, but he did not know what he could say. So he did not. Could not.

He cannot go. He cannot leave.

A sadness like nothing he had felt in many years had filled him. The treefriend did not believe he had what his friend August called a soul, but he wondered if the place in his chest he felt this sadness in the place where those who had souls would feel it.

The treefriend sat up and dangled his legs over the branch. He did not know why he stayed in this form when he could retreat even further into himself, into the roots.

He stopped, for a second.

Roots.

The treefriend blinked.

He, indeed, had roots, and he could make use of them. Hopping down from the branch, he looked down at the dark, cold ground.

He closed his eyes and dissolved himself into the side of the bark. He could feel the things on and around his trunk, branches, leaves . . . and roots.

Using all of his might, he stretched his closest roots forward and up from the grass, while still keeping his deepest roots as a firm foundation. The roots inched along the ground and across the yard, closer to the driveway. The treefriend felt himself continue to stretch, aware of each blade of grass and creature crawling on the roots.

The treefriend felt his branches shift upward a bit, as if they were his shoulders hunching—as he continued to move toward his object of interest: the truck.

His friend August liked to talk about his truck almost like it was another friend. But the treefriend knew that it was not quite the same thing.

If he were in his human form, he would have let out a deep breath. He did not want to hurt his friend August, not at all. But he also knew that he could not let him leave. He did not want him to go, he did not want their time together to come to an end. Not yet.

So the treefriend heaved with all of his might and stretched his roots over and across the vehicle. He would not break the truck—he made sure he held it in place so there would be no moving it. No way that his friend August could get inside and drive it away, far away to the place called Pittsburgh where the treefriend did not live and could not follow.

But maybe keeping the truck would not even work. He was not so sure if anything could keep his friend August from his art . . . not even his treefriend.

Light streamed through August's open bedroom window, a cool breeze awakening him. He laced up his sneakers as fast as he could—Willow was bound to have changed his mind by now.

"Hey, Will," August called as soon as he was a few steps away from the house. Staring at the long willow branches just across the yard, he made his way to the edge of the driveway, heading straight for the tree.

He'll come back today, he'll have to. A bright goldfinch sang, soaring above August's head. He stopped and watched as it flew high, over and across the roof.

August kept his eyes on the sky as he walked across the driveway toward the tree. The clouds spread across the sky in white puffs.

Then his sneakers snagged on something, and he pitched to his knees in the gravel. "Ow . . ." He rubbed his burning hands on his t-shirt. "What the . . ."

He began to pull himself to his feet but froze when he saw what he had tripped on. Seemingly endless, enormous roots stretched the whole way across the driveway from the tree, all the way to the other side.

To his truck.

Willow . . .

Rarely did August feel the urge to curse, but this was one of those occasions. He couldn't stop staring at the roots that covered his beloved 1979 Ford F-150, probably busted. Knees and palms burning, he ran to his truck. He ran his hands over the roots, searching for an opening, but there was none. The roots and branches had sprouted extra leaves, entirely covering the vehicle.

"Willow!" he yelled. Along with his knees and hands, his face burned now too. "Not cool!" he yelled louder. "I seriously can't believe you did this," Groaning, he tried to yank a root from the driver's side door, but it wouldn't budge, no matter how hard he pulled. "And really not a very funny prank, if you're tricking me."

No answer.

"You've gotta fix it. And don't do it again," he called.

Breathing hard, August stopped and thought.

"All right, Willow," he started again, just as loud. "My friend. I need you to . . . not destroy my truck. I need it to get to school, and I, well, I need it to follow my dream, remember?"

He has to be listening.

As he brushed off some pieces of pavement that stuck to his knees from the fall, a realization struck him.

"You don't need to keep me from leaving because, well, you're going with me. Don't you understand that? I'm not leaving you behind." August looked up at the cloudy sky as he waited for the response that might not come. But he had to hope, anyway, like he always had.

This has to be it.

A few of the ends of the roots—or branches, they were so twisted amongst each other, there was no way to tell—shifted on the side of the truck, only holding it more in place.

Willow didn't come back, not for six silent, restless days.

August set a bag on the pavement behind his truck, beside the others he'd already brought out. *Tomorrow's the day.*

He walked to the back of the truck again. Mom and Dad couldn't see the branches—they hadn't said a word about it. They were blind, and this had to have been "that extraordinary imagination of his" that happened to be a whole lot more than imagination. Because he sure couldn't get past those heavy roots.

He pinched his arm—hard—a spark of pain shooting up his veins.

No, all he knew was his truck was busted right now, if only for him.

I can be a man. I've got to be.

As August went inside to grab the last of the bags to put outside, with the buzz of the TV show Mom must've been watching down the hallway, he realized how very scared he had grown. He knew this was what he was meant to do, but he didn't want to do it quite like this . . .Willow had been his home.

Now, he was alone.

Mom had said something about it being a personal experience, getting ready to leave home for the first time like this. She and Dad would be there when it was time to go in the morning.

August wouldn't admit it then, but his heart had entirely sunk in his chest when she said it. He knew all along that they wouldn't be there for him if he'd gone through with art school, but he wished they would've had at least a slight shift in perspective—at least tell him they'd miss him, or that they'd only be a call away, or something like that.

I've got to be a man, he told himself again as he set down the bag, then headed for the grand weeping willow tree.

August stopped in his tracks.

There he sat, leaned against the trunk. His treefriend.

One leg was bent at the knee, and the other sprawled out in front of him. Willow twirled a blade of grass in between his fingers.

August ran as fast as he could toward him without a second thought. He stood in front of his treefriend for a good ten seconds ago to ensure he wouldn't vanish quite so fast this time. "Hey," he breathed.

The boy simply shook his head, slowly, over and over again.

August waited, not so patiently. He had to hold back everything he wanted to say about his truck. He had said enough while Willow had been gone, but there was one thing he decided he needed to say, no matter what. "Don't disappear again. I want you to come along."

Willow kept shaking his head in the same slow way. "I cannot."

August sighed. "What do you mean you can't?" He lowered himself to the ground next to his friend; he wanted to listen closely, carefully, while he still had the chance. "I need you to."

"No, you do not need me to . . . and I cannot." His voice was small. "The magic will not let me."

His treefriend looked as scared as August felt.

"We could find a way, couldn't we? We always find a way."

Willow closed his eyes and shook his head.

"Why not?" August gently squeezed his friend's shoulder. "We could," he repeated.

Willow only exhaled another long, heavy breath as he looked up at August. "Can I tell you a story?"

August nodded. Willow's stories had always been good, if not a little bit odd—Will would remind him that stories were so much better from someone who had a heart *and* a soul, but that he could try his best.

"Many years ago, I was a treefriend for another human," he said, without another second of hesitation.

August's breath caught in his chest, immediate tension falling on his shoulders. This was not at all what he had expected.

"He was a lot like you, before he got older. Except . . ." He trailed off.

"Except what, Will?" August didn't move. "This story's true?"

Something shifted in Willow's face when he blinked his green eyes open again. "Except he forgot. He did not keep the memories we had, and they are gone forever now."

August stared at the ground and whispered, "I would not and will not ever, ever forget." August swallowed. "I care too much about you—about what we've shared—to do that. You've been like the brother I never had." *How will I make him understand?*

"But you want to leave."

August knew Willow wasn't thinking rationally—he had to give Willow the small bit of hope he had left. *We always find a way . . .*

"I want to leave, yes, but I want you to come with me. The magic hasn't ever held you back before, has it?"

Willow's voice got even quieter. "Things are different now. You grew up. Maybe it is because . . . you no longer need me like you once did, like you did before."

August thought for a moment, then nodded. "Do you believe that I would never forget about you, even if we were apart?" He said his words slowly and carefully, enunciating each one with precision. "I won't forget, but I think . . . I think it's time, I think I've got to go."

The songbirds started singing again, but Willow didn't say a word, and August found that he had just about run out of things to say.

"I want you to stick with me, won't you?" he tried. He turned to glance at Willow only to find that he'd vanished just as before.

Then came the silence, all over again.

It hit midnight again, and August knew he had to try—for not just his sake, but Willow's—once more before the morning came. He tightly held his most beloved sketchbook to his chest and padded down the hallway as quietly as he could.

After he slipped his sneakers over his socks, he pushed the screen door open inch by inch, but it still creaked once the space was wide enough for him to slip through. August paused for a moment as he held the door, listening for any sign of his awakened parents before he gently let it close behind him.

Sketchbook still in hand, August headed toward the willow tree, careful to step over the remaining outstretched roots. The air filled with the persistent and rhythmic singing of the spring peepers as he kept going.

"Will, won't you come back? One last time?" He didn't whisper, but spoke in a careful, hushed tone. This time, there was only the smallest bit of hope left, even though he took the time to ask. "I know now that you were right about what you said, all of it...I don't want it to be true, but it is. It's time."

This mattered more than the other fears that had set in along with it after the letter arrived—saying goodbye.

He knew what he had to do.

With that last smidge of hope for his treefriend, he set the sketchbook on the ground, right under the trunk where Willow liked to sit.

Please believe me.

Once he heard the softer slam of the door closing, the treefriend appeared again.

He hopped down to the ground in the moonlight, without any of his normal wild mischief, just a thud, and picked up the sketchbook, his ghostly hands shaking.

My friend August left it for me. For a reason.

As he flipped through the pages, starting in the middle, he found the things they shared drawn in different ways.

There they were, at the swamp, one with them watching the stars. Another one, up in his tree. He kept flipping, flipping, flipping, until he had seen and studied each and every page.

The treefriend noticed the lines and shades, and wondered how long it had taken to draw all of these. He noticed how in every one, his friend August's face was not clear, he was always further in the back—but Willow was close and clear. It felt like looking in a mirror, only better than the swampy water, which was the only other place he saw himself.

He stuck a hand in his curly hair, wondering if it always seemed that wild. He smiled.

The treefriend went through the pages over and over again, locking the pictures in his mind. Though the memories had always been there, they were even more beautiful now.

As soon as he flipped the final page of the book, something fluttered to the ground. The treefriend crouched down to pick it up—a notecard. He was lucky that August had taught him to read so many years ago. It was a good thing for a treefriend to know.

"Dear Willow," the scrawled-out ink read.

As he read the note, tears slipped down the treefriend's cheeks at not only the words from his friend August, but at the drawings. He flipped back to one of his favorite pictures, tracing the painted tree on the page with his finger, feeling the gratitude of his friend August seeping through it to him.

He had to say goodbye.

He would have to believe that his friend August truly would not forget.

With a new sense of strength—even in the sadness, the sadness that even the treefriend without a soul could feel—the treefriend hopped back up into the branches, taking the sketchbook with him. Morning would come soon.

It was time to go.

August stood under the tree again, with the same words he had written to Willow on the tip of his tongue. He wasn't sure whether or not to say them all over again, since he saw the sketchbook was no longer where he had placed it.

But before he could think about it any longer, Willow himself hopped down into the grass.

The sounds of nature made up for his and Willow's silence as they stood there—the wind scattered the leaves and songbirds sang around the corner.

August stared, trying to figure out how and what to say this time. He had given him another chance . . .

The force of Willow's hug nearly knocked August to the ground.

As soon as he regained balance, relief flooded over August. Willow's arms surrounded him with the kind of warmth only a good friend could give.

August laughed when he wouldn't let go. "You came back. Did you see it?"

"Yes, I did. I love your art." Willow's voice muffled, his face still wrapped in the embrace. "I can see now. I want you to go. You need to go, I need to stay."

August stepped back and looked him straight in the eye. He turned around for a short moment, finding that all of the outstretched roots that were once over his truck were back on and under the ground around the tree.

He knew what he had to say. He knew what he had to do.

August embraced Willow again and spoke into his shoulder. "I wish it wasn't like this. But I truly won't forget. I promise."

Willow stepped back. "I have something for you, too." He held out a twig with just little bits of green left on it.

August took the twig and held it close, a sad smile growing on his face.

"Do you know what it is?"

"It's one of your branches. It'll help me remember even better—"

"Not just any of my branches," Willow interrupted. "It is an undying branch. It is filled with magic."

August's mind filled with awe and wonder, his jaw dropping. Willow never joked about the magic itself, though he didn't talk about it often. "What sort of magic is that?"

Willow took back the branch as he spoke about it. "With it, you can feel my presence. You can know I am with you wherever you go, wherever you are—in me, you will always have a home, even when you need to go." He paused. "You do need to go."

August nodded, the words echoing inside of his brain.

"I never could've asked for a better gift, Willow."

Willow handed the branch back to him. "I know. But you can be brave, even if I am not with you there. You will still have me from far away—always have me—your brother." With a tilt of his head, Willow raised an eyebrow, as if asking August if his use of the word was right. He was more than a treefriend now, wasn't he?

"Yes," August felt a smile growing on his face, "Yes, that's right. And you know what?" August looked off to the sky as he clutched the branch again. "In the end, I think knowing that will be enough . . . Willow?"

"What?"

"You most certainly do have a heart *and* a soul."

Two days later, August stood by the one window in his new dorm. His old sketches surrounded him, hung on his side of the wall. Sure, he'd make all kinds of new art here . . . but he had to hang on to these, too.

Goodbyes were hard things, but they're the only way to welcome new beginnings. After all, blank canvases could become something beautiful, August now knew.

He set his branch in the middle of the windowsill.

Willow's voice reverberated inside his mind, tinged with glimmers of something that wasn't quite mischief but wasn't quite a sweet innocence, either—something in between that could only be found in the voice of a treefriend.

You can be brave. You will still have me—your brother.

His treefriend was the brother he never had, after all.

And he knew it was true.

RYAN ELIZABETH

Ryan Elizabeth is the daughter of singer-songwriters and the granddaughter of a master artisan. She writes to remind readers of the extraordinary within the ordinary, crafting contemplative stories that explore beauty in the midst of sadness.

When she isn't working on one of her books, you could probably find her serving coffee as a barista in her Pennsylvania college town, dabbling with one of her many musical instruments, or chatting about theology and the arts.

Achievements

- Wrote three full-length novels, a novella, and multiple short stories.
- Founded Leaf & Light Creative Clubs and taught visual arts and creative writing to over fifty students with five sold out events.
- Upcoming artist management intern with Bragg Management in Nashville, Tennessee.
- Has been published in *Story Warren*.
- Has been published by *Rabbit Room Poetry*.
- Attended Realm Makers Conference in 2022, HopeWords Writers' Conference in 2024, and Write to Publish Conference in 2024.
- Has over 250 email list subscribers and 950 Instagram followers.

Pitches

- A Fredrik Backman-esque literary novel centered on a shy singer-songwriter's mission to save her small-town record store on the brink of closure—all whilst rediscovering her own voice.
- *Gilead* meets *Peace Like a River* in a 1980s-set literary novel featuring an unconventional young priest following his hopes to unite a divided congregation under the guidance of miraculously talkative stained-glass saints.
- *The Midnight Library* meets *If We Were Villains* in an adult fantasy novel about estranged friends who are forced to navigate the notorious Abbott Theater's meddling curses together—a week before the opening of their production of *Macbeth*.

THE WOLF AND THE WILLOW

Rachel North

"Love is in the air—and it stinks." My girlfriend Lexi wrinkles her nose and leans against the trunk of the weeping willow, its branches enclosing us in a chamber of leaves that make a shushing sound in the wind. The message I carved in the bark years ago is visible around Lexi: *J + L forever* encircled by a heart.

Her teasing accelerates my pulse that's still racing from my winning track sprint. "Are you sure it's love and not deodorant?" I pat my face dry with a towel, damp from my quick shower in the boys' locker room.

"I know the difference." The lights from the high school track field behind us illuminate Lexi's blue eyes.

I step closer. Tease a leaf out of her blonde hair. "It's love, right?"

"Mmhmm." Her face is inches from mine.

It's difficult to resist kissing her after years of wanting to. I only worked up the courage to ask her out a few months ago—a game of Truth or Dare gone terribly right when she said "yes."

However, I want to save our first kiss for a bigger moment.

I trace our initials. "Remember when we carved this?"

"When *you* did? Of course. I ran home and told Mom I had a boyfriend."

"You were ten years off." I grin at the memory. We had escaped to the woods after our older sisters' track meet, and it had occurred to my eight-year-old self that vandalism was a surefire way to hit on a girl. With Lexi cheering me on, the willow tree became my target.

Lexi opens her mouth, but her ringtone interrupts whatever she was about to say. "Oh, it's Madi. I should take this."

We do an abbreviated BFF handshake, and my touch lingers on her wrist, not wanting her to leave yet, as she answers her little sister.

Her brow creases. "A wolf in the area? This far south in Minnesota?" She gestures to the forest, as if to ask, *See anything?*

I glance over my shoulder at the woods. Panic stabs my middle, but not because of nonexistent wolves. What if she forgot? "We're still on for Perkins, right?"

Lexi mouths "yes" and saunters to the parking lot.

Jittery nerves race through my body, but I'm too exhausted to do more than walk toward the gym to close for the night.

I text my buddy at Perkins: IS THE PLAN STILL ON?

Waffle Bro: YUP. HEART-SHAPED WAFFLES, EXTRA WHIP.

Freshly mowed grass swishes under my quickened step. I thought about doing a more elaborate promposal—you know, the kind you see on TikTok—but Lexi loves two things: simplicity and waffles. Besides, I'm 99 percent sure she'll say yes.

But what was she going to say before her phone rang?

Opening the gym door, I call, "Anyone still here?"

A startled yelp answers.

I stare at a boy hunched over in the middle of the lockers, an unnaturally hairy hand clutching the strap of a duffel, *Thad* printed on the side. His breathing rattles. Asthma?

"Hey, you okay, man?" I ask.

"I'm fine," he rasps, his voice deeper than I expected. He waves me off as I approach, white chalk floating off his fingers—he must be the pole vaulter from the other team. "You scared me, that's all."

"I need to lock up. You done?"

Thad nods and exits the locker room.

I bolt the door behind us and follow him to the parking lot, the moon's beam cutting across the green like a searchlight.

Thad's breath comes in gasps and starts. Sweat beads his brow, and tremors run through him.

I study him. "Are you okay?"

"R-run." His shoulders contort at an odd angle.

My pulse spikes. Is he having a seizure? A stroke? Lexi kept nagging me to take a first-aid class with her, but I never did. Is he going to die? "Thad, can you hear me? Thad?"

He jerks forward, oblivious to my voice.

I grab his arm.

His body goes rigid. He stares me in the eye, his a mesmerizing shade of yellow. Hair ripples around his eyelids and consumes his face, collarbones, hands. Canine ears press flat against his skull, and fingernails elongate into razor blades that serrate the strap of his duffel.

The Gatorade I guzzled earlier threatens to come up. Is it possible to overdose on sports drinks?

Thad makes a low noise in his throat, like he's attempting to talk.

Blinking, I try to wake up, but this isn't a dream. This is terrifyingly, horrifyingly real. I'm staring at a bona fide werewolf.

At that moment of revelation, I realize my mistake—I'm still holding his arm. Restraining him.

I release his arm, scramble away, but I trip on Thad's shredded clothing. My backpack flattens under me, the Gatorade bottles inside cracking. Four legs pin me down.

My gaze narrows on his fangs, a white flash in the moonlight.

Self-preservation kicks in. I swing my knees against Thad's spine as hard as I can. His jaw, inches from biting my throat and crushing my windpipe, misses. His teeth sink into my shoulder.

I scream like a little girl. My heartbeat throbs in each drop of blood.

Hospital.

Need. Hospital.

Panic surges through my veins. I whack my legs against Thad again. He rolls off me, teeth scraping along my shoulder until they release.

Clutching my wound, I struggle to my feet. Dizziness pitches my stomach.

Thad snarls behind me. I whip the gym key from my pocket and clench it between my knuckles like Lexi does. As Thad lunges, I jab the key into his eye. He howls in pain and collapses. I don't linger to see the damage.

I sprint faster than I ever have before, praying I make it to my car before Thad decides he wants another Jude-sized snack. Why did I decide to park in another time zone?

I glimpse my dazed expression in the zero of the "2024 Grad" painted on my rear window.

Paws thud against the pavement.

Hands slick with sweat, I jam my car's unlock button, cursing the dying fob battery I haven't replaced yet.

Click.

I hurl myself into the driver seat and slam the door shut.

Thad barrels into the door, and my old Toyota shakes on its shocks. I lock the doors. Vision hazy with adrenaline, I turn the key in the ignition and yank the stick to reverse. I slam the accelerator to the floor. The car spins so fast I almost vomit.

Thad jumps back, howling until he disappears in the rearview mirror.

The drive to the hospital blurs. One moment I'm in the school parking lot, the next I'm stumbling toward the triage desk.

Every gash in my flesh screams as my adrenaline gives out, and dizziness causes me to sway on my feet. Why is the line so long? Was it this long the last time I was here? (Thanks, Lexi, for pushing me out of a tree.)

"Mama, that boy is bleeding."

I blink rapidly. Who's talking? My gaze lands on a little girl pointing at me, then trails up to her mom, her face—faces?—green.

I wave. "Hey. How's it going?"

A receptionist launches across the desk, picks up a landline, and barks a code that must translate to "teenager bleeding all over the carpet."

A nurse materializes with a wheelchair. "Sit right here, sir."

Sitting seems like a good idea, but my body opts to slump to the floor, unconscious.

I tilt my head, struggling to look at my phone without the ER lights glaring off the screen.

"Hey, you're supposed to be resting."

I glare up at my brother Jack, who's dared to move from his glorified folding chair in the corner. Mom and Dad are out of town, so I called him. He was far too eager to ditch his college homework to be my emergency contact, although it took some convincing to make him promise not to tell our parents.

"I'm looking something up." I angle my phone away so he won't see my search history: "werewolves," "lycanthropy," "next full moon."

"Nope." He snatches the device from my hand. "Come on. Tell me what happened."

My heart monitor spikes. "Whaddya mean?"

"I know when you're lying—although I never thought you would go to the length of getting a rabies shot. 'Fess up."

still feel Thad's canines sinking deep into my skin, see the feral sheen in his yellow irises, smell my blood with an awareness that chills me to the bone.

I shake my head. "I told the truth. A wolf attacked me." I didn't know how to explain to the police that it was a werewolf. Besides, what would they do to Thad? Jail him for something he probably can't control?

Worse, if the legends are to be believed, lycanthropy is contagious, and my graduation plans do not include becoming a lab rat.

But I have to tell *someone.*

My phone pings and the lock screen lights up in Jack's hand.

"Who is it?" I reach for the device.

"Lexi." Jack holds it above my head. "And I'm not returning it until you tell me."

I growl—an echo of Thad. *Where did that come from?* "Give it to me."

"Not until you talk."

I curl my fists, but that doesn't work well with a pulse oximeter attached to my finger. "Fine. But don't freak out."

"I am the epitome of calm."

I take a deep breath and blurt out, "A werewolf bit me."

Jack drops my phone with a *crack*. "What the heck, Jude?"

"Did you break it?"

He grabs my shoulders. "You were bitten by a *werewolf*?"

"Yeah. Some guy on the other team."

"Whoa." Jack rubs his beard, and it reminds me of Thad's transformation. "So the stories are true, then. Werewolves are coming back."

That's his response? "This isn't a trend like fanny packs."

"No, not like that." He scrapes my phone off the squeaky tile. "You know that cryptid subReddit Allison told me about? There have been tons of stories about werewolf bites."

I usually don't believe his girl-space-friend, but . . . "Really?"

"That's what they say. But are you sure that's what happened?"

"What do you think?" I touch my bandaged stitches, which are throbbing as the painkillers wear off.

My phone rings, and Jack hands it to me. "Lexi."

I press it against my ear. "Hello?"

"Jude? Where are you?" She sounds annoyed.

I fiddle with the hem of my hospital gown. "I'm in the hospital."

"Oh my goodness, what?" Lexi's deep voice rises a notch. "Are you okay? What happened?"

"Um, I was bitten by a . . ." A sudden jolt of fear wraps around my throat and pulls tight. What will she think if I tell her the truth?

"Say it," Jack mouths.

". . . a wild animal at school," I finish.

Jack facepalms and sinks into his chair.

What does he want me to say?

"What? What was it? Does the school know?" Her questions trip over each other.

"I think it was a wolf, but I don't know. It was too dark to see." My foot jitters under the bedsheet.

"Wolves? I thought Madi was joking."

Discomfort building in my chest, I scrounge for an excuse. "Remember that moose last year?"

She's quiet for a moment. "Are you okay?" Her timbre drops. "It's not bad, is it?"

"Just a few stitches in my shoulder and a heckuva rabies shot. I'll be okay." Palms sweating, I switch the topic. "Are you at Perkins?"

"Yes. And Jude, these waffles are *amazing*." Her lips smack, and I can hear her smile. "Was this your idea?"

"Yeah." I ruffle my hair, my face warm. "I was going to ask you to prom. I mean, who can say no to—"

Jack clears his throat. Loudly. I pull the phone back an inch and *shush* him.

"Heart-shaped waffles! Of course I'll go with you." Her voice buzzes with excitement—or a sugar overdose. "Promise me you'll stay away from any wild animals."

My feet do a little happy dance. "Awesome, and yes, I will." A nurse raps on the doorframe, and I motion him to come in. "I need to go. I think they're going to draw my blood. Love you, Lex."

"Love you too." She hangs up.

My heart monitor forms sharp peaks. It's less about the blood draw and more about the fact that I said the L-word, and Lexi didn't skip a beat. But now that I'm cursed? Who can say to a monster "I love you"?

Jack waits for the nurse to leave before murmuring, "Bad move, Jude."

"What?"

"You sure you want to take her to prom?" He turns his phone screen so I can read it: *Next full moon: Friday, May 3.*

It feels like my heart plummets to the floor.

Prom night.

I rake a hand over my face. Prom's supposed to be unforgettable, a night to knock Lexi's socks off, but how can I do that with four left feet? How can I woo her when I'm not even human?

My fingers remember the sticky feeling of my blood dribbling down my collarbones. The image of Thad's crimson-tinged fur sears my retinas. I rub my jaw. Is the hair on my chin longer, thicker? Is the curse already beginning?

Jack leans forward. "Are you going to tell her?"

My insides numb because he's right, and I know when I tell her, Lexi will realize that her childhood crush isn't worth the L-word after all.

"I'll cancel prom." My voice is barely a whisper.

"Good choice." Jack settles in his chair, likely reading his cryptid subReddit.

I sigh, relieved he didn't see through my half truth. I *will* cancel prom, but I won't spill my werewolf guts to Lexi. Not quite yet.

In the meantime, I need a good excuse to bail on her—and a safe room for my first night as a werewolf.

The waxing moon watches me through the sunroof of my car. I yank it closed, the hairs on the nape of my neck standing on end. My transformation isn't for another seven days, yet the three weeks since the attack have slipped through my fingers like slobber from a dog's mouth.

I cruise down Lookout Hill. A shopping bag full of dog toys slides off the backseat, and I pray the economy fridge I stuffed in the trunk survives the bumpy trek to the library. My family thinks I'm adopting a dog for college—there's an ongoing bet on the breed. Jack's the only one who knows the truth: these purchases are the last items I need for the "Werewolf Intensive Containment Unit" (WICU for short).

The other part of the plan—canceling prom—is still a giant *to-do* on my list. I meant to do so during our weekly study date at the library, but first I had my stitches removed, then I babysat my siblings last minute, then I stayed home because of a headache, so I pushed it off to tonight.

My Toyota rumbles into the library lot. Lexi's baby-blue Volkswagen Beetle is parked crookedly as always. I've always teased her that she can write perfect letters, draw perfect lines, and earn perfect grades, but she can't park perfectly to save her life. *And I'll be ruining one more perfect thing for her.*

Opening my car door, I take a deep breath of humid air. *Tell her what she needs to know now and figure out the rest later.*

I enter the library and meander to the balcony where plump couches overlook a swath of forest. Light from a reading lamp turns Lexi's hair gold. She's stretched across a loveseat, her foot bouncing to an invisible beat.

I slow. It reminds me of the Christmas party, finding her reading and challenging her to a game of Truth or Dare. Maybe I can ease into this conversation too.

"Hey, Lex." I set my backpack down.

"S'up?" She swings her legs over the edge of the couch to make room for me and pulls down her long sleeves.

"The ceiling." I sink into the cushions, wishing they would envelop me like my fears. I unzip my backpack and grab a book I checked out a few days ago.

Lexi reads the cover as I crack the aged spine. "*Lycanthropy: The Werewolf, the Myth, the Legend*. What's *that* for?"

I'm leaving sweat marks on the pages. How is she not warm? "I saw a YouTube video about werewolves and got curious."

"Huh." She returns to reading her book: *Hereditary Disorders.*

"Are you studying genetics in bio?"

"Um, yeah." She takes a long sip of water. "I think it's really interesting."

The Lexi Crawford I know has *never* been interested in science, but my throat clenches like a squeezed tube of toothpaste, so I let it slide.

As I read, the strangled feeling only grows worse.

Werewolves put their communities at risk. Under a full moon, they are no longer purely human. Their primitive selves take the reins, intensifying their flight or fight response to animalistic extremes, setting their instincts on high alert, and filling them with insatiable cravings.

However, one thing remains untouched: the soul of a werewolf is fully human. When morning dawns, the damage of night becomes clear. Their uncontrollable fear, anger, hunger is seen in stark light.

A chill courses down my spine and strikes my stomach. *Uncontrollable.*

If I can barely talk to Lexi now, if I snap at my parents every time they mention the dog kennel in my bedroom, if I already have a hankering for meat—how much worse will it get once I transform? What if I go feral like Thad?

I have to confess. Everything. No excuses, no half truths, no pretend dogs.

I clear my throat. "Hey, um, I have a question for you."

"Yeah?" Lexi glances at me through her hair, and out of habit, I tuck the loose strands behind her ear. A leaf floats free from her tresses. Where did that come from?

I shake myself. *Focus.* "What would you think if . . . um . . ." I search for a way to ease into *hey, babe, I'm a werewolf.*

"Yes?" Her eyebrows pinch together.

"H-how would you feel if Madi's date canceled last minute? And-and how would she feel?" Ugh, that is the *worst* intro.

She slams her textbook shut. "Is Marcus standing her up?"

"N-no. It's, um, a hypothetical." I. Can't. Stop. Stuttering.

"Well, he'd be a jerk if he did." She reopens her textbook. Her words are a gunshot, a silver bullet straight to my werewolf heart.

I stare at our reflections in the dark window, unable to look at her directly. "Why do you say that?"

She closes the book again. "Isn't it obvious? It's Madi's first prom. You should've seen her face when she tried on her dress. It'd kill her if she couldn't go."

"Yeah." I drop my head. An illustration of a werewolf, blood coating its teeth as it rises on its hind legs, stares at me with charcoal irises.

Just like Thad.

Just like me. Jerk, werewolf—what's the difference to her?

"Is this really about Madi?" Lexi's voice is far from a whisper.

I wince, unable to look at her, but her gaze pierces me all the same. "No, it's

. . . I meant to tell you sooner."

"Tell me what?" Her question hangs dead in the air.

I twirl the leaf in my fingers, struggling to breathe. I can hear Jack's voice in my head: *say it*. "I have a scholarship interview prom night. I can't go."

My gaze flies to Lexi, and her gaping mouth mirrors my own.

I'm convinced that a few blocks away, at Pizza Hut where Jack works, he would be curled up on the kitchen floor, struck by a disturbance in the Force, crying, *You were supposed to tell her the* other *thing, Jude.*

Lexi sits up straight. Her textbook falls off her lap and thuds on the floor, summoning a librarian's *shh*. "Seriously, Jude? You couldn't have told me before?"

I scramble to salvage this. "I found out this week, I—"

"You *know* how important prom is to me. There was no other day that would work for the U?" Her cheeks are red, her irises bright with fire.

My chest caves in. I knew she would be upset, but not like this. "N-no. There wasn't."

She snatches her textbook off the floor and stuffs it into her satchel. "First not studying for weeks, and now this? I see I'm not a priority to you."

Tears sting my eyes. "Lexi, that's not true."

"Prove it." She stands, hands on her hips.

Why is she being like this? My gaze latches on her long sleeves that have ridden up her arms with the movement, and I flail for a distraction. "Why are you wearing long sleeves?"

"*That's* what you have to say? Because I'm cold." She slings her satchel over her shoulder. "Enjoy your interview. I'll be at prom with people who care."

I launch to my feet. "Lexi—"

A frigid hand touches my shoulder.

I turn slowly and come face-to-face with a librarian, her glasses perched on the edge of her nose and her lips pursed. "If you two want to fight, take it outside or whisper quietly."

"I'm sorry, ma'am. I'll be going." Lexi tosses me a glare. "See you later, Jude."

She doesn't wave goodbye. Doesn't hug me. Doesn't reach out for a BFF handshake. She simply leaves.

The librarian's heels click away into silence.

I flop onto the couch like a marionette with its strings cut, trying to understand the part it played.

The WICU is complete. I canceled prom. Lexi doesn't know I'm a werewolf. It's everything I wanted on paper.

So why is there a gaping hole in my chest?

For the millionth time since the Disastrous Library Date That Wasn't, I check my phone. Nothing. Lexi's gone radio silent.

I flop on my bedroom floor, the bulb of my lamp blinking on and off, glinting off the metal rungs of the kennel like a promise. Seven o'clock was probably too early to close the blackout curtains I installed, but better safe than sorry.

I'm too acquainted with sorry.

I fidget with a chew toy and hit "next" on my rewatch of *The Mandalorian*. Right now, I wish I were in a galaxy far, far away, where my only concerns would be evading bounty hunters and raising a little green child.

Jack knocks on my door. "Jude? Your supper's ready."

"Pass it through the doggy door." A home improvement my parents didn't quite approve of, but they'll understand after tonight.

How many hours are left before my whole family knows?

"Okay." Jack sounds resigned. "Jace, you can't fit through the doggy door. You'll get your head stuck, and I'll have to cut it off like a guillotine. Do you want that?"

The maniacal laughter of our twelve-year-old brother grates on my sensitive ears as I cross the room. Jack passes me a plate loaded with homemade fries and a chicken sandwich. I salivate at the meat. The flap closes, but not before Jocelyn can stick her decorated fingers through.

"Look, Jude! I can do your nails, too, if you come out."

My nostrils fill with the intense chemical smell of the polish, and I force down a gag. "No thanks, Lyn."

"Hey, dinner's ready upstairs. Go eat." Tiny feet scamper away, but I know Jack's still there—I can smell his deodorant, the pizza sauce under his fingernails, the mousse in his hair that does nothing to tame his curls.

I shouldn't be able to sense these things. Am I already changing?

He peeks through the doggy door. "Do you want me to chill with you?"

"Not right now. Go eat."

The flap swings shut, but he doesn't leave. "Oh, I just remembered. I heard from Lexi."

Jealousy stabs my stomach. I tap my phone screen, empty of notifications. "Yeah?"

"Allison told me Lexi's going with Thad, her brother."

"Thad?" My heartbeat stutters. "He's not a pole vaulter, is he?"

"Yeah, although he hasn't been at a meet in a while. Some guy jumped him and stuck a knife in his eye or something." Jack makes a sound of disgust, and it reverberates in my ears. "Why do you ask?"

Adrenaline bursts through my veins. Limbs shaking, I rush around my room, grabbing my wallet, keys, and a hoodie as the world turns upside down. I canceled on Lexi because I knew what tonight meant. Beyond the blackout curtains, the full moon waits. Waiting to rise, waiting for prom to begin, waiting to turn boys into monsters.

Thad should know better. And yet he, a werewolf before I was, the werewolf that bit me, the werewolf that should be hiding, is going to prom with *my girlfriend*?

"Hey, earth to Jude," Jack says.

"Thad is your girlfriend's brother? Why didn't you tell me?"

"Allison's not my girlfriend." Jack huffs. "And what's so wrong with Thad?"

I stuff my hairy arms through the sleeves of my hoodie and throw open the bedroom door, forcing Jack back. "Thad's the werewolf!"

His jaw gapes, but he doesn't make a sound.

I shove past him. The house is sharp, jagged on my senses like a werewolf's claws: dishes clattering upstairs, more chicken charring on the grill, carpet poking through the holes in my socks. It does nothing to lessen the anxiety pulsing through my veins.

If Thad hurt me, what will he do to Lexi?

"Where are you going?" Jack calls.

"To school." I take the stairs two at a time. I can feel my parents' quizzical gazes as Jack and I dart past the dining room.

"They're already in the car." Jack snags my arm in the entryway.

I teeter off-balance, struggling to jam my feet into my sneakers. The sunlight streaming through the front window casts Jack's face in half-gold, half-shadow.

"It's almost sunset," Jack hisses. "You'll be too late."

"Then I'll fight him as I am." My voice quavers. I know I'm not thinking straight—even as a werewolf myself, I don't have the experience Thad has—but I have to try.

Jack's grip on my arm loosens. "What if we called the police?"

"And they'll what? Get bitten, too, while trying to lock him up?" I wrench away from Jack and open the front door. "I'll call you on my way home."

Jack sighs and sticks his hands into his pockets. "Stay safe."

I'm out the door and in the driver's seat of my Toyota before he can say another word.

My tire wheels screech as I tear out of the neighborhood. The left turn arrow for the highway to school blinks yellow, but there are too many cars. I drum my fingers on the steering wheel, nails scraping pleather. "Come on, come on," I beg.

The red light winks at me like the Eye of Sauron.

Cursing, I fish my phone out of my pocket and dial Lexi.

"Hi, you've reached Lexi Crawford," her cheerful voicemail greets me.

The arrow flashes green, and I accelerate onto the highway. "Lexi," I say over the purr of the motor, panic bleeding into my voice. "Lexi, you have to come home. Thad isn't safe. Call me."

Cars zip past on the highway toward the rising moon on the horizon.

After an eternity of driving—are everyone and their grandma's feral cats out tonight?—I whip into the school parking lot. I scan my rapidly darkening surroundings, praying Lexi isn't already inside. Even from this far away, my ears can make out the sounds of "A Thousand Years" playing in the gymnasium.

My body shakes. Prom's already started.

I'm so distracted that I barely notice two girls, arm in arm with a tall boy, striding into the path of my car. I scream and slam on the brakes.

They jump out of the way. A blonde girl in a green dress with flowy sleeves turns, anger clear in her blue eyes as she locks her glare on me. For a moment, I'm transfixed by the waves of hair dancing around her face, her elegant curves, her ruby lips. Lexi looks so beautiful tonight.

"What the heck are you doing?" Her yell breaks me out of my reverie.

I kill the engine and jump out of the car. "Lexi."

"Jude?" She blinks. "What are you doing here? What about the interview?"

"Yeah, what's wrong with you?" Thad steps up beside her. A black patch covers his left eye—the one I keyed trying to flee from him. He crosses his arms. "Wait, do I know you?"

"This is Jack's little brother," Allison offers.

"Can we talk?" I take Lexi's wrist, my fingertips brushing the yellow tulips of her corsage, but I must have grabbed her harder than I thought because she totters on her high heels.

Lexi braces a hand against my chest. "What's going on?" Her sleeve slides down her arm, and something about her skin looks off. Has Thad already hurt her?

Rage surges in my veins. "I'll tell you, we just need some space." I switch our positions—her with her back to the Toyota, me with my back to Thad. "There. That's better."

"Do you guys need a minute?" Allison asks.

"That'd be great, Ally," Lexi says over my shoulder, her gaze fixated on me. "Why are you puppy guarding me?"

My body shakes. There's no way I can say this without implicating myself. Without spilling everything. But it's the only way to protect her.

Even if she never sees me the same way after.

"When I was in the hospital last month, it wasn't because I was bitten by an animal." I rub anxious circles on the inside of her wrist. "I was bitten by a werewolf. Specifically Thad."

"He's a *werewolf*?"

"That's why he wears the eyepatch. I keyed him so he'd be down long enough for me to get help." I swallow, my heart knocking hard against my ribs. "I think I'm cursed too. So I made up an awful excuse and canceled prom because tonight is a full moon, and I don't know what's going to happen."

My throat feels scraped raw. My insides hollow. Everything is out in the open.

And Lexi is staring at me, not saying a word.

She reaches for the scar peeking out from my collar, her touch surprisingly gentle. "Is that why you've been acting so weird? With the library and the dog and everything?"

"Yeah." I study the cracks in the pavement, the twinkling stones of Lexi's bedazzled heels, and huff out a laugh. "I'm the dog."

Thad taps his foot impatiently. "We really need to go—"

"Stay right there." Lexi's voice cuts into him. "You are not going anywhere near that school. Go sit in the car and tell your sister who you are."

"I'll be fine," Thad growls. "There's no moonlight inside."

I cross my arms. "What song is playing in the ballroom?"

"'Enchanted' by Taylor Swift," he answers without thinking.

Ally's forehead creases. "How can you *hear* that? I can't even feel the bass."

"See? Your senses are already heightened. You're changing, like it or not." I snap my fingers, and he flinches. "Now get in the car—or do you want me to report you to the police when you bite another high school student?"

After a beat of silence, Thad and Allison's footsteps shuffle away. The tension in my body eases slightly. But I'm still waiting. Waiting for Lexi to say more.

"Why didn't you tell me?" she whispers.

"I was scared. Of what you would think. Of what it would do to us." I lift my head, and the expression on her face isn't scolding or upset or angry. If anything, it's amused.

"I guess I can't judge you when I have a secret too." She releases my hand and pulls up the sleeve of her dress until it bares her arm.

A pattern akin to tree bark crisscrosses her skin. Curious, I brush my fingers over it. It feels rough and wooden, and I trace it all the way to her upper arm, to a green tattoo: an exact replica of our willow tree carving.

"You got some ink?" I shake my head. "How is that equal to . . .?"

"Doesn't feel like skin, does it?" She smirks, but the corners of her mouth quiver. "My mom's a dryad. I knew, growing up, that there was a chance I could manifest power before my eighteenth birthday, so I chose the willow tree to be mine if I ever turned—but I didn't think the carving would result in a tattoo." She chuckles, sheepish. "After a few years, I didn't think it would happen. Until it did."

I'd think she was bluffing, if it weren't for my own mythological nature. "When?"

"A few weeks ago. I meant to tell you, but you were acting strange, and I guess I was scared too."

I stare at her, limned in twilight. The fading rays of the sun catch on a leaf in her hair, matching the color of her dress. Out of habit, I pluck it free.

She grins, her face mere inches from mine. "See? We don't have to do this whole fairy-tale-creature thing alone, Jude. We can navigate it together. Hand in hand."

I brace my arms on the hood of the car, closing her in. "Hand in paw."

Her eyelids flutter shut. I lean closer, closer, closer until our lips meet. The kiss is sweet and soft, and I never want it to end.

Lexi pulls back with a gasp. "The moon," she blurts, her cheeks pink. "We should take you home. I can stay, if you want. Be there when you transform."

I hesitate. What if I hurt her? But this is her choice to make, and I'd appreciate the company, even if we're sitting on opposite sides of the safe room door.

"Sure." I glance at Thad in his car, where it looks like he's undergoing a verbal lashing from Allison. "Let me ask Jack if the WICU has room for a few more."

"The WICU is a dumb name, by the way," Lexi quips from the other side of the wall we've set up in my bedroom, made of old poster boards and dining-room chairs.

My mouth quirks into a smile between stabs of searing pain in my muscles.

Thad lets out an inquisitive *ruff*. He's already shifted, his long lupine frame curled up in the dog kennel pressed between my bed and the economy fridge, a chew toy between his paws. Although I'm not enthused he's here, he needs a secure place tonight. Turns out he bit me last month because I genuinely startled him in the locker room. He felt the transformation coming on, and he was terrified of being seen, which led to his teeth in my shoulder and my key in his eye.

Still not sure how to explain *that* part of the story to my parents. The least I can do is pay for Thad's optical surgery.

I assess the kennel. How much could I sell it for on eBay?

A tremor splits through my spine, like it's ripping in two. I howl—and honestly? It's kind of a pathetic sound.

"Jude?" Lexi's voice tinges with concern. *Captain America: The Winter Soldier* freezes on my laptop screen; she must have stopped casting from her side of the partition. "Jude? Do you need me to come over?"

I moan in reply, my spine straightening of its own volition, stretching to include a tail. My stomach twists. Fur sprouts from my skin and covers every inch. Muscles bulge, nails sharpen to talons, my clothes shred as I become something other, something inhuman.

And I wait.

For the bloodlust, for another howl, for Avengers-like strength to course through my veins. Instead, I can taste the raw steaks in the economy fridge on my teeth, count each individual pixel of Black Widow's face, and feel an irresistible urge to scratch behind my ear with my hind leg. *Oh, yeah. That's the spot.*

I stop itching, suddenly embarrassed.

This is what I was so afraid of?

A knock sounds on my bedroom door. "Everything okay?" Jack asks.

Lexi stands. A chair creaks, then she's looking over the partition at me, my leg frozen halfway in the air.

She ducks her head into her bark-covered arms. Her shoulders shake.

She's *laughing*.

I yip. She thinks my compulsive need to scratch is funny?

She lifts her face, happy tears in her eyes, the liquid sparkling like fairy dust. "We're fine, Jack," she calls. "Now stop bellyaching and enjoy your date with Allison."

"It's not a date," Jack protests.

Lexi winks at me as he walks away.

Before I can say a word, she's moved the poster boards aside and plopped her laptop next to mine on the floor. She sits crisscross beside me, having exchanged her prom dress for some comfy sweats from my older sister's closet.

My tail tucks between my legs. She's too close. Too comfortable with this version of me. What if something goes wrong?

Lexi holds out her hand to me. Gently beckoning.

I pad closer and sniff her fingers. She smells like fresh dirt and sunshine and the safety of a weeping willow. Our weeping willow.

I close the distance between us, curling up in her lap like an oversized dog, pressing my nose into the *J + L Forever* tattoo on her arm. My tense body relaxes. I paw the laptop keyboard until I hit PLAY.

Lexi scratches under my chin. It feels glorious.

The movie rolls on, my eyelids growing heavy with sleep. And as Captain America says to Bucky, "I'm with you to the end of the line, pal," I feel a soft kiss on my forehead.

I blink my eyes open. Lexi's golden hair surrounds us like the branches of the willow.

"You're a good boy," she whispers.

I woof softly. *A boy in love.*

RACHEL NORTH

Raised as the only girl in a family of boys, Rachel North is used to holding her own. She loves reimagining historical accounts and classic tales with strong YA heroines who fight for hope in a grim world. She lives in Minnesota, where the cold weather gives her the perfect excuse to stay inside and watch *Pride and Prejudice* (2005) for the hundredth time. When she's not writing, she's learning to be gentle with her chronic depression by pursuing her joys of hoarding fairytale collections, trying new anxiety fidgets, and writing indie-folk music.

Achievements

- Drafted four novels and four novellas.

- Received and implemented three developmental edit letters, including one from award-winning YA author Nadine Brandes.

- Attended over a dozen writers conferences, including Realm Makers (2020-2024) and The SCBWI Marvelous Midwest Conference (2019).

- Taught the session "Writing and Mental Health" at the One Year Adventure Novel Summer Workshop in 2022.

- Received interest in multiple projects from editors and agents.

- Placed in the One Year Adventure Novel Student Novel Contest three times: finalist (2020), second place (2022), and winner (2023).

Pitches

- *Pride and Prejudice* meets *This is How You Lose the Time War* in a YA historical fantasy about a cryptographer who must time travel to reverse her ruined reputation—but unless she makes peace with the present, she'll destroy time itself.

- *The Kingdom of Back* meets *The Hunger Games* in a dark academia YA historical fantasy about a girl competing in a magical trial to succeed Vivaldi as the conductor of Italy's only female orchestra.

- *Hoodwinked!* meets *Maxine Justice: Galactic Attorney* in a YA fairytale about a cash-poor defense attorney who fights to win the court case of the century: Cinderella's stepsister vs. Fairy Godmother.

- *Echo North* meets *Romanov* in a YA historical fantasy about a huntress who must save her dying father by capturing a magical bear—but she doesn't know that doing so will unleash a terrible evil on 1360 Norway.

HISTORICAL & CONTEMPORARY

PHONE CALL TO THE WIND

Calissa Ding

Baba's favorite place was the hill where we planted the cherry blossom tree. She used to say that from there, you could see all the way home.

But that's not true.

Even if you hike to the very top of the hill and squint out over the waves that wrestle each other on stormy nights. Even if the sky is cloudless and the sun is bright. Even if you have *the sight of a hawk*, as Mom might say, you can't see Baba's first home.

It's eleven hours across the ocean. Of course you can't.

That's what I told her, but she shook her head and said, "Imagine it, Mari-chan."

My grandmother loved that hill. But if she were still around, I don't know if that'd be true anymore.

It's morning and the air smells like wet earth. I'm standing in the spongy grass and staring at the big crack down the middle of the trunk, and things are definitely looking bad.

I readjust my glasses. The crack seems to widen.

Definitely.

The fancy scientific name for a cherry blossom tree is *Prunus serrulata*, which I learned from Baba's gardening books. Dad wishes I played sports or did something a little more active than exploring my grandmother's library, because I'm twelve and *full of possibility*. But the only possibility I'm thinking about is if the tree will ever bloom again.

Last spring, it spread pink and white flowering branches over us as we sat on the bench and felt the salt sky and sea on our faces. My grandmother would fall silent, which usually meant she was thinking of Japan. It meant she was missing it again.

Right now?

It's almost spring. The sky is clear and blue.

The tree is spindly and dark and bare.

I glare up at the sky.

It's *too* clear and blue, like it's pretending that the storm last night never happened. The big, stupid storm that snapped stems and ripped out tufts of grass.

I curl my fingers. They're cold and stiff from the morning air.

I should've checked the weather forecast. Last night, I was lying awake in bed and listening to the wind howl, and I should've realized I had to cover the tree in a tarp or something.

Baba would have known what to do.

I kick the base of the bench Jiji built forever ago because *no wife of his was going to sit on the wet grass*. It doesn't feel as good as I thought it would.

Actually, it mostly just hurts.

An ache presses up against my throat, and suddenly I'm not thinking about my grandmother sitting on the bench, or helping me plant the tree, or telling stories about home. Instead, I'm seeing her the last night she—

I turn and start walking back down the hill. If I stand here any longer, I am probably going to start crying.

The grass squelches under my feet. The wind tugs at my skin.

At home, it is very, very quiet.

I take off my sneakers and line them up on the rack by the front door, then I slide on a random pair of slippers from the basket. I'm headed to the garage. Dad's at work, and Mom is probably at her book club, since it's Friday. But if I have to guess, my grandfather is in his workshop.

It's not like I feel like talking or anything. Mom and Dad are always trying to start these conversations around the dinner table where *everyone can be open and honest*. Asking all these questions. Asking how I'm feeling. Asking, asking, asking for words when all the words left with Baba.

I only cross through the kitchen and crack open the door because I know Jiji won't do that. I only peek in the garage so I'll know I'm not the only one here.

But then Jiji glances up from the table. His face cracks into a smile, his bushy white brows lifting.

His eyes are bright and blue, and he waves me in.

I step inside. The air is thick with sawdust and silence.

My grandfather flicks a peel of wood away. It lands by his shoe. The floor is covered in sawdust, since he never sweeps. He used to say it was your own fault if you went barefoot in here and got a splinter. This was mostly just to tease Baba, because she didn't let him wear shoes inside the house. She could never make him put on slippers instead, though.

That ache in my throat.

Jiji's hands, wrinkled like old candy wrappers, shake a little as he works. They've been doing that a lot recently.

"What are you making?" I ask.

He shrugs. "Not sure yet."

Jiji usually plans out his bigger projects, like chairs or benches or bookcases. He'll search up references and draw diagrams and make calculations, and sometimes I will sit in the corner of the garage and watch him work. It is precise. It makes sense.

When he's carving, it's different.

When he's carving, I usually leave and do homework instead.

He chisels the block of wood. "You're wearing your baba's shoes."

I glance down. I didn't even notice when I put them on, but they're *her* slippers, the ones with the big embroidered cranes on the straps. Jiji got them for her birthday one year as a joke. Baba loved it. Mom thought it was tacky, but I guess that was kind of the point.

The slippers used to be so big, but now they fit me just right. I don't know when that happened.

I swallow. "I have homework."

He peers at me.

"I have to leave," I say.

"You know, Mari," he says, "her birthday is on Sunday."

Oh.

Somehow, I forgot about that. I line up the dates in my head. It's been eight months since . . .

My grandfather's eyes are usually sharp, but right now they seem soft and worn-out, like Baba's favorite sky-colored apron.

"If you need someone to talk to, I'm here."

"I'm fine." But that's rude, so I add, sort of like an apology, "Thanks."

I hurry back into the house without wiping my—Baba's—slippers off on the mat. I slip them off, pushing them back into the basket at the front door, and I don't bother getting new ones.

Quiet. So very quiet.

I should go back to my room.

I should do my homework.

But my grandparents' room is right across the hall from mine, and before I know what's happening, I'm turning and going in.

My family doesn't believe in ancestral worship, but that doesn't mean we've forgotten Baba. Her hairbrush sits on the dresser, exactly where she left it the last night she was home, glinting with a few strands of silvery hair. And if I stand still on the tatami mat and breathe in, I think I can smell her vanilla perfume.

But the part that reminds me most of my grandmother is the tall bookshelf against the opposite wall.

It's spilling over with every book she has ever collected. It even holds the ones she brought from Japan, before she met and married an American teacher.

Jiji loved her. A lot. My grandfather didn't say it often. But you could tell from the way he looked at her and the hours he spent building that bookshelf and how he held her hand while she was—

Anyway. He loved her.

Baba's favorite was fiction. Most of the shelves are filled with novels.

But I'm not here for a story. I find the section on gardening in the bottom right corner and scan the titles. *The Gardener's Bed-Book. A Horticultural Universe. Mullin's Comprehensive Guide to Tending Trees.*

I choose the last one.

I imagine my grandmother flipping through the same pages, tabbing them with pastel sticky notes from her favorite stationery store. But then my chest tightens, and I focus on the table of contents. On the part about repairing trees.

The section is only a couple pages long. When I finish reading it, I squint out the window at the hill in the distance. Tomorrow is Saturday. No school. I'll do it as my birthday present for Baba. I mark the page with a yellow sticky note, shut the door quietly behind me, and take the book to my room.

When my grandmother went to the hospital eight months ago, the cherry blossom tree was a fluffy crown of pink and white. That's what you call peak bloom.

The petals had just begun to fall the night she left.

On good days, when Baba wasn't too tired, we went up to the hill and breathed in air crusted with salt, and she talked about her old home.

When she told stories about it, she always said to use my imagination. So I shut my eyes and imagined a world where summer storms turned dirt roads into playgrounds, where kids splashed in puddles and ran home covered in mud. I imagined the humidity hanging in the air like wet laundry, and a cherry blossom tree in a neighbor's front yard. I imagined Baba as a little girl, collecting fallen petals from the sidewalk and pressing them between the pages of her schoolbooks, though her parents scolded.

Sixty years ago in a world six thousand miles away. She never said she missed it, but she didn't have to.

Even before Baba went to the hospital, the hike up the hill had been getting harder and harder for her. She had to take lots of breaks, and Jiji or I held her elbow, and even then she was out of breath by the time we reached the top. But almost every day, she went up to watch the sea, and she just rolled her eyes whenever Jiji had anything to say about it.

Standing up here, I get it. I get why she came here every day, for the endless sky and sea and salt wind.

Even if there aren't any cherry blossoms right now.

Even if sometimes, it feels like the ocean took my grandmother and never gave her back.

I shake my head and focus on the book, the page that talks about tree repair. My breaths come out in cold puffs and fog my glasses. I keep wiping at them with my sweater sleeve.

My hands are heavy with the thick gloves Baba always wore when gardening. She always wore a hat with a huge shady brim, too, but I figured I wouldn't need that so much.

I couldn't find the gloves I wore when we planted the tree together, so I'm borrowing Baba's. Only because I have to. I found them in the workshop, tossed on the table and covered in a film of sawdust.

I got a pair of red tree clippers from the workshop too. On my way out, I spotted Jiji's carving project from yesterday. This morning, it looked less like a block of wood and more like a sculpture, though I still couldn't tell what it was.

When we tended the tree together, Baba taught me how to use the clippers. But she always helped me hold them up, guiding my hands. Carrying them up the hill was harder than I thought it would be. I set them on the bench as soon as I could.

Now I only have to hold the book. "It is important to prune back each of the damaged branches," I read aloud. "This will help the tree's wounds close up."

That sounds about right. I close the book and set it on the bench.

I lift the clippers and start with a thinner branch, one of the broken ones. The wind is ice, but soon I'm sweating beneath all my layers of clothes. The handles wobble beneath my fingers. I grip them tighter.

The first branch drops, and I stare at it for a few seconds.

I only clipped it at the area where it split, but the cut is a little crooked. I turn to another branch, also bent. I try to snip more carefully this time. You never want to hurt the tree—just to take away the bad parts. That's what Baba said.

Another branch snaps off and falls.

The buds are tightly closed, not a hint of pink in sight. I work anyway. The sun pulls itself up the sky like it's using the clouds as handholds, and more sweat beads on my forehead.

I keep working. The sun keeps getting higher. Mom would want me to put on some sunscreen, wear a hat. Dad would just be happy I wasn't reading in my room.

Neither of them know I'm up here. If I had told them, they'd have wanted to have another *open and honest* conversation. They'd have asked, "Why? Why are you doing all of this, Mari?" And I couldn't have answered, because I don't even really know why.

I just know that I have to.

I step back and inspect the tree. At least four or five branches litter the ground, but it still has that huge split right down the middle.

The ache in my throat is getting harder to ignore. I should probably check the book again. I set the clippers down on the grass, peel the gloves off my sweaty hands, and push my glasses up.

Then I pick up the book and flip to the right section.

"Sometimes," I read, "a pruning sealer may be used to patch up cracks."

My family doesn't have that.

"Another option is to wrap burlap around the trunk."

My family doesn't have that either. I try not to crumple the page in my fist and keep reading.

"However, in cases of extreme damage, it may be best to remove the tree entirely."

I slam the cover shut.

This time, I am a little less careful when I return the book to the bench. The cover gets bent in the corner, and I sit next to it and try to take deep breaths, slow and steady.

Dad would say to *weigh my options*, so that's what I try to do.

Sealer. Burlap. Removal.

My head hurts. Those all seem like adult things to do, to know. They seem like Baba things.

Big, stupid storm.

Big, stupid, horrible storm.

I have to keep working. I have to do something, or the lump in my throat will only make it harder to keep going and the tree will remain broken.

I stand. My legs are heavy, but I make them carry me back to the tree, to the clippers.

The waves are as wild and gray as the clouds. The sky is the same color as Baba's silver necklace.

It's supposed to be almost spring, but it sure doesn't feel like it.

Maybe I should ask Mom or Dad to help me buy the right materials. But then I'll have to tell them what I'm doing and they'll have so many questions and they'll poke holes in my plan until it falls apart. I take off my glasses and rub my eyes. They're hurting. Probably because I was staring at the same big dark break in the trunk for so long.

My breaths are shaky. If the tree was blooming, I would collect the petals from the grass and press them between the pages of books until they were flat and dry. That would have made Baba smile.

But it's not peak bloom. There are no petals.

My hands are trembling, and I shove them into my pockets. Why is this happening to me? Why can't I make the shaking stop? I try to swallow, but it makes my throat hurt. Everything hurts.

"Mari?"

I turn. It's Jiji, just coming up over the top of the hill, his hands in his pockets. His expression is creased with concern.

For a few seconds, he studies the situation. The pile of broken branches on the ground, next to the clippers, next to me. I imagine how lame it must look. I imagine how lame *I* must look.

I turn away.

Then he walks over to me and says, "Sit down."

"I can't."

"Why not?"

"I . . ." My throat is thick. "I can't."

The words disappeared eight months ago, so instead, I point at the tree Baba and I planted together so she could sit under it and remember home.

My grandfather sighs.

I kneel and pick up the clippers again. Somehow, they're even heavier than before.

"No," he says. "Not right now."

"Yeah, right now." But the clippers are trembling. I forgot to put on gloves. What if my hands are too sweaty and the handles slip from my fingers?

Jiji stares hard at me. "Would your grandmother want this? Would she want you trying to fix the tree alone and probably hurting yourself in the process?"

I don't meet his gaze. I don't care if he wants to have an *open and honest* conversation. I just need to do something.

I set the clippers on the grass so I can pull on Baba's gardening gloves, then I pick them back up. My arms are sore.

I stare at the tree, at the trunk split in half and the branches I cut to the ground and the buds that haven't bloomed, and I think what a big fat mess it all is. What a big fat mess everything is.

"Mari-chan," he says. I flinch. Only Baba called me that. "You don't have to fix it."

"But it . . ."

He doesn't interrupt. Just looks at me, waiting for me to continue.

I press the words back down. I was going to say that the tree belonged to Baba. And if I can fix it, maybe I'll feel a little more like I did when the two of us sat under the tree, and it was blooming in the spring, and the world was full of possibility.

And if I thought about that, I wouldn't have to think about other things. Like Baba in the hospital. Like Baba the last time I talked to her.

I can't tell him all that. It only makes my throat hurt more.

I step towards the tree. Every part of me hurts now, but I try to raise the clippers. They start to slip, even though I'm wearing Baba's gloves.

Suddenly, Jiji is at my side, gently lifting the clippers away from me. He sets them on the grass a few feet away. I try to go to them, but my legs are wobbling and my stupid glasses are fogging up.

"I know," he says.

Right, I think. As in, *Yeah, right*. But when I wipe my glasses clear, my grandfather is staring at the tree. And maybe I'm imagining it or maybe it's just the sunlight, but on the side of his face that's turned to me, I spot a glistening in his eye.

A single shining tear.

I drop my hand. Jiji blinks and turns to face me fully.

"Let's talk," he says softly.

Maybe it's because I'm too tired to argue. Maybe it's because of that single shining tear. But I let him guide me back to the bench, where we sit side by side.

And when Jiji holds his hand out to me, wrinkled and shaking just a bit—the kind of shaking he probably can't stop—I take it.

The last time Mom and Dad took me to visit Baba, I couldn't look at her face.

She lay on the hospital bed, her hands draped over the sheets. She wasn't wearing any gardening gloves, and I could see the blue veins winding like rivers underneath her skin.

"Mari." Mom nudged me. She wasn't crying at the moment, but I knew she had been because her eyes were red and puffy. "Do you want to say anything? Right now?"

I shook my head. But then Mom looked as though her eyes were about to get even redder and puffier, which I definitely did not want, so I took a tiny step closer to the bed.

I stared at my grandmother's hands. Pale even against the blankets, filled with rivers.

Facts. Facts are good.

"The scientific name for a cherry blossom tree," I whispered, "is *Prunus serrulata*."

She didn't respond.

I swallowed. The heart monitor beeped, slow. Someone had closed the curtains. Why was the room so dark? Didn't they know my grandmother loved the sun?

"Mari." Mom put a hand on my elbow, probably about to send me out of the room. I shrugged her away. She wanted me to say something. I was saying something.

"Peak bloom happens sometime between March and April," I said.

I wasn't exactly sure why, but it was important that I remind my grandmother of these things. It was important that she remember.

At that point, Baba couldn't even speak much. I'm not sure if that was because she was too weak or because she just didn't feel like it.

Behind me, Mom and Dad were whisper-talking to each other.

But Baba's hands twitched, just a little. She could hear me. She was listening.

"Some varieties of this tree," I said, "can grow up to . . . up to . . ."

But the facts got stuck. They didn't make it out.

"Mari." This time it was Dad nudging me. Mom was crying again. "Not right now. Maybe another time, okay?"

Okay. Okay. It would be okay.

I blinked quickly. I could feel the facts hardening, twisting, becoming a knot in my throat.

An hour later, the heart monitor showed a single flat line. It might have looked like a river, if a river was a smooth, straight, unchanging line going absolutely nowhere.

But then they hurried me out of the hospital room and Mom went through an entire box of tissues and Jiji held my hand as we waited in the lobby.

I still saw it. That line, going nowhere.

"Some varieties," I said under my breath, "can grow up to fifty feet."

The last time we measured the tree on the hill, it was sixteen. I was about to say that, too, when Jiji glanced down at me. His eyes were clear blue. His grip tightened.

We sat together, quiet, in a room in a world without my grandmother.

We sit together, quiet, on the bench on the hill.

For a little while, neither of us says anything. I'm holding Jiji's hand. It's steadier now.

Finally, Jiji says, "You know that picture at home? The one in the kitchen?"

I nod. It's the only photograph my family keeps in the kitchen, hung up on the wall so you can see it as soon as you come through the doorway. It's of my grandparents when they got married. They're young, all dressed up in black and white and looking kind of stuck-up and stiff, which I guess is what you were supposed to do in wedding photos back then.

"We were so serious," Jiji says, as if he can read my mind. "You know, your grandmother never liked that picture. That's why I kept it there." He laughs, and the sound is like scratching sandpaper.

"Why not?" I ask before I can stop myself.

"Hm?"

It's too late to take it back. "Why didn't she like the photo?"

"Ah. Well, I think it had something to do with her hair. She hated that style."

Now that I think about it, I guess Baba's dark hair was sort of poofy. But what I remember most is the expression on her face. When you lean in, you can see that her eyes are crinkled a little around the corners. Like she knows she's not supposed to smile, but she wants to anyway.

I start to smile, too, but I stop myself.

Jiji lets go of my hand, reaches into his pocket, and pulls out a small wooden carving. I stare at it. Now I know what it's supposed to be. He must have worked on it since I left this morning.

The telephone shape is carved from smooth, unpolished wood, and the handle seems just big enough for Jiji to hold to his ear and pretend like he really is calling someone. But he doesn't do that. He stares down at the pretend phone in his fist.

"For a long time," he says, "I believed in the numbers. The facts. What I could measure and what I knew for certain."

I'm not sure why he's telling me this, but I know what he means.

"And then I met your grandmother."

Here comes the sappy part. I sigh.

"I know. I know. You don't want to hear it. But when I was first getting to know her, I found out she was *terrible* at math. She never could remember her multiplication tables. And you know what? She couldn't care less."

That sounds like her.

"At times, it was frustrating. We were very different." He turns the phone over in his hand. "But eventually, I learned that my numbers and my facts are not the only things in the world. The stories matter too. That's what your grandmother believed."

I stare out at the waves, watching them churn.

"Mari."

"What?" I wait for him to scold me. I'm being really rude. But maybe if he starts giving me a lecture about manners, he'll stop talking about Baba.

"May I tell you a story?"

I breathe in. I count for one, two, three, four seconds, then breathe out for the same amount of time.

"What kind of story?" I ask.

"A true one," he says. "And a sad one."

"I don't want sad."

"I know, Mari-chan. But there's hope too."

I rub my eyes, even though they're dry. "I don't know what that means."

Gently, Jiji reaches out, uncurls my fist, and places the wooden telephone in my palm. My fingers curl around it.

"You will," he says. "Now may I tell it?"

I think about it. I think about how cold and tired I am right now, how my grandfather sat with me in the hospital lobby, and I think about that single shining tear from earlier.

Maybe that's why I whisper, "Okay."

So he tells me.

He tells me a story that is both sad and true, a story that really happened several years ago in Japan.

It begins with a man building a phone booth in his garden. It held a coal-black telephone, but it wasn't connected to a line. It was connected to the wind.

"I don't get it," I say.

"Just wait," Jiji says.

I wait.

The man built the phone booth because of a deep and heavy sadness, for his cousin had passed away recently, and the man needed a way to continue the conversation he had lost when he lost him. He needed to find the words again.

So, the man went into the booth, picked up the disconnected phone, and talked to his cousin.

Of course, he knew he wouldn't hear an answering voice. He knew his cousin was not on the other end of the line. But the wind phone wasn't about that. It was about the imagination. The things you cannot see or hear or measure, but that matter all the same.

A year after the man built the phone booth, the great wave—the tsunami—came. It rose from the sea and swept through the region, destroying homes. Taking thousands of lives.

"I don't want sad. I told you."

"I know," Jiji says. "I know it's not an easy story. I'm sorry. But that's not all."

After the tsunami, many were left mourning.

Then they began to hear about the man, the garden. What he had built. They started traveling to the phone booth, and word spread. More visitors came from all over the world, journeying to the garden to speak to their lost loved ones.

Hi, they would say into the receiver. *I miss you. I love you. It's been a while. Here's how I've been.*

Are you there? Are you listening?

Hello.

Goodbye.

In that phone booth in a garden in Japan, where the wind took up their words and carried them to distant places, people began to set down their loads of sadness. Just a small piece at a time, with each word they didn't get to say before. And, eventually, they started to feel like they could keep living.

Like the man who first built the phone, they did not come to hear a voice through the line.

Instead, they came to find their own again.

And that is the story.

I grip the wooden phone. It's smooth and solid in my fist.

"I don't have a phone booth," Jiji says, "but I have this carving. This hill that your grandmother loved." He points. "This tree."

It all sounds kind of vague and *theoretical*, as Dad would say. It sounds like the kind of story Baba would listen to with her eyes closed.

"Your sadness," he says. "It's not for you to keep to yourself."

The knot is still stuck in my throat. The broken tree's branches sway in the wind.

"I can't," I say. "I can't."

"Mari," he says, "do you know how she loved Japan?"

I nod.

"She loved you even more."

The wind smells like tears. I swallow.

Finally, I lift the phone to the side of my face and glance at my grandfather.

"I can leave," he suggests.

I shake my head. "No. I just feel kind of dumb."

He smiles. "It's okay to feel dumb."

I look out over the gray, gray sea. I imagine a world sixty years ago, six thousand miles across the ocean.

"The tree is dying," I tell the phone. I tell the wind. I tell my grandmother. "I—I'm sorry. I can't fix it."

My cheeks are wet. It's weird to realize that silent tears are dripping from my chin.

Jiji doesn't comment or point out my crying or even try to comfort me. Maybe he knows it would only embarrass me more.

I let the salty air fill my lungs.

After a few more breaths, I start talking again.

Baba told me lots of stories about when she got married. She and her new husband, an American teacher who built benches and bookshelves in his spare time, found a house by the sea so she could look across the waves whenever she missed home. They papered paisley on kitchen walls and hung up their black-and-white wedding photo.

And below that, on a table from a secondhand shop, they installed a cherry-red rotary phone.

I don't know where it is now, and no one owns phones like that anymore.

But back then, my grandparents used it a lot. Mostly to talk to each other, which might seem kind of silly because they lived together. Jiji always said that it was for Baba's sake, because she would get lonely while he was at work and want to talk to him.

Baba rolled her eyes at that. She said he was the lonely one. Dialing home when he was supposed to be working, chatting instead of grading tests. Meiwaku, she called him. Nuisance. But he kept the phone ringing.

And she picked up. Every time.

The breeze drifts. The waves toss below me. They're not wrestling today. Instead, it almost seems like they're playing.

I sit cross-legged on the hill in the grass, Jiji's wooden phone in my hand.

"Hi," I whisper into the receiver.

Daisies poke out of the grass around me. I loop the stem of one around my finger. Even with the bench here, Baba preferred to sit on the ground. At least, whenever her *joints didn't complain*.

"Jiji and I replanted the tree," I say. "We used a clipping from the old one. It's really small. No petals or anything. It looks kind of lame."

I stare at a strap of black Velcro that's peeling off my sneaker. The knot in my throat feels a little smaller these days.

"But it'll live."

Six years ago, Baba and I planted the cherry blossom tree on this hill. The sapling she had bought from the nursery an hour away didn't have a single petal, and I said it wasn't supposed to be like that. We must have gotten the wrong plant.

She told me not to be silly. She told me it would bloom. Not right now, but someday.

The clipping Jiji and I planted today is even smaller. It definitely doesn't have any petals. But I scoot closer to it and watch a ladybug climb over the mounds of fresh dirt we packed around the scrawny trunk.

Someday feels like a promise.

Yesterday, I visited her room again. I was putting away *Mullin's Comprehensive Guide to Tending Trees* when I found one of her old schoolbooks. I didn't understand the characters—Mom never could get me to learn Japanese—but I didn't really care. Because the book held traces of Baba's perfume, and when I cracked it open, I found some dried cherry blossom petals, pale and thinner than tissue paper, folded between the pages.

I wonder how old they are, and I wonder how old Baba was when she collected them.

It's spring. The sky is clear and blue.

"I miss you," I say.

I imagine the wind carrying my words all the way home.

CALISSA DING

In middle school, Calissa Ding was the kid constantly holed up in her room with a book. Now a young adult, she draws on her Chinese-American heritage and fresh perspective on growing up to write whimsical, real-world stories kids can see themselves in.

When not writing, Calissa can be found hunting for matcha soft serve, touring the local thrift stores, or playing Chopin's nocturnes on repeat. She also enjoys working with youth, both as a piano teacher and as a ministry volunteer.

Achievements

- Drafted six full-length novels, two short stories, and a novella
- Received three professional manuscript assessment letters and practiced editing on deadline
- Received and implemented numerous rounds of developmental feedback from professional editors
- Started a piano teaching business to practice in-person/online marketing skills and has taught over a dozen students
- Won writing competitions within The Young Writer's Workshop in 2020 and 2021
- Attended the Write to Publish and HopeWords conferences in-person and virtually in 2024

Pitches

- *The Labors of Hercules Beal* meets *Front Desk* in a middle-grade contemporary about a girl who tackles the school project of the century—fixing a hot air balloon—in order to remain the model student her parents love.
- *The Thing About Jellyfish* meets *Jennifer Chan Is Not Alone* in a middle-grade contemporary where a girl uncovers the mystery of her missing best friend through original fairytales he left behind as clues.

SAILBOAT OF DREAMS

Kristianne Hassman

Tears stream down my face, nearly blinding me as I stumble down to the cove. Thorny caper bushes scratch at my legs, but I hardly register the pain. *I have to get away.*

I duck around cactuses as I follow the familiar twists and turns of the path, one I've walked a thousand times. When I reach the red boulder, rising like a sentinel along the cliff, I cut down to the bluff overlooking the cove. There, I throw myself on the grass and bury my head in my hands as sobs shake my body.

Today was the day I was supposed to leave. To finally go on a grand tour of Europe with Mamma. To finally see what lies beyond the horizon and experience the glittering cities from Mamma's stories. To finally fulfill the dream I've had for thirteen years, ever since Mamma first told me about the adventures she took as a young woman from New York.

When I was only five years old, I'd declared with one hand clasped over my heart, "I'm going to go to all those places someday, just like you."

Mamma laughed, claiming I was born with her restless wanderlust in my blood. "On your eighteenth birthday," she'd always say as she tucked me in bed, "I'll take you to all those places, Flore. Just you and me. I'll show you the grandeur of Rome, the romance of Paris, and the arts of Vienna. I'll show you what the magic of a city can do to you."

And after years of saving and scrimping and planning, that dream was finally going to come true. Mamma and I were going to embark on a two-week cruise to some of Europe's finest cities. Until Mamma's sickness came back.

When she called me into her and Papa's room this morning, I took one look at her face and knew it wasn't going to happen. Even after all my late-night prayers to God, it was futile.

"I'm so sorry, my flower," she'd whispered, reaching up to cup my cheek. "We'll do it next year, *sì*?"

I'd swallowed my disappointment and attempted a smile. "Next year, Mamma."

But now, tucked in my favorite hideaway place away from my family's eyes, the tears flow freely. I suck in a shuddering breath and kick at a pebble lying near my foot. It bounces down the side of the cliff a few times before settling at the bottom among the yellowed rocks. Dull and bland. Like everything else about Lipari.

I've never understood how the tourists that flock here yearly can be so enraptured with this island. Then again, they haven't lived here their whole life. They've never longed to see beyond this little world, to experience wondrous places of adventure and excitement outside the island.

I gaze out at the ocean, breathing in the salty air. The ocean is the only thing I could never be tired of. A kaleidoscope of greens and blues, it's constantly changing. Never predictable.

A flash of white amid the waves catches my eye.

I squint, shading my eyes from the sun, and try to make out the shape bobbing beyond the breakers of the cove. Too big to be a buoy. Besides, buoys don't have sails. *What is a sailboat doing all the way out here?*

Curiosity compels me to scramble down from my perch and make my way down to the beach. *No one brings their boat all the way out here. Not this far from the village . . .*

But my eyes don't lie when I reach the shore. Sure enough, it's a boat, sails limp in the wind and its white sides gleaming in the late morning light. Even from here, I can tell it's a fine boat. And it appears unmanned, no trace of life inside.

Strange. I bite my lip, propping a hand on one hip. What should I do? I can't leave such a beautiful craft out there exposed to the elements. Suppose someone's searching for it?

I glance down at my blouse and overalls. I'm not quite dressed for a swim.

Mamma would probably be appalled if I swam in these, but then again, this is a unique situation.

"Why not?" I mutter to myself as I roll up my overalls and tie my hair back. Then without a second thought, I dive into the warm waters of the Mediterranean Sea and let them engulf me.

It takes me a few minutes of vigorous swimming to make it past the waves and reach the boat. I grip the side and peer inside, looking for any sign of its owner. But it's empty. Nothing to indicate to whom it belongs. Now that I'm up close, I can tell that it was once a beautiful boat, with its red oak sides and delicate trim. But the elements have worn away the paint and siding, leaving it a little worse for wear.

With a grunt, I haul myself inside the boat and use the one oar to row it closer to shore. Once I reach the shallows, I hop back into the water and tow it up onto the beach, careful to avoid the sharp rocks protruding from the sand.

There! With one final push, the boat skids onto the rocks and I collapse beside it. Once I've caught my breath, I take stock of the damage.

Some of the planks are broken and rotting. And water sloshes in the bottom. While the mast appears sturdy, the mainsail is completely shredded.

But despite all that, it's still a beautiful boat, evident by its level of fine detail. Whoever made this was a master craftsman.

I frown, tapping the side. Who would be so careless as to leave their boat untethered to drift out to sea? I know all of the fishermen's boats in the village, and I've never seen this one before.

I trace the outline of a boat in the sand as an idea swirls in my mind. *Imagine all the places you could go with a sailboat . . .*

With this boat, I could sail to Milazzo, the mainland, or even France. Mamma and I could still take our trip together, without needing any of the extra money that's going to Mamma's medicine.

Is this from you, God? For a moment, I half expect to hear a whispered reply in the wind. It's certainly a strange coincidence, if that's all it is.

But that still leaves me with a dilemma. Suppose it really *is* someone's boat? I can't very well just take it.

I'll ask around the docks. I pull myself to my feet. *If no one claims it, then I'll keep it.*

I drag the boat up so that it's sheltered behind the rocks. Then I roll up the legs of my soggy overalls and head for home. With the sun pushing midday, my siblings will be looking for me soon.

When I reach the house, I yank the screen door open. Judging by how quiet it is, the younger ones must be playing outside. I head upstairs to the room I share with Sophia. As I pass Mamma's closed door, I remember to be quiet and tiptoe past.

Sophia wrinkles her nose when she sees me. "What happened to you?"

She's a whole year younger than me, but she acts like she's ten years older.

"I went for a swim." I rummage around in the dresser, searching for my other pair of overalls.

Sophia makes a noise in the back of her throat as she goes to pick them up. She hates messes. "This early in the morning? Are you crazy?"

I roll my eyes. "Some of us actually *like* to swim, Sophia. Did you forget we live on an island? Aha!" I hold up the missing pair of overalls triumphantly. "I knew it was in here."

"You're making more laundry for me," she grumbles as I head to change behind the screen.

I pop my head out. "I'll take the twins and Giorgia down to the beach for the afternoon if you'll take care of the laundry. Please?"

She sighs. "Fine. As long as you don't track water into the house again."

"Deal." I finish changing and emerge from the screen. I toss my wet overalls to Sophia and give her a quick hug as I pass. "You're the best, Soph."

"I won't always be here to do your cleaning," she shoots back, but I can hear the smile in her voice.

I head down the hall toward the stairs, stopping when I notice Mamma's door is ajar. *She must be awake.*

I peek my head in. She's propped up in bed, reading a book. She's pale and thin, dark hair clinging around her face. But she must be feeling a little better, if she's awake reading. "Mamma?"

She looks up and smiles. "Flore, come in." I settle onto the bed beside her. "Where are you off to now?"

"I'm taking the younger ones to the beach, so Soph can get some work done."

"Ah, trying to get on her good side, are you?" She raises an eyebrow and I laugh sheepishly.

"Maybe." A bottle of pills on the nightstand suddenly catches my notice. "What are these?" I pick it up.

"Those are some new pills the doctor gave me for the pain. He stopped by earlier this morning."

I jerk my head up, heart in my throat. *Is she getting worse?* "He did?"

She smiles gently as she takes the pill bottle from me and replaces it on the nightstand. "It's nothing to worry about, my flower. He just wanted to make sure I was following his instructions."

I search her face, noticing how gaunt and pale her cheeks look. "Feel better soon, Mamma," I say, resting my head against her shoulder for a brief moment.

She brushes a few tendrils of hair from my face, her touch as soft as a butterfly's, before I get up. "I'm trying my best, love."

At the door, I pause and watch her for a moment, worry tickling the back of my mind. *She has to get better,* I think fiercely. My gaze drifts to the painting above my parents' bed of the lights of Paris, the Eiffel Tower rising in the background. One of Mamma's favorite paintings.

Her face always lights up when she's talking about her travels, and she seems so happy and full of life in those moments.

Maybe the boat doesn't have to only be for me, I think as I turn away. *If I can keep it and fix it up, I bet a trip with Mamma would be just the thing to help her get better. It would give us both something to look forward to!*

I send up a silent plea. *Please, God, let me keep the boat.*

A few minutes later, I head out with Giorgia and the twins, Marco and Matteo, in tow. At the fork, I lead them down the path to the village. As the dusty-colored houses of the village appear on the cliffside, Giorgia puckers her brow in confusion. "I thought we were going to the beach."

"We will," I promise. "I have a quick errand to run in town first."

At the docks, I ask around to see if anyone's heard of a missing sailboat. But when I describe the craft, the fishermen shake their heads. "We've never seen such a boat," they all say.

Once I've talked to every last fisherman I can find, I guide the kids back through the village toward the beach.

The twins run ahead down the street, shouting and jostling each other to be the first to get there, and I can hardly keep from grinning ear to ear. *I can keep the boat! Mamma and I can take our trip after all. Thank you, God.*

Giorgia sticks close to my side, chattering on about her friend Bianca's birthday party in a few weeks and all the wonderful things they're going to see at the cafe in Milazzo, Sicily.

I pass Salieri's Hardware, and the front display window catches my eye. I stop in my tracks and stare in wonder at the beautiful piece of sailcloth. The color reminds me of the cloudless blue sky on a sunny day. *It would be perfect for the boat.*

"There's going to be games and lots of cake and tea, of course," Giorgia chatters on, oblivious to the fact that I've stopped walking. "Oh, and Bianca said there's even going to be three kinds of gelato. *Three kinds,* Flo. How am I ever going to choose? Flo?"

She finally stops talking, but it only lasts for a brief moment. "What *are* you looking at?"

"Will you tell Marco and Matteo to come back?" I say. "I need to go inside."

"But what about the beach?" Giorgia whines.

"It will only take a moment," I say firmly.

She huffs but does as I ask. Once she corrals the twins back, I march inside and head straight for the display window. I finger the finely woven cotton, marveling at how firm yet flexible the cloth is. "It's beautiful," I murmur.

Giorgia wrinkles her nose. "What's so special about a piece of sailcloth?"

I ignore her and make my way to the counter before I lose my resolve. Signor Salieri glances up as he finishes wrapping a customer's order.

"How much is that piece of sailcloth?" I point to the display window.

He raises an eyebrow, but answers my question. "That would be twenty-five lira."

I gulp. That's a lot of money. More than I can afford.

I bite my lip. *I need to do this for Mamma. I can't give up on my dream.*

An idea forming, I turn to Signor Salieri. "Would you let me work for you in exchange for the sailcloth?"

He strokes his mustache thoughtfully. "I suppose there is some cleaning to be done around here, if you can come after closing."

Once we reach a satisfactory arrangement, which includes doing some extra tasks to pay for the other supplies I'll need, I manage to coax Giorgia and the twins away from the candy counter and leave the shop with a triumphant grin on my face. My plan is coming together.

Giorgia looks perplexed as we leave the village. "Are you really going to buy that sailcloth?"

I nod. "I arranged it with Signor Salieri. I'll work to pay for it."

"But why?" She stops in the middle of the road, planting her hands on her hips. "Does Mamma know?"

"Mamma doesn't need to know," I say carefully. "Look, this will be our little secret, okay?" I lower my voice to a whisper, glancing to make sure the boys are out of earshot. "No one but you and me know about it in the whole world. How special is that?"

Giorgia's eyes are huge, and I can tell she's tempted. She loves being privy to family secrets—especially when she's the only one who knows. Finally, she shrugs. "Fine, I won't tell Mamma." She shoots me a look. "But you can't keep it a secret forever."

"I will as long as I can," I murmur to myself as she runs ahead.

After the chores are done that evening, I sneak away while my siblings are occupied with a game of hide-and-seek in the backyard and grab some of Papa's old tools and scrap wood he won't miss from the shed. Then I take the path to the cove, eager to start my project.

First, I fix the broken slats and patch the holes in the bottom. As I yank up rotting planks with Papa's crowbar, I silently thank him for his insistence that we learn the basics of boat building.

Fishing and boat building have sustained this island for hundreds of years, he would say. *You're not a true Liparian unless you know both.*

By the time I've removed all the broken planks, sunlight is fading fast and my muscles are screaming in protest. I set my tools aside and lie back against the sand, my muscles protesting. Above me, tiny stars twinkle, gradually starting to appear amidst the dusky sky.

I tuck my hands behind my head and let out a sigh. If only one of those stars was a ship, coming to take me and Mamma away into the horizon. To escape this tiny island and leave Mamma's sickness behind forever.

Someday soon.

I jump up, suddenly realizing how late it's getting. *I'd better head home before someone notices.* I place the tools inside the boat and pull it back into its hiding spot. *Thank goodness no one else ever comes down here.* Just in case though, I drag a few branches in front of the boat.

Then I head back over the dunes toward home, the lantern swinging in my hand. Sophia is already in bed by the time I sneak upstairs. She turns over as the door groans behind me and frowns. "Where have you been?"

I shrug. "Out looking at the stars."

Sophia is silent as I change into my nightgown. "Mamma doesn't like it when you're out past dark."

"It was only just getting dark when I headed back," I retort. "Besides, I can take care of myself. Mamma doesn't need to worry."

"She's not well, Flo," Sophia says, her expression grave.

I hop into bed and pull the covers over me. "I know that."

"I mean really not well." I can feel Sophia's gaze in the dark. "She's getting worse."

I let out my breath in a huff. "Where are you going with this? Somehow, I sense a scolding coming."

"I don't want Mamma to be more worried than she already is."

I prop one hand against my head, holding Sophia's gaze. "There's nothing to worry about, Soph." I drop my gaze to the floor, debating how much to share with her. "Look, I have a plan to help Mamma get better. That's why I was out late tonight. I promise it's something good. Trust me."

Sophia sighs before she tugs the covers closer under her chin. "I hope you know what you're doing."

Oh, I do, I think to myself with a smile. I can't wait to see Mamma's face when she sees it. She's going to be so pleased.

Over the next few weeks, I spend every free moment down at the shore fixing up the boat. I manage to wrangle Papa's scrap wood into some semblance of a deck, although I end up with bruises from the hammer slipping. Next, I patch the holes in the hull with pitch. By the end, I'm covered in the stuff.

Sometimes, I'm so tired from the long days that I fall asleep working and jerk awake to darkness around me. Those nights, I hardly have the energy to stumble back home and collapse into bed fully clothed.

Sophia finally gives up lecturing me about my late nights. She shakes her head when I come back, covered in sweat and grime. Several mornings, I wake up late and stumble down to breakfast still half-asleep. But thankfully, Papa is so preoccupied with work he doesn't seem to notice. He's been awfully worried lately, trying to support all of us and have enough for Mamma's medicine.

My stomach twists. *I need to finish the boat soon.*

The next week, I work enough hours to bring home a bucket of white paint. Each afternoon, I dutifully sweep and clean the hardware store before working on the boat. *Soon that sailcloth will be mine,* I think to myself, imagining it billowing in the wind. *I can practically feel it, it's so close.*

Another week later, Signor finally hands me the sailcloth, packaged up neatly. "You've done good work," he says, patting me briefly on the shoulder.

"Thank you, Signor," I call as I head toward home, a bounce in my step.

Later that evening, I spread the heavy cloth on Papa's worktable. First, I measure and snip it to the right dimensions. Then, I pin up the edges to be sewn. I pull out one of Mamma's heavy duty sewing needles and start stitching.

The heavy fabric resists the movement of the needle and I grit my teeth. Finally, it pierces through the top, and I plunge it back into the cloth for the next stitch. I'm not nearly as good as Mamma at a needle, but I can hold my own.

After several stitches, I stop to examine my progress. *Oh no.* I groan at how crooked they are. *I'll have to start over.*

It takes hours of laboring by lantern light to even make a few presentable stitches.

I wish Mamma could help me, I find myself thinking as I prick my finger for the thousandth time.

No. I won't ask Mamma to help. She's tired enough already.

When I can't keep my eyes open anymore, I set it aside and head back to the house. I'm asleep as soon as my head hits the pillow.

When I finally make it downstairs the next morning, my siblings are already long gone at school. Mamma looks up from where she's reclining on the sofa.

"Are you ill, Flore?" she asks in soft concern. "You've slept a long time." She presses a hand against my forehead.

"I'm fine." I hold back a yawn. "I stayed out late last night gazing at the stars."

Satisfied that I don't have a fever, she removes her hand and pats the seat beside her. "I feel as though I've hardly seen you lately."

"I've been busy," I say, laying my head against her shoulder.

She smooths my hair with lily-white fingers. "My dear, hardworking girl," she murmurs. "I wish you didn't have to do so much. It's not right."

I glance up at her, noticing a sheen of tears. "Don't be sad, Mamma." I take her hand. "You're going to get better soon, and everything will go back to the way it was before."

She smiles, but it doesn't quite reach her eyes. "That's what I pray for every day. Despite it all, you've handled the disappointment of the trip so well and helped Sophia take care of things around the house." She squeezes my hand briefly. "I'm so proud of you, my flower."

Warmth fills me and I squeeze her back. "Soon this will all be a distant memory, Mamma. Someday, you'll be out there on grand adventures again, as though this never happened."

She chuckles. "My Flore, ever the sunny optimist. I can't wait for that day."

Noticing her empty teacup, I jump up. "I'll brew you some more tea, Mamma."

"That would be lovely, dear."

That afternoon, the children burst into the house after school. The boys immediately head out to play, but Giorgia wanders over to Mamma, dragging her bag along the ground.

"What's wrong, love?" Mamma asks.

"Bianca's sick, so we're not going to the tea shop tomorrow." Giorgia sniffles.

"Oh, love, come here." Mamma wraps an arm around her as Giorgia buries her head in Mamma's shoulder.

"There was going to be all kinds of gelato." Giorgia's voice comes out tearfully muffled. "And now I'll never know what they taste like."

"I'm sorry, Giorgia. That is disappointing." Mamma brushes tendrils of hair back from her face. "But you know, you don't have to go to Milazzo to have a tea party. What if you have one here, down by the shore?"

Giorgia shakes her head. "It won't be the same."

"Well, we can certainly try." Mamma straightens. "Why don't you ask Sophia to make some cakes and brew up a pot of tea. You can put on your best Sunday clothes and set the table with my china. And I can help you make invitation cards for each of your siblings."

Giorgia's eyes start to widen in excitement. "Can I ask Sophia to make little cannoli?" She smacks her lips. "They're my favorite. And we can have whipped cream to go with our scones. Oh, and strawberries too." She jumps up. "Sophia!"

She scurries off to the kitchen, still chattering about all her ideas. Mamma and I look at each other and chuckle.

"That was a simple enough fix." Mamma winks. "You'd better be prepared for your invitation to Giorgia's fancy tea."

"I can't wait," I say, laughing.

It takes me days, but eventually I start making progress on the sail.

One evening, after pricking myself again, I'm pressing a cloth to my finger when I hear footsteps outside. *Someone's coming.*

Heart racing, I scoop up my tools, including the sail, and shove them behind a stack of boards. I spin around, plastering an innocent look on my face, right before Papa steps inside.

"Flore." Surprise flickers across his face. "What are you doing here?"

"I was . . . uh . . . searching for something."

His brow creases, and I hurry to explain. "I was . . . looking for a screwdriver. To fix my mirror. The handle, I mean."

I hold up a screwdriver. "Found it."

Papa folds his arms over his chest, his expression anything but convinced. "What are you up to, Flore?"

"Nothing," I say quickly.

His gaze narrows, but he doesn't say anything. I avoid his gaze and edge toward the door, trying not to glance toward my hiding spot. "I'll go fix that mirror."

Once the door shuts behind me, I breathe a sigh of relief. *That was close.* I'll have to find a new hiding spot for the sail. And I'll need to be more careful next time. What if Papa found out I've been using his tools and supplies? He might make me give up the boat before Mamma and I can take our trip.

I can't let that happen. When I'm sure the coast is clear, I sneak to the back deck and tuck it deep underneath where no one will see it.

The night finally comes when I finish the sail. I'm so tired that I hardly feel a sense of accomplishment. *Tomorrow, I'll take it for a test run,* I think to myself as I crawl into bed.

The next morning, I rise bright and early and retrieve the sail from my hiding place. Then I sprint down the path to the cove. The sun is beating brightly by the time I reach the boat's hiding spot.

As I drag it across the sand and into the water, I notice the blank space on the stern, reminding me that I still haven't thought of a name for it.

I thought of using something like *The White Lady,* but that's too dramatic.

Maybe Mamma's name? *No, that's too obvious.*

I push those thoughts away for later and row until I'm beyond the waves. Then I raise the sail and secure the rigging, gritting my teeth with the effort. *Am I doing it right?* I scrunch my forehead, trying to remember Papa's instructions on how to catch the wind. I turn starboard so I'm ninety degrees off the wind. Then I gradually trim the sail until it's taut.

I release the rope, sit back, and let the boom swing to the other side. My breath catches. *Is it going to work?* Doubt niggles in the back of my mind that maybe all my work was for nothing. Maybe the boat is too far gone. Maybe it won't hold in the wind.

For a moment, the sail hangs limply. Then with a whoosh, wind fills it and the boat jerks as it's pushed forward. It skims along the waves, riding the wind.

I laugh breathlessly as water sprays into my face, hardly able to believe that I'm sailing. *It actually worked!*

The feeling of cutting through the waves sends energy coursing through me. One hand on the wheel, I spread the other out in the wind. All those hours of exhausting work, the aching muscles, the detail work on the sail—they were all worth it for this.

Once I'm satisfied that the sail holds, I pull the boat back to shore and scramble up the path toward home. Now that it's ready, I'm bursting to tell my family about it. *Mamma, Papa, all of them—they're going to be so surprised.*

My bare feet slap a rhythm on the sandy path. *I did it. I did it. I really did it.*

I turn the corner onto our driveaway and stop. The doctor's automobile sits like a dark omen, casting a shadow over the morning. My heart drops. *Not Mamma.*

My lungs scream for air as I race toward the house. When I don't find anyone on the first floor, I bound up the stairs, taking them two at a time. I nearly run into the doctor at the top.

He reaches out to steady me. "Flore. Your father was looking for you." He doesn't say anything else, just gives me a pat on the shoulder and a sympathetic glance before brushing past me.

Dread rising inside me, I round the corner to find my siblings gathered in the hallway outside Mamma and Papa's room, the door shut. "What happened?" I ask.

"Mamma fainted this morning, and it took awhile to revive her," Sophia says, biting her nails nervously.

I look up as Papa opens the door.

"Is she all right?" I ask, trying to peer around him at Mamma.

Papa nods as he closes the door. "She's sleeping. We need to let her rest after the doctor's visit."

The knot in my stomach untwists a little, but I know there's more going on. "What's wrong?"

Papa doesn't answer. "Leo, Flore, Sophia, we need to talk." He turns to the younger children, gentling his tone. "I want you three to play in the backyard for a little bit."

My heart drops. *What could possibly be so terrible that he can't say it in front of the younger three?*

I watch as they obediently head outside, as though they sense the seriousness of the situation. Sophia, Leo, and I file down the stairs and into the living room. Papa settles in his big chair and leans forward, his expression sober.

"You know that Mamma's been sick for a long time."

The three of us glance at each other and nod.

"Doctor Gallo says she's getting weaker every day. He doesn't think she's going to get better." His jaw tightens. "And as much as it pains me to tell you, I can't keep the truth from you." He closes his eyes briefly before opening them again. "Your mother . . . won't be with us much longer."

I feel as though all the air has been sucked from my lungs. *That can't be true. Mamma's been better lately. He's wrong.*

It takes me a moment to register that Papa is still talking.

"The younger ones might not understand what's happening, so I need your help. I need you to help me comfort them." He searches our faces. "Can I count on you for that?"

"Yes, Papa," Leo says solemnly.

"Mamma's *fine.*" I hardly realize I've voiced my thoughts aloud until I see

Papa's surprised expression. I rush ahead. "She needs more rest, that's all. She needs more fresh air and better food—"

"Flore," Papa interjects gently. "She's been resting for two months now, and there's been no improvement. We've done everything Doctor Gallo recommended, but it isn't enough."

He runs a hand through his hair, suddenly looking haggard beyond his years. "I'm afraid there's nothing more we can do."

Anger rushes up inside me. *Is he really giving up on her?*

"I don't believe that." I stand abruptly. "I'm not giving up on Mamma." I flee the room, ignoring Papa's calls to come back. I run out the back door, down the path, passing the red boulder in a blur. By the time I reach the cove, I'm gasping for breath, but I don't care.

I stare out at the sea, trying to calm myself as thoughts whirl through my mind. *Mamma can't be that sick. She can't. We still have to go sailing.*

My eyes catch on the little white boat—the boat I never named—lying on the sand.

Mamma's never going to ride it, I think bitterly. *We'll never take our trip. We'll never see the world together.*

Red swirling in my vision, I march over to the boat. I shove it as far as I can out into the water. The sail flaps loosely in the wind, and in dismay, I realize that my clumsy stitches must have loosened. It only makes me angrier. "Go," I shout. "Sail far away. You're useless now."

But it sits there, bobbing innocently in the waves. I slosh out into the water, not even caring that I'm soaked through. I grit my teeth and push with all my might, but the boat doesn't move.

Exhausted, I give up and collapse onto the sand. Worse than getting my hopes up once was getting my hopes up twice and still getting them crushed. All those hours spent on the boat were for nothing. *Wasted.*

Then one thought breaks through with startling clarity.

Mamma's going to die, and there's nothing I can do about it.

As reality sinks in, the floodgates open until I'm sobbing so hard I'm shaking. I hardly register when a strong arm encircles me, followed by Papa's soothing voice. "Shhh, Flore. It's all right."

I cry until I can't cry anymore. I cry for my lost dreams, for how unfair the world is, for the unnamed boat that will never be sailed.

I cry for Mamma most of all.

When I'm done, Papa offers me a handkerchief. I mumble my thanks.

"How did you find me?"

"Well, I was coming down here to think and pray after the doctor's news. Finding you here was a surprise." He smiles, though it's pained. "This little cove has always been special to your Mamma and me. We used to come here and talk for hours after we first got married. There's something about this place that clears your head."

"I didn't know you knew about it." I lean against his shoulder and lapse into silence for a few moments.

Papa points to the boat bobbing in the waves. "Why is there a boat all the way out here?"

"That's the boat I was fixing up for Mamma," I say, my voice flat.

Papa cocks his head. "Where did you find a boat like that? And what do you mean it's for Mamma?" He holds up a hand before I can speak. "Why don't you start at the very beginning and tell me everything."

And so I do. I explain how no one seemed to know where it came from, and how I've been working to pay for supplies to fix it up. I feel silly as I tell him my plan for sailing to the mainland with it, but he doesn't laugh at me.

Understanding dawns on his face. "So that's what you were up to all those nights in the shed."

I duck my head. *He knew about that all along?*

"I wanted it to be a surprise," I say sheepishly. "I was hoping to show it to Mamma—and all of you—this morning."

Papa's silent for a moment before he starts taking off his shoes and his shirt.

"What are you doing?" I ask.

"I'm rescuing the boat," he replies before diving into the water.

He tows the boat back to shore and runs a practiced hand over the paneling. "This is quite the beauty. You've done a good job, Flo."

I flush at his praise, but my voice is bitter. "It doesn't matter. Not when Mamma can't take the trip anyway."

Papa doesn't respond as he returns to his seat beside me. He pulls something out of his pocket and twirls it around in his hand. "Remember Giorgia's tea party the other day?"

I nod, unsure of how this relates to the conversation.

"She talked for days about that fancy tea shop in Milazzo. She couldn't wait to try all the cakes and teas and gelato." He bumps my shoulder. "That was her dream, just like yours is to travel Europe. And like you, her dream didn't end up working out when her friend got sick."

I frown. "I know. But what does that have to do with Mamma?"

Papa's lips quirk up in a smile. "Let me finish. Instead of giving up on her dream of having a fancy tea party, she reimagined it. And—with Mamma's help—she created her own version of a high tea party, right in the backyard." He holds up what he's been playing with, and I recognize it as one of Giorgia's homemade invitation cards. "And even added her own twist with those cannoli." He smacks his lips. "Mhmm. I don't believe I've ever tasted something so delicious in my life."

I laugh. "Soph really outdid herself."

"She certainly did," Papa agrees. "You might not be able to take Mamma to see Europe," he continues. "And I'm sorry for that. Truly." He smiles sadly. "But what *can* you do to bring Mamma joy in these last few months? How can you bring a little bit of that wonder of traveling the world right here to Lipari, to Mamma?"

I pull my legs up to my chest. A part of me is tempted to give up on my dream entirely and give in to self-pity. It's the easier option. But Papa's right. This isn't all about me. Just because something didn't turn out exactly the way I envisioned doesn't mean I should throw in the towel altogether.

I turn to Papa, the beginnings of a plan forming in my mind. "I have an idea . . ."

The next few days are a bustle of activity as we work to bring my plan to fruition. Papa and Leo put the finishing touches on the boat, doing a far better job than I could have done. They even help me decide on a name for the boat and paint it on the side in careful strokes.

Sophia spends an entire day baking special treats. And Giorgia and the twins help me decorate the boat with all the ribbon and flowers we can find.

The day before the surprise, there's one more thing I have to do. Papa helps me remove the tattered sail and fold it up carefully. Then I bring it up to Mamma's room and lay it on the bed beside her.

"I have something special for you, Mamma, but I need your help first. Can you fix this?"

Curiosity flickers across her face, but she doesn't ask for more explanation. She bends to examine the torn cloth with a careful eye. "Of course I can." She gestures to her sewing basket by the dresser. "Can you hand me that, love?"

She murmurs a thank-you when I return with it. "I'll have it ready in no time," she assures me.

"Thanks, Mamma." I linger at the door, noticing how she seemed to perk up at the prospect of a project. There's even some more color in her cheeks.

Smiling to myself, I leave her to it.

Sure enough, she presents me with a good-as-new sail later that afternoon.

"I can't even see the patch, unless I hold it up to the light." I admire the tiny perfect stitches.

"Now." Mamma arches an eyebrow. "Are you going to tell me what this is all about?"

"Tomorrow, Mamma," I promise with a teasing smile. "Just be patient."

The next day, Papa carries Mamma down to the boat, me running ahead to lead the way while the others flock around us. The twins can't stop bouncing up and down like they have the biggest secret in the world.

"Don't look until I say, Mamma," I warn her as we reach the cove.

"My eyes are closed," she assures me.

We stop in front of the boat. I take in a deep breath, trying to still the butterflies in my stomach. *What will Mamma's reaction be?* "You can open them now."

She opens her eyes and gasps. "Oh, Flore. It's beautiful."

"This is *Dream Maker,*" I say proudly. "Your own luxury sailboat." I explain to her how I found it and decided to fix it up.

Then Papa helps her onto the seat, arranging the Afghan and pillows around her. She reaches a hand to touch the flowers Giorgia and I tied around the edges of the boat. "You did all this?"

I nod, my heart swelling. "With a little help from everyone else. Papa and Leo put the finishing touches on the boat, Sophia made the picnic, and Giorgia and the twins helped me with the decorations." I point to the sail. "But we couldn't have done it without the sail. So you were really part of it all along."

Mamma presses a hand to her mouth.

I clasp my hands behind my back and beam. *Now for the best part.* "I know it's not the same as a real cruise to the mainland, with the three-course meals and entertainment and all, but I thought we could have our own little tour of the island. And I thought—maybe—you could show me all your favorite places. You know, the places Papa took you to when you first met."

Mamma's eyes shine with tears, and she reaches up to wipe them away. "What a beautiful idea, Flore."

Papa shepherds the others out of the boat, so it's only Mamma and I. I take the wheel.

"Ready?" Papa asks.

"Ready."

He and Leo push us out into the water, and I row beyond the waves. Once we're headed into the wind, I unfurl the sail and hoist it. Then I turn the boat and start trimming the sail.

When it's just right, I stop. "Watch your head, Mamma."

We both duck as I let go of the beam and it swings to the other side. The sail fills, propelling us forward.

Mamma's laughter drifts in the breeze. I turn back to see her with one hand on her hat, the other gripping the side of the boat, her eyes closed. "This is spectacular," she calls over the rush of air.

I grin, keeping a firm grip on the wheel so that we remain parallel to the shore, and mimic a captain's deep voice. "Where do you wish to go first, *mia signora*?

I am at your service."

"Hmm." She taps her chin. "Let's visit the fisherman's wharves first. I hear they are some of the finest in the world."

We both laugh. Lipari's wharves are nothing much to look at, but Mamma can make anything sound as exotic and exciting as some faraway land in Asia.

At the wharf, I dock the boat as Mamma watches the fishermen working. "This is where I first laid eyes on your papa," Mamma says, a smile playing on her lips. "We had just disembarked from the cruise ship when I saw the most handsome young man, sleeves rolled up to his elbows as he hauled in the biggest catch of fish I'd ever seen. He threw them over his shoulder as though they weighed no more than a sack of feathers. That's when I knew I had to find out who this strong, burly fisherman was."

I smirk as I sit next to Mamma, imagining her as a lovestruck teenager. "So what did you do?" I've heard this story dozens of times, but here, nestled beside Mamma on the seat and watching the sunlight sparkle on the fishermen's nets, it's like I'm hearing it for the first time.

"Why, I marched up to him and told him what a fine catch he had. Except, I ended up using the wrong Italian phrase and telling him what a fine catch *he* was."

I giggle. "And that's how it all started?"

Mamma nods, her eyes dancing. "He finally managed to understand what I was trying to say, and then he offered to give me a tour of the island. 'You cannot come to Lipari without seeing the sea caves it is famous for,' he said. And so I stayed."

A fisherman friend of Papa's calls a greeting from the wharf, and Mamma pauses to raise a hand in reply. A soft look enters her eyes. "And never left."

Next, we visit the crumbling castle where Mamma and Papa first confessed their love for each other. From there, we sail around the island to the sea cave where Papa proposed to Mamma after they nearly drowned from getting trapped inside. As Mamma's strength starts to wane, I anchor the boat near the lookout point where Mamma and Papa got married—not far from where Papa built their house with his own two hands—so we can eat the lunch Sophia packed.

We eat our sandwiches, and I listen in rapt attention as Mama spins tale after tale, her eyes alight with an energy I haven't seen in a long time. So many places . . . so many stories . . . so many memories.

Some I've heard, many I haven't—or I've forgotten. And as we circle the island, I begin to see Lipari with fresh eyes.

Suddenly, it doesn't look like the tiny island I've known all my life. The one I could trace like the back of my hand. The one I've seen day in and day out for eighteen years. Instead, it's a hidden paradise full of adventure and magic and treasure.

When Mamma's eyelids droop with exhaustion, I know it's time to call it a day and turn the boat back toward the cove.

As we near the beach, Mamma sits back against the pillows with a happy sigh. "What a lovely day this has been. Thank you for this gift, Flore. I will never forget it." She reaches across to squeeze my hand.

"Of course, Mamma." I scoot closer to her and rest my head on her shoulder. "Mamma, what made you stay?" I ask, glancing up at her. "I mean, besides falling in love with Papa, of course. What about your dream of going back to New York and starting a family there?"

She's quiet for a moment, the only sound the wind and the waves and the flapping sail. "I suppose . . . I suppose my dream changed," she finally says. "As I saw how much your papa loved Lipari and talked about how he wanted to raise a family here, gradually, his dream became my dream."

She gazes down at me, her expression thoughtful. "That's the thing about dreams. They don't always stay the same. They change and grow as we mature, and that's a good thing. Dreams are a gift from God, I think, to brighten our lives. They're beautiful things to hope for."

A smile tugs at her lips. "Someday, you're going to travel the world, Flore. Someday, you'll get to see Paris and London and Rome. I know it."

"But Mamma, I don't want to. Not without you." My throat clogs, and I struggle to swallow.

Mamma draws me close and strokes my hair. "I know, my love." Sadness bleeds in her voice. "My heart aches to be leaving you. But I'll be there with you in spirit. I'll never be far away."

She pulls away and clasps both my hands in hers. "Promise me something, Flore."

The earnestness in her voice startles me. "What is it?"

Her deep blue gaze captures me. "Promise me you'll embrace whatever adventure comes your way . . . even when I'm not here. Promise me you'll chase joy even in the midst of sorrow. Promise me you'll follow your dreams, even if they look a little different and take a little longer to reach. Because dreams—they're what make life worth living. No matter what, I want you to never give up on them. Promise me?"

I search her face, noticing the moisture glistening on her cheeks and yet the peace that seems to radiate from her. I want to say *yes.* I want to make her proud. I want to embrace life, even in all its confusion and messiness, with the same wild abandon Mamma has.

I blink away my own tears and nod. "I promise, Mamma. I won't give up."

She pulls me close and I cling to her, burying my face in her arms. "I am so proud of you, *mio fiore*," she murmurs against my hair. "So very, very proud."

And for a long moment, we simply hold each other, rocking gently in the tide as *Dream Maker* brings us home to shore.

KRISTIANNE HASSMAN

Kristianne Hassman grew up exploring the highvelds and mountains of South Africa as a third-culture kid, which fed her love for books—and adventure—from a young age. She writes historically inspired stories, infused with themes of hope and belonging, about young heroines discovering their place in the world.

When she's not writing, you can usually find her getting distracted by new classical music she's discovered, drinking copious amounts of chai tea, or visiting a new country on her bucket list.

Achievements

- Drafted two full-length novels and multiple short stories.
- Received and implemented a professional edit letter.
- Started two pop-up businesses (K Social Designs) and practiced online marketing skills.
- Published on *The Rebelution* blog, *The Young Writer* blog, and the *TCKs for Christ* blog for third-culture kids.
- Gained 100+ subscribers to email list in a month and has over 900 Instagram followers.
- Attended the Write to Publish conference and pitched to agents and publishers in 2024.

Pitches

All the Lost Places meets *The Butterfly and the Violin* in a YA historical novel about Sabrina, an impoverished violinist who is thrown into high society and must face the secrets of her past when she discovers that the father she's never known is the famous musician Niccolò Paganini.

DETAILS IN THE BUTTERCREAM

Juliet Artman

The mixer whirs, turning confectionary sugar and butter into a fluffy frosting. Sunlight pours through the high widows and reflects off the industrial tables, ovens, and fridges filling the bakery kitchen. Beside me, Aunt Tina gives the turntable a final spin.

"How's the frosting coming, Vanessa?"

I shut off the mixer. "Ready to add the coloring."

Aunt Tina nods. "Alright, dye it light blue and then we will separate it into three bowls for the darker shades."

This birthday cake will easily be finished before closing today. Aunt Tina fetches three offset spatulas as I drop in dots of blue food coloring, and watch the buttercream transform. I'm not excited to practice the spatula technique again, but Aunt Tina insists I practice one more time before she leaves.

Before she leaves.

Spring is slipping by too fast. I'm glad she gets to move closer to her son, but Washington is so far away. From middle school till now, my senior year of high school, I've spent my free time baking and decorating cakes with Aunt Tina here in Dad's bakery. I love working alongside her. The dream has always been to work full time at the bakery once I graduate high school, but until last year I didn't think it would be alone. Can I really fill her role as head cake decorator?

I push away the heavy dread with a deep breath of the sweet sugar dust that floats through the air.

Aunt Tina sets down her bowl and settles onto a wooden stool. "Alright, Vanessa, show me what you remember."

I sigh dramatically. Even with her "testing" me, warm joy fills my chest.

"Don't rush it," Aunt Tina sips water, "and remember, doing teaches you a lot."

Picking up the widest offset spatula, I face the cake. Here goes.

With a glob of frosting on the edge of my spatula, I spread it up the side of the cake with quick wrist motions. Slowly, I spin the cake with one hand and continue to pull more frosting up the sides with the spatula. Once all three colors are on, I grab a smaller spatula and blend the colors together. Lastly, I add ridges in the frosting, making the whole cake look wrapped in ribbon.

Well, the trickiest part is done. Now what?

Is there anything I missed? I give the cake two spins on the turntable.

"I think that's everything." I push the cake towards Aunt Tina.

Her face breaks into a wide grin. "It looks great. Remember your first try at this?"

The mangled mess appears in my mind's eye and I laugh. "Oh, don't remind me."

"This does look really good." Her voice takes on the serious, proud tone I've grown to love. "I think the only feedback is don't be stingy with the frosting. There are a few spots on the side where the buttercream could be thicker."

My shoulders fall as reality hits me. I still haven't mastered this technique, and I'm running out of time. "I noticed that when I was blending."

"Always make sure to have a clear plan before you start. Did you know what order you were going to do the colors before you picked up the spatula?"

"Kind of . . . I could have thought through it more."

Aunt Tina's eyes twinkle as she picks up a spatula. "You have grown to the point where you don't need the whole plan written out, which saves time. Now the trick is to think through the plan before you start." She scoops up the frosting.

I know that she is teaching, and I'm thankful for it, but my shoulders feel heavy. I should know these things. I shouldn't have made simple mistakes.

"I know what you're thinking." Aunt Tina's voice takes on a note of humor. "You should know these things. It should be easy now."

I laugh at how direct her words are. She's always been able to read my mind.

"Vanessa, you have skills. You have gifts. Keep practicing, and also don't be afraid to lean into your strengths. This cake design is my strength, but it doesn't have to be yours."

I smile. "Yes, good reminders." I take a deep breath. What am I going to do when she leaves next week?

When Aunt Tina's phone rings, she stands to answer it.

I carry the buttercream bowls to the sink in the back corner of the kitchen and fill it with hot, soapy water. Aunt Tina walks past me into the office on my left, her eyebrows pinched together in worry. I hope everything is okay. I gather up the rest of the dishes, and Dad comes through the door in the front wall that leads to the store front, turning off the lights as the door swings shut, and then clipping the keys to his belt. A long day of work is over.

Aunt Tina steps out of the office and stands between the ovens Dad is shutting off and the sink where I am washing.

"Daren called. Mercy is having some pretty serious contractions." Aunt Tina's voice is tight, but excitement laces her words together.

Mercy's due date isn't till the end of May.

"That's earlier than expected," Dad says, untying his black apron.

Aunt Tina smiles and I relax. "Yes, but baby will be okay this far along, and Mercy should be able to deliver safely too."

I swallow hard. Trying to push down the lump so that I can speak. I know what this call means. Aunt Tina is moving to be closer to her son, daughter-in-law, and grandchild after all.

"I think I am going to move out there this weekend." She folds her hands together.

I drop my eyes to the white and black tiles. I knew it. Aunt Tina has been packed for a week and already has a condo in Washington under contract. She is really leaving and I'm going to be left to run the cake department of the bakery alone.

The day to step into Aunt Tina's shoes is here. I just hope my feet are big enough to fill them.

I unlock the bakery and turn on the lights, illuminating the industrial kitchen. My footsteps echo against the red brick walls. It's too empty. I feel the void of Aunt Tina, and she hasn't even left yet.

I knew one day would be her last, and I would fulfill orders and serve customers by myself.

I just didn't expect *one day* to be today.

Lord, I'm scared. I'm so scared of not living up to all Aunt Tina has trained me to be. I know that you, Lord, have good plans in the middle of this. But I still feel so scared.

With weak arms, I pull out flour and cocoa powder for a batch of cupcakes. Not only does Aunt Tina leave tomorrow morning, but I graduate high school today too. This is all too much. I need to bake to clear my head.

I start the mixer spinning. As I focus on the recipe I've memorized, my thoughts hush.

"What flavor are you working on?"

I jump, dropping the measuring cup into the mixer, and jerk to turn it off as it bangs against the bowl. Aunt Tina's bubbly laugh makes my fluttering heart slow.

"Oh sorry, I didn't mean to startle you." She leans back against a stool.

I pull the measuring cup out of the batter and clean it off with the spatula. "It's okay. I was too focused, I guess."

Aunt Tina bites back a smile and tucks her side bangs behind her ear. I stare into batter, and meticulously scrape the side.

The hum of traffic can be heard as normal, but today isn't a normal day. My chest tightens; she's here to say goodbye. Maybe if we don't say anything the time will never come.

Being the bold leader she is, Aunt Tina sighs and her stool scrapes as she stands. "Hard to believe it's already time to say goodbye."

Tears sting my eyes. I won't cry yet. I focus on the cupcake batter.

"How are you *really* doing today?" Her words are spoken in a soft tone, almost a whisper.

And here come the waterworks.

I lift my blurry vision to her face. "I wish we had one more week together."

Aunt Tina rubs her hands on her jeans. Her eyes are full of warmth and sadness, and she puts her arm around my shoulders. "Me too. I am going to miss waking up early to bake with you." She pulls me tight as my shoulders shake. "But, Vanessa, you don't need another week of study to do this alone. You've been ready for months."

I pull back to see her chocolate brown eyes; they add another layer of confidence to her words. She takes her arm from my shoulders and grasps my cold hands with her warm ones. "There comes a point where baking the cake or trying the new design alone is going to teach you better than listening to me talk about it."

I laugh, even as tears fall from my lashes. "I know. You've always made me try things before I felt ready."

"Yes." She smiles. "And you learned more by doing it, right?"

I nod. *Every time.*

Aunt Tina squeezes my hands. "God has been preparing you for this longer than I have. Just like when I was helping you establish your techniques with buttercream, God's going to give you exactly what you need when you need it. He won't let you down as you step into this new role."

I sniffle. Even on complex designs, she never overwhelmed me with feedback. She always knew exactly where I was stuck and how to help. Can I trust God to do the same for me now? I want to, but it'll be hard.

Still, Aunt Tina believes in me. If she thinks I'm ready for this next step, I'll be okay.

Aunt Tina pulls me back into a hug, and I feel her chin tremble against my shoulder. "Teaching you has been one of the happiest seasons of my life. It's time for new things, both of us need them, but man . . . I'll miss this. I'll miss you."

"Me too." I close my eyes, and melt into her firm arms.

We don't often hug, but this embrace lasts forever. Aunt Tina is sturdy, arms around me, soft hair presses against my cheek. This season of joy and preparation is a gift. I'm ready to bake cakes without Aunt Tina. Come growing pains and all, today *is* the day, and I will step forward.

In the matter of a weekend, I'm a high school graduate and the head cake decorator.

No big deal, right? How does one move on from a weekend like that?

All morning I have to remind myself to take deep breaths. My emotions have gone through the wringer, and my lungs haven't kept up.

After my lunch break, I work the cash register while my sister, Ashely, eats. I slide cash into the register and wave as the customer leaves. When the phone rings next to me, I jump. Man, I get scared way easier than anyone should. Maybe it is a sign of emotional fatigue.

I put on a smile to brighten my tone and answer the phone. "Hello, this is Coldwater Bakery, I'm Vanessa, how can I help you?"

"Hi, I'm Cortney Stratton, and I'd like to order a cake for my baby shower on June 20th."

Ooo... my first cake order. This will be fun. I pull out paper and pen from under the register. "Wonderful. We would love to serve you. Do you have an idea of how many people the cake will be for?"

If only I could hold the pen without my hand shaking. I scribble down the numbers fifty to sixty. Aunt Tina isn't here to help with the details. This is all on me.

I gulp. "And do you have any design ideas, color schemes, or flavors in mind?"

"Yes, I ordered my wedding cake from you guys a few years back, and I was wondering if we could replicate the design."

"Of course." I move through the kitchen, past the ovens and step into the office nestled by the back door.

Thankfully, we keep a picture of past orders on the computer, and I don't have to remember the cake she had last time.

Her voice rushes forward with excitement. "We're doing a forest, tree themed nursery, so a green leafy pattern for the frosting is what I'm hoping for."

"That sounds neat. I'm sure we can do that."

Typing her name into the folder search bar, I'm only half listening as she gushes about her wedding cake. This shouldn't be a problem. I can do this. I've made hundreds of cakes with Aunt Tina.

With a little smile, I open the picture.

My shoulders fall.

There is no way. This has to be a joke.

Her wedding cake has a layered ombre buttercream. The design requires the spatula technique Aunt Tina is so good at and I struggle to pull off.

Why? Of course, it would be the hardest design on the planet.

"So do you have room in your schedule?" Cortney asks.

Her question pulls me out of my spiraling panic. I click over to our calendar and scan the openings in June. "Yes," my voice squeaks.

That is not enough of an answer. What do I tell her though? Her design makes me want to run away.

"Yeah, yeah . . . uh, we've done this design before, so I'm sure we can make it work."

"Fantastic! Thank you so much. Is there anything else you need from me?"

I blink and look back at my paper. "Huh, yes, we should discuss flavors for the cake."

"Oh yes, well, I love unique flavors! That is the reason I bought my wedding cake from you guys. What are your popular flavors?"

Flavors are my thing. I can recommend those. I rattle off our top cake flavors: espresso, chocolate mint, peanut butter, banana cream, and salty chocolate. Then some of the fruity fillings that go well with plain chocolate or vanilla. She selects a combination of salty chocolate cake with caramel filling.

"I'll work on putting together a quote for the price and send that to you this afternoon. Can I get an email address?"

We complete the final steps, and I end the call. Cortney Stratton is a very excited customer.

But what if I can't pull it off? I've never done this without Aunt Tina.

Dad steps into the office and switches on the coffee pot. "New customer?"

I close the tab on the computer. "Returning customer. She bought a wedding cake and now wants a baby shower cake. It's a tough design, but I think I can do it."

My stomach tightens at the lie. I want to feel confident, so maybe if I say I can, I'll start to feel it?

Apparently, Dad hears the false confidence in my voice, too, because his eyebrows pull up in a question. "Really? Are you ready to take on a hard design? Did you offer her any other designs you're more comfortable with?"

"No, but she was really excited about this design. I think I can pull it off."

Aunt Tina has been preparing me for the complicated designs. And practicing them is the only way to improve.

"Alright." Dad's voice has a hint of skepticism. "In the notes of the quote, make sure to let her know that it won't be Tina making the cake this time."

"Right, yeah, I'll do that."

Dad slides a coffee mug across the table. "You care so much about people, Vanessa. I couldn't think of a better partner to fill Tina's role."

I blush, feeling like a grown-up, not just a daughter.

Dad takes his mug of coffee back to the kitchen, and I pull up the document to make the official quote for Cortney's baby shower cake.

The bell over the front door jingles all day. Warm June sun has thrown our small town into tourist season, and our bakery is barely able to keep up.

Hikers spend the night in the valley and wander through the Appalachian mountains all day. Hiking works up an appetite for cupcakes, breads, and cookies.

The first two weeks of tourist season are exhausting. And this year is worse because I'm in charge of all things cake. Finally though, I've figured out my rhythm with the cupcake demand, and I will start on the baby shower cake today.

Normally, I give myself more than four days to finish a cake. But I might not have taken into account the start of tourist season when I told Cortney I could make it by the twentieth. But her party is booked so I have to keep the timeline. Today I will bake and tomorrow, decorate.

Pulling another tray of cupcakes off the cooling rack, I carry it to the prep table. With thick vanilla frosting, I make a swirl on top of the fifty cupcakes then push three raspberries on top.

I carry raspberry cream cupcakes to the storefront for walk-in customers. Ashely stands behind the cash register running a regular customer's card.

Balancing the tray on one hand, I open the display case and arrange the fresh cupcakes inside. A family with four little kids admires the case of cookies, cupcakes, breads, and muffins.

Ashely calls them to the register and the kids jump around their dad with more suggestions as he orders. As Ashely fills a box with the requested cupcakes, the kids watch in awe.

"Do you make the cupcakes?" the mama asks, balancing a baby on her hip.

I smile and straighten to see over the display case. "Yes."

"They're fantastic. We love all the options, and each flavor is such high quality."

"Awe, thank you." My face warms.

"Every year we come up here to visit my parents, and this is our first stop before heading to their house."

My heart melts in my chest. "Thank you so much. Making the different flavors is my specialty."

"Well, I hope you continue to lean into that. I think the flavor matters more than the decorations. I remember the taste even after I leave."

Ashely prints the receipt, and the parents corral the kiddos to the door.

As I step back into the kitchen, I'm floating. Her kind words fuel me with energy to keep working, and I pull out the ingredients for the baby shower cake.

For the first time in two weeks, the shop is quiet, except for the rattle of the old fridge.

Dad, Mom, and Ashely are at the monthly farmer's market, so the shop is closed until they arrive back. Hopefully, the silence will help me finish this baby shower cake.

The white crumb coat frosting is in a bowl, the piping bags are ready to make borders for the caramel filling, and the spatulas are out for decorating.

Now that I am almost ready to start, it's too quiet.

What if I can't pull this off?

No. No, I won't dwell on that. Aunt Tina always taught me not to listen to that voice.

Push through what you think you can't do. You are often more capable than you first realize.

I shake out my hands and roll my neck. Time to get to work.

I cut the domes off the top of the four cakes and throw them in a bowl for cake pops later. Carefully, I lift the first spongy confectionary delight off the cooking rack and onto the cake board. One down four to go. I rim the brown cake in buttercream and fill the center with caramel. With thoughtful motions I lift the second cake in the air. It bounces back against my fingers like a pillow, and I rest my fingertips on top to steady it.

Inches away, the moist cake cracks.

No! How?

Pinching it back together with my thumb, and I rest it on top of the first cake.

Heart racing, I examine the crack. How did this happen? I haven't had a cake crack on me in ages.

I bite my bottom lip, and take a step back. The crack is visible even from here.

This is so bad. Hopefully, frosting will fix the problem. It should work as a glue, right?

With a deep breath, I reach for a piping bag. I circle the edge of the cake then fill the middle with caramel.

Well, it doesn't look awful. The crack only lets a tiny bit of the caramel leak through and I fix that with more icing. I slide supports into the middle of the delicate cake and add the last three cakes to the top. Maybe it will all be okay.

I transfer the cake into the freezer to chill and try to keep my mind and hands busy. The silence makes thoughts buzz in my head, so I scrabble for my phone and connect it to the speaker. Instrumental piano music should help me breathe normally, right?

Retrieving green food dye, I begin to mix the three shades of leafy green buttercream, and carefully cut a tree trunk out of fondant.

Clanging echoes over the music as the timer vibrates on the counter. Time for the decorating.

Lord, would you please guide me in the details of this cake? Please?

With the cake on the table, the spatulas seem to glare at me.

I look at the paper with design details, but I've forgotten everything. I need silence again to concentrate, so pause the music. What in the world am I supposed to do first? I should have the muscle memory for this.

Angling my wrist, I slowly pull the frosting up.

It globs. What? Why am I having so much trouble?

I clench my teeth. Maybe it's too much frosting? With a smaller amount, it goes on smoother, but it's patchy.

I bite my lip and stare at the page. What am I doing wrong? I *have* to pull this off.

I take another breath and pray silently. If the Lord wants me to make this work, I'm going to need strength and patience that only comes from Him. It's too late to give up, but as I add layers of frosting, the cake tilts towards the crack.

My hands shake. The spatula slips in my fingers. Breath catches in my throat.

In slow motion, the layers separate. "No, no," I gasp.

I grab anything within reach. Frosting does nothing to glue it back together. Spatulas only make it worse. Buttercream smears up my arms, and in one final attempt to prevent the collapse, I support it with my shaky hands. Caramel leaks over my fingers, and the cake caves in on itself.

My shoulders deflate, my hands trapped under the melty, sticky mess. Gingerly, I pull my hands away from the cake. I've failed.

A tear slides down my sweaty cheek. I can't pull off this cake design. Maybe I can't pull off a cake at all.

A buzzing on the table behind me pulls my eyes from the toppled cake to my phone. I wipe my hands on my apron and work to free my voice from the tight hold of tears. The caller ID reads Aunt Tina.

More tears spring to the surface. Do I have to answer? There is no way to hide the emotion in my voice. But if I don't, she might call Dad, or she'll keep calling me.

I hit the green button and hold the phone to my wet cheek. "Hey," my voice quivers.

"Vanessa." Instant worry fills her voice. "Are you okay? Is everything alright?"

How do I answer any of that? I don't want to tell the whole story. I don't even want to be on this call! Aunt Tina taught me so much, and she expects me to fill her shoes. What do I have to show for it?

A cake, cracked, crumbling, and in pieces.

"I can't do this." A sob overcomes me as the weight of the words fall on me like a bag of flour. "I've failed, and I have no idea what to do."

There's a moment of silence. Aunt Tina must be so ashamed of me. I squeeze my eyes shut against the tears. *She* doesn't even know how to get me out of this mess.

"Well, I know you can do this. I never would have left if you couldn't." Her words have the sharp edge of truth, but the gentleness of love. "Tell me what's going on."

Breathe catches in my lungs. Aunt Tina can help me figure out a plan. She is best at that. I take a deep breath to pull the emotions together. I debrief her, while staring at the horrible cake.

My throat constricts again as I finish. She must be so disappointed. I'm sure she sees now how I've failed her.

"Why did you take this order?" Her voice is calm, collected. "What drew you to this client?"

I look down at my hands and rub dried frosting off my fingers. That was not the question I expected, but I know the answer instantly. "Because I wanted to serve the client. I didn't want to try to pull this off, I just wanted to serve her well. Like you would have."

A quiet "hmmm" is the only reply.

"I wish you were here," I mumble into the phone, with a huff.

"Hmmm . . . a part of me wishes I was there, too. But, Vanessa, as I'm sitting here listening, I am glad you're in this place of failure."

I blink and shake my head. "What?" I hope the harsh tone makes her rethink her words.

"Yes, I know, but hear me out." She takes a deep breath, and it makes my defenses drop a notch. "When I was there, I was your safety net. You never got to figure out how to move forward after failure. And remember what I told you before I left? Learning by doing is what you need to do. Well, here's your chance."

I sigh, soaking in the calm of her tone. It's going to be okay. I feel it even in how breath leaves my lungs. "I liked it better when you were my safety net."

She laughs gently. "I'm sure, but Vanessa, God is intentional. If He is forcing you to reevaluate where you are, He has a good plan."

"But how do I know what I'm supposed to do?"

Dad and Ashely bang through the backdoor with boxes in their arms. I turn so they can see the phone to my ear but not my tear stained face. I'll fill them in later.

"How many years did you work with me?" Aunt Tina asks.

"Five . . . six."

"And you know what you gained in that time?" She pauses, really expecting me to know the answer.

I close my eyes. I can't think right now. "No, I don't know."

"You gained your own skills and talents. You have unique ways of working with cake. God has given you the talents and wisdom you need to face this failure and move forward."

My throat squeezes. Those words soothe my heart. Deep in my soul, I feel the truth of her words.

Dad and Ashely turn on the lights in the storefront and I hear the click of the open sign being turned on. Immediately the bell over the front door rings and Ashely welcomes a guest.

I've heard that bell since I was twelve, and for all those years, I longed to bake cakes and bless people. How can I do that even after a failure like the cake next to me? What else can I do to serve this customer well?

"Vanessa." Aunt Tina pulls my attention back. "Lean into your strengths, face the reality of failure, and overcome it."

I rub the cold remnant of tears off my face, replying Aunt Tina's last words over in my head. I can breathe again, and my world doesn't feel so heavy. "Thank you. When I saw your call, it seemed like the worst timing, but maybe it was actually the best."

She laughs.

Dad walks into the kitchen from the storefront and stands at my side, watching me. After ending the call with my aunt, I face Dad expectantly.

Dad smiles and says, "Cortney is here to finalize her payment. Do you have a minute to ring her up?"

Whoosh. There goes all of the confidence and strength and courage acquired from talking to Aunt Tina.

Dad must see my legs wobble, because his brow wrinkles. "What's wrong?"

I force a laugh and tilt my head towards the work table covered in buttercream, spatulas, and a cake that looks like a tornado hit it.

"Oh, that's her cake?"

I nod. I will not cry again. Just state the facts. "I don't think I can pull off the design she wants. It's Aunt Tina's specialty, not mine."

"Okay, well, what can you do?" His voice isn't chastising, but it has a firmness to it.

Everything inside of me wants to run out of the bakery and never come back.

Face the reality of failure and overcome it.

"I'm not sure, but I think she needs to know, right?"

Dad nods slowly. "Maybe you can offer a different design."

Maybe? But baking, cooling, and decorating a cake in twenty-four hours sounds exhausting. What if I mess that one up too?

"You're creative, just like Tina." Dad winks at me, and moves over to the racks of finished cookies and cupcakes.

I wash my sticky hands in the sink, discard my messy apron and redo my ponytail. It's going to be okay. I step into the store front and take in the sunny room. Standing behind the cash register, Ashely bags a loaf of bread for a customer. Cortney leans against the wall, a hand on her round belly.

I blow air through my lips. I hate this. All I wanted to do was serve her well. And now my failure is going to hurt her too.

"Hey, Cortney." My voice is somehow full of cheer I don't feel.

"Vanessa, so good to meet you." She extends her hand over the counter and I shake it. I hope she doesn't notice how sweaty my palm is.

I go over to the computer next to the register. "How are you and baby doing?"

Small talk is the key to giving me time to figure out what to do. She shares how far along she is, that they are waiting to find out if it's a boy or a girl, and how upset her mom was about that.

I nod and smile, then look down at the computer. Her invoice is open. But I can't fulfill it. I can't charge her for a cake I failed to make.

What would serve her best? What *else* could I offer her that she would love?

Dad comes through the doorway with a tray full of banana cream cupcakes.

"Those cupcakes are so pretty. What flavor?" Cortney gushes.

I straighten my shoulders. "Banana cream. One of our most popular flavors over the weekends."

"I love the frosting color. It's identical to a real banana."

"Thank you," I smile. "They're fun to make. I love making rosettes with that piping tip."

As the last word rolls off my tongue, it hits me. Like sprinkles, ideas and plans fall into my mind.

What has Cortney always loved about our cakes? All the flavors.

She wanted a similar design to her wedding cake, yes, but she was drawn back to our cakes because of the unique flavors.

I could offer to make cupcakes for her baby shower. I know the piping techniques, and I can do something similar to what she wanted on her cake, but I won't have to fight gravity in order to do it.

I open my mouth at the exact moment Cortney asks, "So how is the cake coming?"

My cheeks warm.

Breathe. It's going to be okay.

I do have to tell her. Maybe that is what Aunt Tina meant by facing failure, and the cupcake solution is overcoming it.

"Well." Something inside of me yells to just lie, and figure it out later. But no. I drop my eyes to the counter. Telling her is the only way to make it right. I twist my fingers tightly together and raise my gaze back to her face. "It isn't going very well. I'm not going to be able to complete it for the party."

Do not break eye contact with her.

Her eyebrows go up. I explain what happened with the cake, even admitting I knew it was going to be a challenge from the beginning.

Her eyes are wide, her shoulders tense. "The party's Saturday. I need a cake."

I flinch, my face growing warm again. "I can't make the cake, but I could make cupcakes instead." My voice trembles. "I'm committed to making you a sweet centerpiece. When we talked, you said how much you enjoyed all of our flavors and wished you could pick more than one."

Her eyebrows lower and she rests her hands on her belly again. That fuels me to keep going. "We could pick a whole bunch of different flavors for cupcakes, and I can do similar piping to your wedding cake on the top of them. We have a display tower I could bring, and your guests will love it."

Cortney nods slowly, but bites her bottom lip. "I was really hoping for cake."

"I know." I look down at the counter, before lifting my eyes again. "But it would be a challenge even for my Aunt Tina to pull off in a day. A tower of cupcakes is more doable and would still be an amazing centerpiece for your shower. And I'll obviously cover all of the costs, because none of this was your fault."

Cortney looks down at the case of baked goods, lips pressed together. What if she says no? My fingers are ice cold. I'm out of options if that happens.

"You know what"—she looks at me and smiles—"I actually really like this idea. It's unique, which is one of the reasons I loved my wedding cake so much. But will you really be able to have them done by tomorrow?"

Relief floods my veins, warming my fingers and giving life to my voice. "Yes, I will stay late. And I can still deliver them too."

"Alright, that sounds good to me."

She agreed. She actually wants cupcakes. My heart flutters, and my hands untwist from each other ready to work again.

"Would you like to try some samples of our flavors to pick for the cupcakes?"

She grins and her bubbly personality rises up again. "I would love that."

For the next twenty minutes, Cortney and I sit at a table eating cake and drawing up plans for her cupcake centerpiece. She is a fountain of ideas, and once I get her talking, she doesn't stop.

By the time she leaves, we have a whole plan with five flavors, three decorating styles, and so much excitement. I hug the notebook filled with details to my chest, close my eyes, and breathe deeply.

Thank you, Lord, for being so intentional even in Cortney's personality. I'm so thankful she was willing to let me try again. And Lord, You have given me everything I need. Even an opportunity to pivot and reevaluate.

I step into the kitchen, and fill Dad in as I gather ingredients for the cupcakes.

Ashely has cleaned up some of my work table. All that's left is the discombobulated cake. It still makes me want to cry. It would have been a huge step of growth to be able to do it alone. But switching to something new doesn't mean I failed. I pick up the cake and move pieces into a bowl for cake pops.

Aunt Tina never had to discard a whole cake. It's a lot of time and ingredients lost, but I'm not Aunt Tina, and this will still go to good use. Plus moving forward is the best path.

I open my notebook again and begin to work on Cortney's cupcake tower.

Maybe cupcake towers will become a long-term thing. Maybe this is my specialty.

"I need the whole story." Aunt Tina's energetic voice fills the van.

I set my phone down on the cupholder and put both hands back on the steering wheel.

"Yes, so after we talked, the customer, Cortney, came into the shop to make her final payment. Dad wanted me to go talk to her."

"What timing!" Aunt Tina laughs.

I already texted her that part of the story, this next part though is the big news I waited to call her about. "Right? I was still trying to figure out what to do. And to make a long story short, I offered to make her a cupcake tower instead of a cake. She jumped on board with the idea, and we planned it out together."

"Awe, Vanessa."

Excitement bubbles inside of me. Telling Aunt Tina makes this all even more amazing.

"Yes, it's so incredible. Minutes before talking to Cortney, I felt like it was all falling apart. I mean, it kind of was."

Aunt Tina snorts a laugh.

"But God lined up all the details so perfectly. Talking to you encouraged me, then Dad walked in with the new cupcakes, and Cortney admired them, and yeah!" I take a breath to slow my joyful heart. "God was so intentional in all of the details, and this order is now probably my favorite order ever."

"I am so happy for you, Vanessa. I knew you would find your exact role in the bakery once I left, and I think you have discovered it."

As I bump into the church driveway, we say our goodbyes. I park the van and hang up the phone.

I step out of the van and slide the keys into my pocket.

I made it. The cupcakes are done, and I actually enjoyed the process. Even with the late night, I feel like I can conquer the world.

As I step onto the sidewalk a middle-aged woman carrying balloons waves to me from the side door of the church.

We exchange introductions and she introduces herself as Cortney's mom. "Follow me. I will show you where to set up."

I step into the multi-purpose room, it's full of pastel colors, centerpieces of ferns, and wooden accents everywhere. It all radiates joy and excitement.

Cortney's mom shows me the dessert table, and I begin the slow process of bringing all of the boxes of cupcakes and tower pieces inside.

When I hear Cortney's bubbly voice arrive, I'm turning the final cupcakes to showcase their best sides.

A forest green dress falls over her baby bump, and her jaw drops when she sees the cupcake tower. I bite my bottom lip, but I can't stop my wide smile.

"Wow"—she steps closer—"this is amazing."

I smile at the curving three foot tower, full of all different shades of green and flavors of cupcake. "Thank you. I really hope it makes today a little more memorable and a whole lot sweeter."

Her eyes sparkle. "I'm sure it will. Thank you for all your work."

Guests come through the door, and Cortney hugs each one. I slide the final box under the table and pat my pocket for my keys. As I walk to the doors, I hear not only Cortney exclaiming about the cupcakes, but her whole host of girlfriends as well.

My heart is going to explode.

As soon as I slide into the driver's seat, and slam the door shut, I cover my face with my hands.

This feels like a dream. What an incredible ending to a "failure," and what joy to serve others with the skills the Lord has given me. How intentional the Lord is in every single detail. Down to the design of a cupcake and the details in the buttercream.

JULIET ARTMAN

Juliet Artman strives to be everyone's big sister and cheerleader. She writes contemporary fiction for young women, where characters seek the joy of the Lord despite everyday struggles. Juliet writes to encourage a weary heart to keep smiling.

When Juliet isn't in her purple bedroom writing or practicing chords on the piano, she is pouring into young people. Juliet has built her own house cleaning business where she employs teens to clean with her, and in the evenings, she interns at a local worship ministry where she helps students grow in musical skills and love for the Lord.

Achievements

- Drafted two full length novels, three novellas, and eight pieces of short fiction.
- Attended over 100 high-level coaching calls with industry professionals, to get feedback on her stories with The Author Conservatory.
- Received and implemented both developmental and line edits from professional editors.
- Attended Blue Ridge Christian Writers Conference in 2022 and Write To Publish in 2023 & 2024.
- Built a house cleaning business that fully provides for her financially, allowing her time to pursue her writing goals and practice the marketing and networking skills needed to be an author.
- Spoke at The Young Writer's Workshop Conference in 2022.

Pitches

- In a YA contemporary similar to *Walk Two Moons,* Arianna tries to keep her grandparent's fruit farm running, but as their health declines, her dream of keeping the farm in the family fades.
- In a family-oriented YA contemporary novel with Hallmark charm, a 17-year-old girl rallies her small town to save the local florist shop and ends up saving a lot more in the process.

KINDNESS IN COLOR

Bailey Gaines

May 1870

Two Springs, Nebraska

Nineteen-year-old Winnie Fallon tilted her head back to relieve some of the tension in her shoulders. She closed her eyes as though that would help her hear Ruby Douglas's whispery recitation.

Poor, shy Ruby.

Timidity had to be overcome if these children were going to make anything of themselves. The world wasn't kind to timid people. Winnie knew that well enough.

Ruby's voice trailed off, and Winnie opened her eyes. The younger girl stood with her hands clasped in front of her, her expression silently pleading for Winnie to allow her to sit down.

"Thank you, Ruby. You may sit." Winnie came out from behind her desk, eyeing her students. "Class, your recitation should be clear, confident, and loud enough to reach the back of the room. Remember that as you study. All right, you may be dismissed. Please file out in an orderly fashion."

Swishes and whispers filled the schoolhouse as the children gathered their belongings, but the sounds quickly turned to laughter and joyous whoops as the schoolhouse door closed behind the last child.

Winnie sank into her chair, stretching her legs out underneath her desk and wiggling her toes in her worn chestnut-brown boots. Her feet almost sighed in relief, but none of that relief went to her head as she surveyed the rows of empty wooden benches.

None of the children had said goodbye to her. Was she a horrible teacher?

What was wrong with her that she couldn't get them to recite any louder?

Winnie pinched the bridge of her nose and massaged it gently as she leaned over the desk. She paused to listen to the laughter of her students outside in the yard, then opened one of the textbooks stacked on her desk, and slid out the tri-folded piece of paper that had haunted her since she'd received it last week.

Dear Miss Fallon,

Congratulations on your appointment to Two Springs School. As you are one of the county's newest teachers, and in light of your previous position, the board has asked me to visit before the customary two months to gauge your progress with the children and your suitability as their teacher. I am writing to inform you of my intent to visit your school on the 6th of June. Please prepare your students accordingly.

Sincerely,

Edward Dwight, Superintendent of Schools

Winnie's knees quavered as she reread the letter. Two weeks until Mr. Dwight's visit. Two weeks until her teaching dreams were crushed . . . again.

She would have to leave Two Springs and go back to her family, burdening her mother and father again, robbing them of the money she sent from her teaching.

Winnie blinked fiercely to stifle tears.

Should she even try? Maybe the Lord didn't want her to be a teacher. Maybe that was why He was making it so difficult. Why would He have given her that challenging group of students back in Graceton and not let something good come from it?

Winnie's throat tightened. At least *here* there were no big husky farm boys who swaggered around as though they were the ones in charge.

A shout rang from outside. Winnie jumped, and her heart pounded as she blinked quickly and swallowed hard. The door thumped open, sending a rush of terror down her spine. Only the older boys made noise like that. She gripped the edge of the desk in preparation for a battle of wills over the work she'd assigned.

Eleven-year-old Albert Perry raced down the aisle, his tow-headed, porridge-bowl-cut hair bouncing. He skidded to a stop, surprise radiating off his suddenly-still limbs.

"Hey, Miss Fallon," he murmured. The copper toes of his boots wiggled inward.

Winnie blinked, then pushed herself up from the desk. It was just Albert. She didn't have any boys older than twelve at this school, and none of them ever argued with her. She forced her voice to stay steady as she asked, "Hello, Albert. Did you forget something?"

Albert sidestepped to the bench he normally sat at. "Just my reader." He fumbled on the bench without looking at his hands, somehow came up with his McGuffey reader, then backed down the aisle.

"I'm glad you remembered. See you tomorrow, Albert." As the words came out, Winnie felt her face stretching into an unexpected smile.

Albert's mouth quirked upward in an awkward half grin as he walked backward out of the door. He pulled it closed behind him.

Winnie gathered up her own books, tucking the superintendent's letter back into the cover of her arithmetic book, and exhaled slowly. Albert was a good boy. A little like her brother Brendan in the way he grinned.

Homesickness twisted her insides, along with a pang at the thought of leaving the children of Two Springs.

I have to try.

There were too many reasons not to try: the income for her family and the wellbeing and education of the children.

As Winnie pulled the schoolhouse door shut behind her, she glanced up and down the boardwalk that lined the dusty main street. Today the children had dispersed quickly. Was that another indicator of how they felt about school? Were they so eager to escape from the schoolhouse that they rushed straight home to chores?

Winnie shook her head. Instead of being so gloomy, she ought to be planning [illegible] tomorrow. She could fill the day with recitation practice, but that would [illegible] children behind on their sums, which were arguably more important [illegible] a farming community.

[illegible] Fallon. My condolences."

Winnie paused midstep to meet the gaze of Mr. Nelson, the general store owner, who swished a broom up and down the porch of his establishment. She blinked. "I beg your pardon?"

Mr. Nelson frowned. "Oh. I'm sorry. I thought—" He gestured jerkily at her. "If no condolences are in order, then—have a fine day."

"Thank you, Mr. Nelson." Winnie frowned as she continued down the boardwalk to the Douglas's house. Why would the storekeeper assume someone she knew had died?

The hearty aroma of corn, flour, and butter filled the cozy house. Winnie sat on her bed with her legs crossed beneath her and her teaching books in her lap. Although the curtain the Douglases had hung in the corner of the house gave her a little bit of privacy, the sounds and smells from the rest of the house always traveled through.

A heavy clunking noise of cast iron on cast iron reached her ears. Likely Mrs. Douglas checking on the cornbread.

Winnie fumbled for the chain where her watch hung and pulled it from the waistband of her skirt. Flipping the brass case open, she squinted at the tiny hands in the dim light. Nearly time for Mr. Douglas to be home.

She slid across the patchwork quilt Mrs. Douglas had spread over her mattress and brushed the curtain aside. Ned and Ruby glanced up from their books, and Mrs. Douglas paused in ruffling Ned's hair to give her a smile. The children immediately focused on their books.

No "Hello, Miss Fallon." Maybe that meant they thought of her more as a family member when they weren't at school.

"What can I do?" she asked quietly as she came to Mrs. Douglas'

"I got some peas that need shelling." Mrs. Douglas wi

sleeve across her forehead and pointed to a tin bowl fil

Winnie grabbed the bowl and slid into a chair at the table, soon losing herself in the repetitive motions of splitting the shells and emptying them back into the bowl.

Her head jerked up as Ruby slid out of her chair and carried her slate over to her mother. "Ma, I don't know this one."

Winnie blinked. Why hadn't Ruby asked her for help?

Mrs. Douglas turned around, her face pink from standing over the stove. She wiped her hands on her apron before patting Ruby's shoulder and nudging her back toward the table. "Ask Miss Fallon. She's your teacher."

Winnie smiled at Ruby and beckoned her closer.

But instead of returning the smile, Ruby hunched her shoulders and trudged to her chair. The girl stared at her slate with a bit of chalk poised over the surface.

Winnie pressed her lips together, and a little knot formed between her brows as she tried to ignore the twinges of pride and pain that pricked her heart.

The memory of Albert backing awkwardly out of the schoolhouse flashed in her mind. If the children couldn't even bear to be around her outside of class, no wonder they performed so horribly in class. But why? And how could she remedy it . . . soon?

"Cornbread." Ned stuck his hand out toward the skillet, which sat on the oilcloth in front of Winnie's plate.

As Winnie reached to slide the skillet down the table, Mrs. Douglas *tsked* her tongue.

"How would a gentleman say that, Ned?" She leaned forward and touched Winnie's hand gently.

Ned rolled his eyes good-naturedly. "*Please* pass the cornbread?"

Winnie cut her gaze to Mrs. Douglas, who nodded. "Thank you, Ned. That's much more gentlemanly. That's how your father would say it."

Winnie slid the skillet across the table to Ned.

Mr. Douglas coughed and lifted his glass to his lips. He slurped the buttermilk, set the glass down with a *thunk*, and swiped his napkin across his mustache. "When I'm remembering my manners, anyway."

Ned and Ruby both giggled. Winnie almost smiled at the little huffs of the children's laughter. But were they really laughing? She caught the little dimple in Ned's cheek and the impish upturn of Ruby's lips. The laughter was real, but so . . . quiet.

Winnie counted each bean she stuck onto the tines of her fork. Maybe it wasn't possible to go against her students' quiet natures.

But no, the children were plenty loud when they weren't in school. Even during recess, the squeals and shouts of the boys and girls pierced through the windows.

So what was it about the schoolhouse?

Winnie's confusion had gathered into a knot of tension between her eyebrows by the time Ned rose to collect the dishes.

"Come on, Ruby. Help me." He nudged his sister's side.

Ruby stuck her lip out. "Do I have to?"

Mrs. Douglas cleared her throat. "The dishes are your responsibility, too, Ruby. You know that, love."

"Yeah." Ned nudged Ruby again. "I don't wanna do them either."

Mrs. Douglas raised an eyebrow. "We all have to do things we don't want to, my dears. That's part of life. But the Lord says that whatever we do, we ought to do heartily."

Mr. Douglas's chair creaked as he turned from his place by the fire, his pipe stuck between his lips. "It also says children should obey their parents in all things. So get them dishes up, please."

Ned rolled his eyes again, this time less good-naturedly, and stacked Ruby's plate on top of his. Winnie folded her hands in her lap and stared at them to keep from smiling. Mrs. Douglas's tenderness was so like her mother's, and Mr. Douglas's pragmatism so like her father's, that the Douglas house often felt like home. Mrs. Douglas had exceptional self-control. She would continue to be the same gentle, loving mother even if Ned turned out to be like one of those rough older boys from her first school.

Winnie stiffened instinctively. Her jaw clenched, the muscles in her legs tightened, and her spine straightened.

You're not at that school anymore.

Ned, Ruby, Albert, and her other students weren't anything like the students from her first school. So why was she acting like they were?

She rose slowly, collecting herself enough to murmur "Good night" to Mrs. Douglas before taking shelter behind her curtain. The ropes beneath her mattress sagged as she sat down, then she flopped back onto her pillow.

Why was she treating the Two Springs students the same way as her old students? The little girls of Two Springs didn't whisper about her behind her back. They were scared of butterflies sometimes. And the boys like Ned and Albert would rather take a licking from their fathers than challenge her in the classroom.

Ruby's quiet giggle floated through the curtain, and Winnie propped herself up on one elbow to stare at the curtain—as if she could see through it.

What would it take to get the children to giggle like that? They hardly ever laughed in the schoolhouse.

Maybe she needed to help them see that it was all right to laugh. They needed to see she wasn't an ogre.

She picked up the tiny mirror beside her bed and stared at her shadowy reflection. No wonder Mr. Nelson had offered condolences. With her hair pulled back into a low, severe chignon and her dark clothes, she really did look like she was going to a funeral.

That had to change.

Winnie pushed herself up from the bed and opened the chest at the foot of her bed. She dug past a navy blouse like the one she wore, past the brown flowered calico of her Sunday dress, until her fingers swiped the bottom of the chest and pulled a lavender-colored skirt into the light.

"Why haven't I worn this?" she whispered, looking down at the dull dark gray of the skirt she wore.

There was an easy answer to that. Gray, black, and navy were somber colors. Colors that helped her look dignified. Not that looking dignified had helped her at her first school. But the Two Springs children would love this purple skirt.

The girls might even come up to her to gush about it, just like she and her schoolmates had gushed about things like the colored ribbons her teacher had worn and given out to the girls as presents.

Winnie smiled at the thought. She dug into the chest again and grabbed a white blouse.

Be kind. With every stroke of her hairbrush as she readied herself for bed, she repeated the thought. *God, help me to be kind.*

As she tied a ribbon around the end of her braid and slid under the covers, she shivered in excitement. The Two Springs children deserved the best she could give them. The brightest clothes, the warmest smiles, and the most kindness Winnie Fallon could muster up. And perhaps she could actually get the children ready for the superintendent's visit.

Winnie grabbed her skirt and hurried up the steps of the schoolhouse in front of Ruby and Ned. The lilac fabric against the faded mahogany brown of her boots eased her heart a little.

Hopefully it will make the children's thoughts brighter too.

She marched down the aisle to her desk and turned around to face the few children already in their seats. No, not face. Greet. She needed to greet them.

She glanced down at the bright white of her blouse, the peaceful purple of her skirt, and a smile spread over her face.

"Good morning, children."

Hetty Bridges's and Ida Gregory's eyes widened as they stared at her from the first row with the other five-year-olds, but when Winnie met their gazes they broke into shocked smiles. "Good morning, Miss Fallon."

"Good morning, Miss Fallon." A chorus of echoes drifted back to her desk. Even eleven-year-old Elmer Jameson, sitting on a bench near the back of the room, echoed her greeting.

Well, that was something. They were talking. Quietly, but talking just the same. She might as well forge ahead and have them do recitation first.

"I'd like to hear your recitations from yesterday," she announced, listening to the way her voice rose and fell. It sounded pleasant enough, but some of the excitement drained from the children's faces.

Winnie raised a finger, keeping the smile on her face. "There were just a few things we needed to get right. You all have done well."

That wasn't too much of a compliment, was it? If she went overboard, the children wouldn't believe her. Children could often spot hypocrisy or dishonesty faster than adults. But Hetty and Ida's round, innocent faces were filled with trust as they tiptoed to the front to recite.

The children didn't recite much louder than usual, but they could work on that later. The important thing was that she was being kind.

"Ouch!" A sputtering cry followed the high-pitched exclamation, which came from the second bench where six- and seven-year-old Billy and Serena Dillon sat. Serena choked on a sob as she rubbed her side.

This would put her gentleness to the test. Winnie hurried over. "What's wrong, Serena?"

"He elbowed me!" A tear leaked out of Serena's eye.

Winnie squeezed her eyes shut. *Why today, Lord?*

This was the first time she'd had to consider real discipline. The way she handled this incident would set the tone for the rest of the school year . . . if she was around to see it through.

Please give me wisdom. Help me know what to say. Help me remember why I'm teaching.

Her school was meant to be a place of learning, a place where learning was loved. If she set down a harsh punishment for Billy, it would destroy his love of learning instead of foster it.

"Shh. It's all right, Serena. I know it hurts right now, but it'll be better soon."

She folded the younger girl's hands in her own. "Take a deep breath."

Serena inhaled shakily. "S-sorry," she gulped.

Winnie squeezed Serena's hands. "It's all right." She took a deep breath and sought out Billy's gaze. He was looking everywhere but at her, fiddling with his suspenders.

"Billy."

He met her eyes with a hangdog expression.

"It wasn't right for you to hurt your sister. The Lord made men to protect women. And you hurting your sister isn't protecting her. It's not kind, and it isn't honoring the Lord."

She watched Billy's face, which melted into regret. "Sorry, Miss Fallon," he muttered.

"Please ask your sister for forgiveness. Then we'll say nothing else about this." Winnie pushed herself up, giving Billy an encouraging smile and patting Serena's hand.

She returned to her desk and surveyed the rest of the class. Downturned gazes. Lips pursed in concentration. Movement caught her eye as Elmer propped his forehead on his arm and scowled.

Unease flitted through Winnie's stomach. If even easygoing Elmer was having trouble preparing for recitation, her day was doomed to fail, no matter how kind she was to everyone.

She gnawed on her lip and paced to one of the windows, where the branches from a few pine trees swayed, dappling the patches of sunlight that spread over the ground.

Winnie found herself clapping her hands. "Children!" They all looked up at her, eyes wide and . . . apprehensive.

She let her gaze fall on each of the children in turn. "Let's try something new. We're all going outside for a while."

Winnie waited for the flurry of chatter and eagerness that normally accompanied recess, but the children just stared at her.

She spread her hands. "Come along. Let's make two lines. Elmer, you lead one, I'll lead the other." She walked backward to the doors and flung them open, beckoning to the children. "Come on!"

Elmer slid off the bench and sidled over to her, a grin starting to form on his face. Another child got up, then another, and then they were all rushing for the door. Even Hetty and Ida pushed through the throng.

Winnie backed down the steps, waving her arms. "All right, everyone. Follow me! Two lines, remember?" She grinned down at Elmer, who walked beside her with his chest puffed out, turning every few steps to make sure his line was straight.

As they rounded the schoolhouse and headed for the shelter of the pine trees that ringed a grassy grove, Winnie turned to the children. "Now, you can walk, run, turn somersaults, whatever you'd like to do. But I want you to notice one thing about nature. It can be as small as a ladybird or as big as a tree. One thing. That's all."

The children drifted out of their double lines slowly, glancing at Winnie from the corners of their eyes. Gracious, did they think she was going to yell at them if they did what she said?

Ned darted across the grove, and Elmer followed him with a *whoop*. Soon the grove echoed with the chatter of children. An occasional shriek of laughter or surprise broke through the air. Elmer, Albert, and Ned crouched at the trunk of a tree, poking an anthill with a stick. Hetty and Ida had planted themselves in a growth of bluets, plucking handfuls of the tiny purple flowers.

Winnie leaned back against the rough bark of a pine tree. Her limbs felt so light it seemed she might float into the sky like a feather. But at the same time, uncertainty lurked in the pit of her stomach.

Would her changes, both inward and outward, be enough to help the children? It didn't feel like enough, but she could prove herself to the children through her actions.

Winnie clapped her hands. "All right, children, gather 'round!" A few of the children looked up and drifted over, but others didn't seem to have heard her.

Elmer jumped up and zigzagged around the grove, tapping children on the shoulders. Thankfulness flooded Winnie's heart. Having such a dedicated helper like Elmer was just one more difference from her old school.

When all the children had gathered in a semicircle around her, Winnie held out her arms. "Now that we've been outside for a while, let's head back inside to work on our recitation. Two lines again!"

The children's faces drooped, and a few sighs escaped from their lips, but they began forming two lines. Their obedience tugged at Winnie's heartstrings. They were such good children. Maybe God had sent her to these children to bless them, but what a blessing they'd been to her!

Winnie spun around to face the children, taking backwards steps as they followed her back to the schoolhouse. "Now, as we go in, tell me one thing you noticed while we were outside."

"The lion bold, the lamb doth hold." Hetty screwed up her face. "The . . ." She shrugged helplessly.

Winnie nodded and laid a hand on the girl's shoulder. "It's all right. What letter comes next?"

"I don't remember." Hetty threw her small hands into the air.

Ida leaned over and cupped her hand as if she were about to whisper the answer, but Winnie held up a finger.

"Wait. Let's figure it out together. Say the letters with me. *A* . . ." Hetty and Ida both echoed her as they listed the letters of the alphabet. ". . . *K*, *L* . . ."

Winnie paused. "What comes next?"

"I still don't know!" Hetty twisted her hands together.

"Well, I think Ida knows. Ida?"

Ida nodded and reached over to give Hetty's hand a squeeze. "*M*. Right, Miss Fallon?"

"Right. *M* for what?"

"Moon?" Hetty's shoulders hunched, but her eyes sparkled hopefully.

"Good. The moon gives light in time of night. Keep working on it." With a smile, Winnie rose from her kneeling position on the floor and glanced over the rest of the classroom.

When lunchtime came, Winnie ventured outside where some of the girls sat on the schoolhouse steps. The girls' conversation died down as she approached. Winnie gestured to the top step. "May I sit here?" She sought out Ruby's gaze, hoping her connection with the girl would sway the scales in her favor.

Ruby glanced at two of the other girls, who shrugged slightly, and nodded. Winnie folded her skirts beneath her and lowered herself to the top step, clearing her throat as she opened her lunch pail.

"What did you all bring for lunch?"

Ruby grinned. "The same thing as you," she said softly. The other girls laughed and one leaned forward to showcase what was in her own pail.

Winnie raised an eyebrow. Ruby was beginning to feel more comfortable around her if she was willing to speak up in front of others. That was progress.

Winnie's knees ached from kneeling beside the children's benches, and her cheeks hurt from smiling encouragingly at the children, but being more involved made the day speed by. When she finally had a moment to fish her watch out of her waistband, its hands pointed at ten minutes past two.

She tucked her watch away, hurried back to her desk, and clapped her hands. "I'm sorry, children. I've kept you longer than I ought. But you've done wonderfully today. You are dismissed. I will see you tomorrow, Lord willing."

Today the children's journey for the door was less restrained. Lunch pails clanged, boots clomped, and conversations jumbled over each other. But in the midst of the retreating children's backs, Hetty's gaze caught hers. The younger girl wiggled her fingers in a tiny wave that almost got lost between all the other arms and hands of the children making their way outside.

But Winnie's heart warmed.

It's working.

She waved back at Hetty.

Thank you, Lord. Thank you for blessing me with that wave today.

Winnie's stomach tumbled over and over like the earthworm that Ralph Smithens had shown her the day before.

Lord, please help me not to be sick. Help me not to faint.

Superintendent Dwight sat in a chair beside her desk, his back ramrod straight. Winnie straightened her own spine. Her jaw ached from clenching it so much already today.

And, Lord, help me to relax.

She took a deep breath and rose. A tense silence had replaced the quiet conversations she'd become used to in the last few weeks, as though the children were feeling the same nervousness she was. Would presenting a calm façade would help them?

As her gaze swept over each aisle, her heart swelled. When she'd attended school, a superintendent's visit had always been an occasion for dressing up, and so it seemed to be here.

Serena Dillon fiddled with the blue ribbon that topped her hair, and Elmer gingerly touched his palm to the top of his slicked-back hair. He might have used just a little too much slickum. Albert had just spit on his hand and was polishing the toes of his boots.

The unexpected sight, combined with nervousness, almost made her break into laughter. That would certainly put the children a little more at ease. But it wouldn't look good in front of Mr. Dwight.

Taking a deep breath, Winnie walked to the first aisle and knelt next to Hetty and Ida. "You girls will recite in just a moment. Are you ready?"

Ida and Hetty exchanged glances, clasped hands, and nodded.

Winnie grinned. "Good girls." As she rose, a movement from one of the other benches caught her eye.

Ruby waggled her hand half-heartedly, but with a look of desperation in her eyes. As Winnie approached, Ruby leaned forward. "Miss Fallon, I think I'm going to be sick," she whispered.

Frustration flitted through Winnie's chest, but then her heart clenched. Dear, quiet Ruby, whose trust it had taken so long to gain, had confided in her. How could she brush aside the girl's worries that so closely matched her own and undo all the work they'd accomplished in the past two weeks? She knelt down and held out her hands. Ruby closed her fingers around Winnie's, staring at the floor.

"It's all right to be nervous, Ruby. I'm nervous. I thought I was going to be sick too. But it'll be all right. I know how hard you've been working. I see you working every night." She smiled, squeezed Ruby's hands, and was rewarded when a smile crept onto Ruby's face.

"All I'm asking is that you try your best. And I'm sure that's all Mr. Dwight expects." Winnie could feel the superintendent's sharp gaze on her back. She kept her spine straight but smiled at Ruby again. "But no matter how well you recite, know that the Lord sees all of your hard work."

She rose, squeezed Ruby's hands one last time, and walked up to Mr. Dwight. "The children are ready, sir."

"They may begin." He gave a slight nod of his rusty, red-bearded chin.

"Thank you, Elmer. You may be seated." Winnie watched as Elmer walked back to his seat, chest puffed out with pride.

He had done well. All the children had. Even Ruby, whose face was just beginning to regain its color, had managed to recite with only a few pauses to gulp or draw a shuddery breath.

Winnie pulled out her watch. A little before noon. The children deserved an early lunch. She tucked her watch away again and clapped her hands. "Well, done, children. It's a little early, but you may take your pails outside. And walk, please."

As the children filed outside, Winnie turned to the superintendent. Anxiety swirled in her stomach, but she breathed a quick prayer.

Help me to trust you, Lord. Give me peace.

She folded her hands in front of her. "Well, Mr. Dwight, it is time for our lunch. Will you be rejoining us later?"

Mr. Dwight was polishing his glasses with his handkerchief.

Winnie bit her lip. Had she made a blunder? He hadn't brought a lunch pail. Maybe she was supposed to have brought a lunch for him.

"Or . . . would you like to join us for lunch?" she ventured.

Mr. Dwight finally tucked his handkerchief into his pocket and settled his glasses back onto the bridge of his nose. "Thank you for the kind offer, Miss Fallon, but I have a lunch engagement with the mayor. I've seen all I needed, so I won't be rejoining you later." He stood and strode down the aisle, hat in hand.

Fear sliced through Winne's insides. To keep her mind from jumping to the worst conclusion, she focused on the noise her shoes made as she followed Mr. Dwight to the door.

"Y-you've seen everything you wanted to see?"

Mr. Dwight paused on the top step as he covered his thinning red hair with his hat and looked back at her. "I will inform the state board that you are fit to teach for the rest of the school year. Your students recited admirably. That speaks to your dedication, Miss Fallon. Good day." He descended into the schoolyard, nodding at the children as he passed.

Winnie sagged against the doorframe as relief swept through her body and left weariness in its place.

Thank you, Lord.

She wasn't going to be sacked. She could keep teaching the children.

She wiped her sleeve across her forehead then made her way back to her desk to retrieve her lunch pail and join the girls on the steps.

Ruby was about to bite into an apple, but she dropped it into her skirt as Winnie sat down. "Miss Fallon, how did I do?"

Winnie smiled and pulled out an apple of her own lunch pail. "You did very well, Ruby. I asked you to try your best, and I think that was the best you'd ever done." She let her gaze fall on each of the girls on the steps. "All of you did."

Murmurs of "Thank you, Miss Fallon" floated back up to her, as welcome as the sweet scent of flowers on a spring day.

Serena broke off half of a cookie and handed it up to Winnie. "Here, Miss Fallon."

Winnie took the cookie and nibbled a bit off the edge. Her mouth watered at the tart but sweet taste. "Mm, molasses."

"I like molasses," Ruby volunteered.

"I don't!" One of the other girls wrinkled her nose, and the rest of the girls dissolved into laughter.

When lunch was over, Winnie rang the bell to gather all the children by the stairs. They held their lunch pails in their hands, looking with puzzlement at Winnie blocking their way.

"You all did so well that I'm letting you go home early." Winnie grinned as she watched elation dawn on the children's faces. "But before I do that, I want to tell you something Mr. Dwight told me. He said you all recited admirably. That means very well." She winked at Hetty and Ida, whose faces had scrunched in confusion.

"And I want you to know that each and every one of you has made me proud today, and I'm looking forward to spending the rest of the year with you." Giddiness swept over her as she stood back to let the children by. "You may collect your schoolbooks now. Don't get into trouble on the way home."

The children flooded past her. Winnie squeezed through a gap in the children, then hurried to her own desk, where her books awaited her.

As she reached out to scoop them into her arms, someone cleared his throat behind her. Winnie jumped, then forced herself to relax. None of her students would be confronting her, especially after they'd gotten through such an important day together.

As she turned around, Ned and Ruby sidled up to her, Ruby beaming with quiet pride and Ned holding out his arms.

"Can I carry your books for you, Miss Fallon?"

Winnie's throat tightened up, but not with worry. With joy. "Yes, Ned. Yes, you may." She handed him the books with a smile.

Ned grinned sheepishly. "Thanks, Miss Fallon." He and Ruby followed Winnie to the door and waited while she locked it.

"I'm glad we didn't do our times tables today." Ned frowned at the arithmetic book on top of the stack. "I can never remember the nines."

"We'll get the nines. Don't worry." Winnie squared her shoulders and grabbed her skirt in one hand to keep it from dragging on the ground too much.

Anything felt possible now that she had overcome this hurdle with the children.

Anything is possible with you, Lord. Thank you.

BAILEY GAINES

Bailey Gaines is always searching for random facts like the salary of an FBI agent in the 1930s or the routes stagecoaches took across London in the 18th century. She writes historical fiction focused on redemption and reconciliation to help people find hope in the stories of those who've gone before. When she isn't researching obscure details to make her stories come alive, she's cooking recipes from her stories, sewing period costumes, or helping people find their way out of escape rooms.

Achievements

- Worked closely with industry professionals to draft and edit three novels, a novella, and to develop multiple short stories.
- Received Columbus State University's Creative Writing Award in 2020.
- Worked on deadline to develop, draft, edit, and market a novella as part of an anthology with Wild Blue Wonder Press.
- Studied abroad at Oxford for six months and earned a bachelor's degree in Creative Writing with a minor in Professional Writing from Columbus State University.

Pitches

- *Sarah, Plain and Tall* meets *Quigley Down Under* in a Civil War era mail-order bride romance where an ex-soldier and a childless widow team up to raise a child who represents both their deepest longings and heartbreaks.
- *The Book Woman of Troublesome Creek* meets *Lawless* in a Depression-era action/romance about a moonshiner's daughter who falls in love with a federal agent whose mission is to arrest her father.

A Note from the Instructor

When I was asked to work at the Author Conservatory, it was honestly a dream come true. Teaching talented new authors and guiding and mentoring them? Sign me up! There is so much to be shared by people farther down the path than you, especially when they want what's best for you. They help you learn to spot and avoid pitfalls that maybe swallowed them whole. They equip you with tools they wish they'd had sooner on their own journeys. They come alongside you on this trek so you're not alone. At least that's the heart behind what we do here at the Author Conservatory.

But my mother-in-law—a teacher—said something to me when I excitedly shared about my new job that became an unexpected focal point. She said *They're going to teach you as much as you teach them.*

And she was right.

(At least I hope my amazing students learned as much from me as I have from them.) The hours spent brainstorming thousands of spaghetti-ideas, thrown at the wall (to see what sticks), listening to creative minds and hearts pour out their thoughts and sort through their ideas, and digging deeper into every story's soul with these writers have been some of the most rewarding of my career.

Because YOU guys taught me so much.

Through watching you learn and grow and tackle not only stories but also LIFE as writers, through listening to your thoughts and ideas and hearts, I learned more about perseverance, patience, humility, faith, and gracious love. I went into every lesson hoping to encourage you, but I walked away from so many of those conversations feeling encouraged on my own journey.

I know I speak for all your instructors when I say these things. You teach us all in your own ways.

Your ideas blow us away. Your talent and creativity inspire us. Your desire to learn and ability to be humble spark courage in those around you. You all inspire. Your voices, your words, your *stories* are worth hearing. I hope and pray you reach many more hearts as you take this journey as writers. I hope many more people are as blessed by you as your instructors are. As I am. I am beyond proud of each of you. I am proud of the stories in this collection and of the ones you're creating even now. I can't wait to see what you dream of next. Keep inviting God into every part of your creative process. He is the heart of your passions. Hold tight to that. And write on.

S.D. Grimm

Author of the *Children of the Blood Moon* Trilogy

On behalf of all the Author Conservatory instructors

Though ultimately Sarah felt called away from the Conservatory to pursue other career paths, we will forever be grateful for her kind encouragement of all our students, particularly those featured in this anthology. We're delighted to invite her to share the instructor note and once again encourage all of us to be creative and follow God's leading both in life and in our stories.

A COLLEGE ALTERNATIVE FOR WRITERS
Build the writing career of your dreams
the Author Conservatory
CHARACTER. CRAFT. CAREER.